A VOW WORTH BREAKING

A
Titan Group
ROMANTIC SUSPENSE

AMY COLE

A Vow Worth Breaking: A Titan Group Romantic Suspense

Theo and Hensley

Amy Cole ©2024

Gasp Media LLC

All rights reserved

Cover and Layout: Mayhem Cover Creations

Edited by: EJ Lounsbury of EJL Editing

Proofread: Emilie Nelson-Mortati of Glitter Penned Edits

This book dives headfirst into complex grief, forgiveness, loneliness, and guilt. I knew Theo's story would be filled with pain and yet as the words came to me, it was worse than I expected. He's been through it, and the guilt was poisoning him. His grief had come to define how he viewed himself, it became his vow.

Then he met Hensley. Hensley carried the weight of her world, the legacy, the shattered life she was meant to live, and she carried it alone. She could have easily slid into crippling grief at what never was. Hensley's strength came to me all at once in the writing process. She was going to save him as much as he had saved her, yet in a vastly different way. She was complete and amazing on her own, yet with Theo, she was unstoppable.

This is a love story tackling two humans who have both lost so much, but with so much love to give. They are sustained by friendship, by their own grit in Hensley's case, and ultimately, by one another. I thought about puzzle pieces often while writing this book. When viewed alone, each puzzle piece can appear jagged, or incomplete, perhaps even inconsequential. One singular piece can be pretty and bring joy while standing alone. And yet, each piece makes the whole more beautiful when connected. Pieces lock together, they are stronger pushed into place, they become more complete.

I think we are like that as humans in a small way. We can be happy, feel complete, and yet we are best when we are in community with more.

When we are giving of ourselves to our loved ones, our friendships, our partnerships, our families both born and found, the causes in our hearts, our pets.

This book is dedicated to my puzzle pieces. Those who have edges that line up beautifully and click into place with all of my jagged edges. To Jeremiaha especially, who has often felt like my perfect puzzle piece, the calm in my raging storm.

I hope you find your puzzle pieces.

Hensley Richard works tirelessly to balance corporate interests with humanity at Richard Companies, the global enterprise she and her brother inherited. When Hensley's life is threatened, she flees toward France and hires the elite security team of Titan Group.

Little does she know, she will get much more than the protection she expected.

Theo Rossi had always been a charmer, in the before times. After the destruction he'd caused his team, Theo made a vow, one that ruled his life. Rescuing an unconscious woman from the English Channel wouldn't change that, he wouldn't let it. However, he is immediately drawn to Hensley's strength and resilience. Unfortunately, she is now his newest client, and he has sworn to protect her, with his life if necessary. As Titan Group and Theo investigate the threats against Hensley and the danger around them escalates, their bond deepens, but is it enough to save them both?

My job is you. Only you.

A Vow Worth Breaking is an adult romantic suspense for fans of brave women, protective heroes, and the adventures that bring them together. A Vow Worth Breaking is part of the Titan Group Romantic Suspense series, a collection of interconnected stand-alones that each feature an HEA.

PROLOGUE

THEO

Mosul, Iraq 2022

THE SUN STILL HELD THAT MELLOW MID-MORNING COLOR, A HAZY golden wash over the Tigris River and the surrounding market. This was the time of day I didn't mind as much; it hadn't yet gotten hot enough to suffocate you as a wet blanket held over your face would. I knew that was coming later in the day, it always did here.

Right now, the ancient desert city was lively, especially along the edge of the bustling market, where the café was situated. The smell of roasting lamb and that unique blend of freshly ground spices was already pungent in the air, the savory-ness of it hitting my nose and making my stomach growl. To my left, baklava was already baking in an open-air oven. I loved baklava—the flaky, yet somehow still gooey layers between my fingers, the crunch of the pistachio. The food was my favorite part of this deployment, aside from the brotherhood I had as part of this team. I surreptitiously scanned the crowd again, starting and ending with Max.

I'd leaned against the wall at my back, the gypsum of the old town building still cool in the shadows of the morning, and drank my own coffee, pretending to read the newspaper I'd bought from the barefoot child selling them to café patrons. Newspapers were crucial in surveillance; looking at your phone just didn't give you the same ability to remain alert, all while seemingly engrossed.

The early morning crowd was thinning out in the café around Max and his informant. Mostly men, fueled by the dark, thick coffees served. Coffee culture had come later for Mosul than other cities, moving from what was once something drunk only while in mourning, to more commonplace, everyday normalcy. I was glad for that, because although I'd do whatever I needed to do to blend in, drinking coffee in the morning was among my favorite things to do.

Max was still holding the 'all good' signal. I was tucked into the shade, my own coffee delicious, and yet, something was off in my gut. I pretended to clear my throat and in doing so, scanned around us again. Exit points were still open, no threats seen, no change in the aromatic air. The same ancient woman street vendor was selling dates from her little wooden wagon. A few women with their colorful headscarves shielding their faces were buying the last of the morning's fruits and vegetables along the water. The din of the big city around us offered the unique song of Iraq. I sifted through the checklist in my head, clearing everything I could analyze, but the slightest twinge persisted.

We'd been business as usual all week. Recon, gathering information and waiting for the signal. Hopefully, Max got something good this morning and we could get on with it. It was heating up now, the cool shadows dying along with the sharpness of the rising sun, and I could sense there was fuckery afoot. I couldn't place it, which I hated. It made me uneasy.

I scanned the crowd again over the edges of the thin newspaper in my fingers. Nothing amiss. Folding the thin paper, I laid it on the table in front of me and polished off the last drops of my coffee.

Max was still good, but wrapping up. Good. The linen shirt I had on was already sticking to me slightly, the sun off the river blazing along my tanned skin. The golden haze of earlier burned off. I shifted, seeing the informant at Max's table stand and shake his hand.

I pulled out a few dinars and dropped them on the table to cover my cup and stretched, killing a moment of time to follow the informant as Max stayed. He'd picked up his own cup, the signal for 'still good,' and pulled out his phone. Okay, my turn.

Turning to follow the man who had been reliable in his intel thus far, I bumped into an arm. Glancing up quickly to apologize and keep moving, I was surprised to find a woman's eyes meeting my own. Incredibly beautiful eyes too.

Women didn't typically meet men's eyes in Iraq unless they knew them, and I did not know the woman before me. From the little I could see of her face, she was stunning. Dark, wide eyes regarded me, the absence of laugh lines framing them. Her eyes were bright, with maybe a sliver of calculation.

I'd place her in her early- to mid-twenties. She had smooth, somewhat fair skin for this part of the world. Although I couldn't see much of her face under her floral scarf, I knew she was smiling at me.

"Good morning, handsome." Her voice was melodic, and her words were said in English, with only the slightest tint of an accent. She'd reached up to steady herself when I'd turned into her, placing her delicate hands on my chest, also an unusual move for a woman in this area. Interesting. Deciding quickly, I defaulted to Italian. I was, after all, undercover.

"Buongiorno, bella ragazza," I replied easily, flashing a hint of a smile. MARSOC training included mastery of four languages, yet that one, Italian, was the one my mom had drilled into my head from the moment I'd opened my eyes in her arms.

I couldn't remember that moment, but I could speak the language with the fluency of a native Italian.

Her pupils widened slightly, which was interesting, but before I could think about that too deeply, her nails scraped against my chest lightly through the thin linen I wore. "Forgive me, sir. I thought perhaps you were American."

She had yet to release me, or to retreat even a breath of distance from me. She was beguiling, and I allowed myself a moment to grin more fully at her, throwing that Rossi charm her way. My team was always giving me shit for that charm and dimple, yet I couldn't help it.

"No, yet for you, I wish I were." The compliment, said in English with an Italian accent, was given freely, and yet there was something in this woman's eyes that unnerved me the longer I studied them. She was almost hauntingly beautiful, starkly attractive in a way that suddenly ensnared me. An image of being in a thickly woven web of sticky silk flashed through me. Was I the prey of this gorgeous spider? Now wasn't the time though, sadly.

"Fortunately for me though, alas, I am Italian. Pardon the bump, bellissima." I smiled at her fully then. I was intrigued, but not right now.

It was time to get moving quickly and quietly right now. Although this woman was beguiling, I was on an op, and a professional.

"Oh, but sir, you are too kind. Spare me a moment, won't you?" She peered back up into my eyes again, still practically flush to me, that lilting voice warm against my throat. Her body brushed against my chest.

Damn, I sincerely wished I could stay and talk with her. She was my type . . . beautiful, engaging, bold in her own confidence. It had been too long for me if that was all it took. Maybe the guys were right, and it was time to settle down?

Also, damn, that was a thought for another day. I wasn't ready for that yet, but I did need to get my ass in gear if I was going to catch up to Max's guy. I flashed her a real smile again, allowing her to see the note of real regret in my eyes as I moved to step past her.

Our bodies were evenly aligned when she shifted again, this time into me more purposefully. I'd already lost sight of the informant, yet I knew his most likely path. I'd pick him up quickly, but needed to get on that.

"Bellisima, forgive me. I must leave you to it. Ciao." This time, I didn't allow the hint of regret for a moment lost to show on my face. I needed to move. I squeezed her hand gently, which had still been lying on my chest, and pulled it away from me, moving to shift past her more fully.

She couldn't pursue me, not in an open-air coffee shop in Mosul, a place where women had almost zero rights. She may be bold and confident, but she had intelligence in those bright eyes too. I glanced back at Max.

He had his own paper pointed unobtrusively toward the direction the informant had gone, his eyes intense as they briefly met mine. Max continued perusing the paper, giving no indication that we knew each other or that he'd just shown me which direction to take.

I knew my part, knew I needed to get eyes on their informant and follow him. The guy had been reliable, yet we always planned contingency plans. Trusting the informant without doing our best to verify was not going to happen. I studied the busy street ahead of me, scanning for the guy we'd come to know over the last few ops. No sign of him.

Damn! Something deep within me tightened. That twinge cramped in my gut again, curdling the coffee. A flash of foreboding streaked along my skin, and yet nothing appeared amiss. I couldn't see anything off, even though I didn't see the informant. There hadn't been a single shift in the environment, yet I sensed a change in the energy on the horizon. Something had made the hairs on the back of my neck stand up, and I spun around, ensuring that Max was still good.

Seeing him sitting there through the crowd as if nothing had happened, I shook myself and turned back around as quickly as I could while not appearing to chase someone. The date vendor was still showing shoppers the fruit. There was no one new in the café area. The barefoot boy was eating one of the baklava, having sold all of his newspapers earlier. Everything appeared as it had seconds ago, and yet still no visual. Fuck. I'd lost the informant.

ONE

HENSLEY

Two years later

THE HEAT FROM THE FLAMES WAS LICKING AT MY BACK. THEY WERE raging all around me, trapping me within their fiery and jagged edges. Frantic, I ran my hand along the narrow hallway toward the stairs, doing my best to keep my eyes closed against the sting of acrid smoke. The fire was growing, engulfing me and my boat, scorching the fine hairs along my arms. My boat was groaning and splintering around me, the flames grasping at my heels as if a beast was chasing me, trying to wrap its hand around my ankle and drag me down inside of itself. My vision swam, the smoke stinging my eyes, making it hard to see anything as I made my way along the hallway. Popping sounds were all around me as the electrical went out, giving way to the beast.

I pushed down the fear that was trying to help this hideous beast of fire and continued my way along, knowing the route by heart.

If I could get to the stairs, I could get above deck to much-needed fresh air. A few more steps, and I could hope to get into the water before the fire consumed me, or trapped me in this watery grave off the northern coast of France.

The boat was shuddering now, and beams were glowing as the fire raged almost completely through them, but I was almost there. My lungs were burning in my tight chest, every breath getting harder and harder to bring in. I could barely even open my eyes at this point, and my heart—my heart was broken. There was only one person who could have done this. Only one person knew where I was or would have hidden away. Only one person had everything to lose.

I wasn't going down without giving every last breath in my body though. If he thought he could take this from me, he was dead wrong. I grabbed again with one hand, sliding along the wall as I tried to keep my other hand firmly pressing the wet shirt to my mouth to prevent more smoke inhalation.

Yes! Right there! My fingers were trembling badly, yet I was able to finally grip the smooth handrail, rewarding my renewed strength. Not today, beast! I pulled myself up the rough stairs, the specialized grip to prevent falls now scraping at my arms and legs as I dragged myself upward.

My first breath of fresh night air almost knocked me out; it was foreign to my desperate and aching lungs. I was dizzy and raw as I crawled to the side of the boat. The boat—my beautiful sanctuary—had turned into a deadly inferno. I had to get off it before that was no longer an option. It was getting tough to breathe now, even above deck, and spots were encroaching on both sides of my peripheral vision. I had to work to pull breath into my starved lungs and push it out. I dropped my hand and the wet shirt I'd been using as a mask so that I could pull up on the polished railing of the boat. My strength was waning, dammit! I could do this; I had to.

I had no choice now. It was die here, or take my chances in the dark waters churning beneath me. There was nothing I could do to save the boat. I'd be lucky to save myself at this point.

That, I realized, couldn't happen. Not if there was any chance in hell that I could stop whatever was happening to my family legacy.

Mentally girding myself to continue fighting, I hoisted myself up to go over the railing, my fingers slipping on the smooth wooden railing. I took one last peek back at my entire world burning and used the last of my strength to heave myself toward the dark water, just as the explosion rocked the night. My body was flying through the air, and I knew the hit of icy water was coming, but I was too exhausted to brace for it. My lungs were already too taxed to take a deep breath before I hit the water, and my limbs weren't listening to the commands in my brain.

Was I watching myself die? It felt like it. I expected the surface of the water to be hard when I hit the waves, as it had been when I'd been water skiing and fell unexpectedly. The dark waves were certainly hard, yes, but not the same as a sunny day of skiing, in the before times. No, this water was shards of glass that exploded into my skin, embedding me in millions of slices of pain, then engulfing me wholly, stealing into my lungs and tugging at my limbs, dragging me down. I'd exchanged the beast of fire for the beast of iciness, and it had gotten me. He'd done it; he'd won. My own brother had managed to kill me after all.

TWO

THEO

I heard the explosion before I saw the boat. Well, that was one way to quickly locate this Hensley Richard. Fuck! I hoped I wasn't too late, that boat had flames shooting out in every direction. This was not a great start to a new op and definitely not what I'd expected when Luke and Tad had sent me to go meet a new client in the charming seaside village of Lion-sur-Mer.

I picked up my pace, foregoing stealth for speed now that this was no longer going to be a quick and quiet extraction. The flames shooting from what had likely been *Le Petit Coquelicot* lit up the night sky like a good old-fashioned Independence Day party back home.

There was no way she survived that wreckage if she had been in her cabin. I'd gotten there as soon as I could, but it had been one delay after another making my way from Paris without being followed. Security had been everywhere in anticipation of the Olympics.

There! Thank God. I'd rounded the cobblestone boat ramp in time to see a woman disappear in the mass of dark, swirling water from the side of the sailboat, but she was dropping like an anchor and parts of the boat had gone down with her. I calculated I had less than thirty seconds to get to her or she'd likely be lost forever in this harbor.

I did the only thing I could. I dove, slicing through the waves. The cold, dark depths didn't phase me, as I'd had hours of time in the water in my active duty days and drownproofing had taught me to manage the environment, never fear it.

Panicking underwater would always kill a person. For a Marine, it was second nature. What stunned me was that she was sinking like a stone, arms limp. This was going from bad to worse, because to be sinking like that, she had to be unconscious, which didn't bode well.

I kicked my feet harder toward where I saw her go down; time was not on my side. If she sank much further, I'd lose her in the darkness of night and these deep, frigid waters of the English Channel. The firelight from the boat was her saving grace. It was the overhead lighting I needed to make another dive for her, this time the woman's hair entangling in my fingertips. I kicked again, propelling against her. Banding my arms around the woman and kicking again as hard as I could, I popped us both back up, breaking above the inky waves.

Whoever she was, she was damn lucky. She had a pulse, fluttering at her neck, yet her skin was already cold from the frigid waters of the Channel. That cold skin was awfully pale too, and I knew I needed to get her out of the water, and undetected. If this woman was Hensley, whoever blew up her boat wasn't going to stop until she was dead. If it was who she had told Tad it could be, he had the resources to be watching to make sure the job was done.

I needed to get us both out of the water, assess her injuries and get us to the safe house Luke had arranged along the coast, closer to Bernières-sur-Mer. It would take us less than twenty minutes to get there by car if the goal was speed, if we could get away from our current location without being seen. It would take longer to double back and lose anyone who could be trying to give chase, which would not be ideal. Car chases through foreign countries typically meant things were not going according to plan. Before I decided that though, I needed her alive.

Spying another dock, I swam that way, using the darkness to my advantage. Parts of her boat were floating in the water now, with only the hull left burning in the water. I stilled alongside another sailboat, listening. The explosion had awoken the towns-people and the harbor master, the local *capitaine de port*.

I could hear shouting and the distinctive French sirens getting louder and louder, but so far, no gunfire or sounds around the sailboat I'd swum us to. Yet anyway. No gunfire or sounds of a chase *yet*. I didn't know if anyone else had seen her going over the side of the boat, or had seen me go in after her. I'd gone in dark, but she'd been highlighted by the flames around her as she'd gone in. If I'd seen her, anyone else watching could have also seen her.

Continuing on, I pulled along the side of the sailboat with one arm while the other dragged the woman, keeping her head above the dark water. Once I got to the swim deck, I paused again, ensuring that it was still clear on that part of the dock. Still quiet in this part of the harbor. Breathing out a moment of thanks for that, I heaved her up onto the teak platform as quietly as I could, kicking my legs powerfully to keep my own head above the water.

Following her up, I crouched down to her and started CPR. She had likely ingested a good deal of the English Channel, and I needed her alert. I tried mouth to mouth, molding my lips to her own, desperate to push the air into her slight frame. Warmth to ice. Within moments, she quickly came to, coughing up seawater and thrashing her arms and legs, fighting against an unknown assailant.

"Stop, you're going to hurt yourself! *Arrêt!*" I commanded. "Tad sent me. I'm Titan Group. *Coquelicot. Je suis avec Tad.*" I was whisper-yelling at her, my hand coming up around her back to tilt her slightly while she coughed up the last of the ocean water in her lungs. Deep coughs were racking her lithe body while she got the water out before turning slightly to face me. Kaleidoscope brown, enormous eyes in a pale face held mine, studying me. Instinctively, I rubbed my hand gently across her cold back, trying to work some warmth back into her bones. Her eyes still held mine, considering. I saw the moment she decided to trust me wash over her, bringing a sense of solidarity to her delicate features.

It was as if I'd pulled my own personal siren from the sea, stunned immobile by those dark, arresting eyes delving into me. Pale face, perfect bow lips, which quivered again, her cough breaking whatever spell I had stumbled into. I shook myself, blinking back into focus. The very last thing I deserved was a moment to appreciate her beauty. That would get us both killed. I had learned that the hard way.

Holding up my index finger in front of my mouth, I gave her the universal sign for 'be quiet.' I didn't want her to accidentally expose our location to whoever had bombed her boat. I knew Hensley Richard to be bilingual, so I tried first in English, my own preference.

"My name is Theo, and Luke and Tad sent me. If you're Hensley Richard, I came for you, to help you." I still had one hand on her back, and something deep within me compelled me to sweep it along her reassuringly again. "Poppy," I added the code word she'd given Tad to ensure she could trust us when she met us. Standard protocol for us with our clients, but we didn't typically cut the timing so close.

Her coughing had slowed, those bottomless eyes huge on her still pale face regarding me, but as soon as I said the agreed upon safe word, 'poppy,' that sense of solidarity from before hit me again in the chest. I'd saved many people in my life, and not once had one inspected me so thoroughly, as if she saw my inner thoughts. Hell, I'd also managed to do the opposite of saving many people, and none of them had ever looked at me in the same way.

"I'm going to move my hand, okay? You aren't going to scream, are you? *Vous comprenez? Coquelicot?*" I asked, unsure if she had understood the English explanation. She'd been quiet and still up until this point, and I wondered if she was in shock, or even spoke English. Hensley Richard would, but I still wasn't sure if I was dealing with my target. The likely answer was that it was her, but I made it a point never to assume shit would be straightforward. That was always a good way to get someone hurt or killed in my line of business.

"Oui, yes, d'accord," she replied, her teeth chattering. "*Coquelicot.* That's me. Hensley."

Relief washed over me, momentarily making me light-headed. I'd managed to get to her in time. Thank God. "I'm not going to hurt you. I'm Theo Rossi, from Titan Group. Do you think you can stand on your own? We need to get out of the water and to the safe house about twenty miles from here without being seen. Are you okay?" I asked her.

It seemed as if her shock at waking up in a stranger's arms with his lips pressed to hers, after being dragged alongside a sailboat in a dark ocean, was wearing off. Her pupils weren't dilated to a dangerous degree, which was reassuring. She was likely still in shock, but okay to move. Nodding her head in the affirmative, her brow furrowed as if considering me the best option from a long list of options. She had delicate facial features, and held against my body as she currently was, she felt small but strong.

"*Oui*, yes. I'm Hensley. I did call Titan Group for help. Just in time, it appears, *oui*," she replied, a tiny upward curve of her bowed lips. Her voice was low and hoarse, likely from that giant gulp of seawater, and the smoke and subsequent coughing.

"*Oui*, good timing." Her pluck made me chuckle, which

rattled from rust in my own throat. I hadn't laughed in a while. This certainly wasn't what I expected, but at least she was with me now and safe—for now. I took my job seriously and already felt enraged on her behalf. It was a good thing that she seemed to be able to make a joke, no matter how small, at a time like this. If she were going to survive, she'd need to be able to keep her wits about her. She'd mostly saved herself so far, which was also a good sign. Perhaps this little siren was stronger than she looked.

"Let's get out of here, and then we can talk about how you got off your boat." I was still whispering, but the ticking clock in my gut told me it was time to go or we'd lose our window.

She nodded again and together, we pulled ourselves up to crouch on the teak swim platform of the boat we were hiding on, as quietly as possible. Once there, I held out my hand and motioned for her to stay quiet, even though she had to understand we were in stealth mode. She'd gotten herself away from a pretty hellacious experience; she wasn't an idiot. I'd been damn impressed when I'd read the file Mila had sent me from command central as I made my way across the French countryside. Hensley's philanthropic work was changing communities in deep and meaningful ways, something the heiress clearly worked hard on. Even more impressive, that was in addition to the role she held with her family empire leading mergers and acquisitions. She was smart; that I knew already. She'd need to be for what was coming, I was also certain about.

The explosion was indeed the distraction we needed. Carefully and as quietly as possible, we picked our way onto the dock the boat was tied to and along the shadows. We moved silently to where the crowds of people were coming down to the harbor to see what had happened. Crouched down, I turned back to her, finding her right against me, her face a hair away from my own, those solemn eyes on me.

"I have a car in the lot next to the entrance to Sword Beach, up the docks from here. I'll lead the way, and you need to stay behind me. My gun should still work, but I don't want to engage and push it with only that and a knife on me. I don't know who we're dealing with, or how many of them. Stay close. We are going to act like concerned tourists who were awakened by the blast, just like most of this crowd. We should be able to get to the car from this area easily with everyone coming onto the docks to see what's happened. We'll blend in as soon as a larger group comes our way. *D'accord*?" I'd spoken fast, but she had nodded as I went, alert and focused on me.

"Yes, *bien*," she replied in a matching whisper.

Nodding again, I set my hand on her lower back, stood and motioned for her to do the same. I was glad the darkness of the night would perfectly conceal the fact that we were drenched in seawater. The attack on Hensley had come at the darkest part of the night, which told me someone had known what they were doing. I glanced down at Hensley at my side, striding forward toward the throng of other people who were all nervously heading along the docks.

I'd just allowed myself the first visual scan of her from head to toe, which stopped me in my tracks. I damn near stumbled. Holy shit. The darkness would do nothing to hide those curves. A flush was blooming up my neck, heating my cheeks as I dropped my hand from the dip at her back. I swallowed hard. Hensley was a smoke show and every delicious curve was visible through the wet tank top and sleep shorts she'd been wearing when she made her way off her boat. I had always been a lover of women, of all shapes and sizes, and never before had I been slammed speechless like I was in that moment. My once-legendary charm was nowhere to be found. That guy was long since dead.

She was also barefoot. Fuck. That had to hurt, but she hadn't said one single thing; not one complaint had left her pretty lips. Waves of protection rose within me, unbidden and urgent. For the second time in seconds, I swallowed back the fierceness of the new sensation and unzipped my hoodie.

"Here." My voice was gravel scraping out of my throat, and ended up sounding more like a growl as I shrugged out of the hoodie and handed it to her to put on. I felt like such an ass, and tried again, clearing my throat first this time. I may have been the ladies' man of the group for years, but my mom had raised me better than to ogle her. More notably in my life, I had learned my lesson on how even seconds lost in the eyes of a woman would end up killing someone. I was also an elite operator, I reminded myself. I didn't need to learn that lesson twice. The first time had practically gutted me, and it *had* killed people, people I loved. I focused on those watchful eyes again and did my best to keep it as clinical as possible.

"Sorry, Hensley, I'm sure you're freezing. And I'm sorry about your poor feet. I'd pick you up and carry you, but that would make us obvious," I said.

My hand grazed hers as she took the hoodie from me, a spark lighting along my fingertips as her chilled skin touched mine. Frowning, I pulled my hand back from the sizzle. First time for everything with this stranger, apparently.

"It's okay, I understand. I'll warm up once we are free of here." Her lilting words carried on the breeze to me, with only a small accent noticeable. She shivered and pulled the sides of the zippered material around her shoulders, its size dwarfing her smaller frame.

"I promise I'll warm you up when we get to Bernières-sur-Mer." My voice had gone low again, a throaty growl making a promise in a way that I hadn't intended, but the thought made my mouth water before I could tell myself not to go there mentally. My body was clearly sending signals to my brain before I could filter them from my words. Another blush flamed across my face, and I gave her a small smile, clearing my throat yet again. "We'll get you warm again. You'll have the entire suite at the safe house, complete with a hot shower."

Shit, I was being awkward right now as she kept her serious eyes glued to mine. Her lips twitched again, the little bow ticking up at the side. Fuck, I used to be the team charmer, but now, I had no idea who I was anymore. Prince Charming had died outside of Mosul two years ago. In his place, a cynical and apparently awkward shell.

THREE

HENSLEY

THE DARKNESS DIDN'T HIDE A RUDDY BLUSH CREEPING UP THEO'S tan neck, and the onslaught of his scent enveloping me in the warm fleece hoodie was divine. He was cute, alternating between blushes and the growly words. I shivered again, but not from the cold this time. Theo was gorgeous.

He wore what I guessed was his Mediterranean heritage well with dark brown hair, olive skin and deep, dark brown eyes. He was tall and solid, everything a woman could want when she'd fled all she'd known and called the proverbial international, *m'aidez*, Mayday signal.

I supposed that if I was caught in the crosshairs of an assassin, at least I had gotten Theo as my rescue squad. Good thing he could swim.

I placed my frigid hand in his larger, warm one. The heat instantly made me feel safer and more alert, like sinking into lush, warm grass in cold shade. His calloused fingers squeezed mine briefly before tugging me in to join the larger group of tourists exclaiming over the burning sailboat in the water. My sailboat, a precious jewel of a haven, part of my family legacy.

My *Le Petit Coquelicot*. That hard shelf of tears was working its way up my throat again, nearly choking me. Rage was also curdling in my belly, edging out my despair. I couldn't cry now; there was no time, but *mon Dieu* I wanted to. If I lived to see this through, I'd make him pay for this. I needed to choose my rage over my heartbreak, a choice I'd made time and time again.

I kept my head forward, locked on the crowd gathering. I didn't think I had it in me to watch her burn into nothing as the water swallowed her. I was hanging on by a thread, my anger driving me more than anything, yet watching the flames eat at my haven, the only home I'd ever loved? No, I didn't have that in me right now. Not if I wanted to keep it together.

I focused on Theo as he exclaimed in French and smiled back at me, putting on a show for anyone watching. We were blending in, and almost to the parking lot where he'd said he had a car. Briefly, I wondered how he'd gotten there so fast, but that was another question for later. First, survive to get to a safe location. Then, there'd be time for talking and, hopefully, figuring out who and where that asshole would strike next. And some pain medication hopefully, I felt every bit of the last hour everywhere in my body.

We made it to his little car without mishap, throngs of villagers and tourists alike gathering on the dock, the beach and along the stone sea wall. Thankfully, it was practically the middle of the night, and no one really looked askance at my outfit or bare feet. No, everyone we encountered was too shocked by the boat sinking in a mass of fiery waves, the blaring sirens adding to the chaos around us all.

The authorities were keeping everyone back from the ramp and clearing the docks as we walked to the car. Once inside and with the engine running, he cranked the heat as he backed out of his parking spot. My own gasp shot out involuntarily as the warm air hit my skin. I hadn't realized how cold I'd gotten while in survival mode. Now that I had, now that the numbness of shock was wearing off, I couldn't stop shaking and my teeth were chattering so hard I'd be surprised if I didn't break them. That definitely wasn't going to help my splitting headache.

Before I could say anything, Theo had the little car on the frontage road. He reached behind him, pulling a small duffle bag to the front seat and handed it to me as he maneuvered along the winding stretch. "Dry clothes. You can change now if you want. I'll be a gentleman. If you don't feel comfortable, at least wrap something around your legs and feet."

I nodded at him, teeth still chattering and shivers still making my movements jerky. My hair was sopping wet and dripping down my back, so I twisted it back and up to wring as much of the ocean water out of it as possible. Once that was done, I pulled out an old sweatshirt from the bag he'd handed me and removed the now also-soaking hoodie he'd given me on the dock. The old sweatshirt looked heavenly, and most importantly dry, but I had just met this man. Changing in front of him in this tiny space was intimate, as if we existed in a cocoon of our own.

Shrugging off the oddity of that thought, I realized that he'd already saved my life at least once in the last half hour, and I had called Titan Group for help. I needed to get warm, and I needed to do so now. I also trusted him already, although I wasn't quite sure what it was about him that made me that level of ease. It could have been the safe word he'd whispered, the fact I had called them, or maybe it was that underneath his handsome demeanor, he had a depth and kindness in his eyes that reassured me. Regardless, the one thing I thought I was excellent at, my own brother withstanding apparently, was reading people, and Theo Rossi was trustworthy.

Making that decision quickly, I whipped my soaking top off and dropped it to the floorboards of the car behind my seat with a splat as it landed. The car swerved slightly, and I shot my eyes over to Theo as I held the sweatshirt to my freezing chest.

"I thought you said you were a gentleman," I accused, narrowing my eyes in his direction.

"I am, I just didn't expect you to come to that decision that fast. I'm sorry, truly, I am . . ." His low voice trailed off as more flames shot up his neck and across his face. He had turned deeply red, enough that I could see the flush on his darker skin, even in the darkness of the night. He was being pretty wonderful, and I did trust him, and I did come to that decision quickly. It was what I did, assess and move quickly; that was my MO.

He reached his arm up to rub nervously the back of his neck, his arm muscles bulging as he did. The man was seriously ripped. Those biceps were incredible, and his forearms? Gah, the man definitely fit the hero aesthetic perfectly. I'd heard of the term "arm porn" on social media, but I hadn't ever understood it until now.

I rolled my eyes at myself thinking about using these moments of my life to focus on a set of biceps, no matter how fantastic. Theo was all alpha male, with a wildness in his eyes, but deep kindness too. Even if he had peeked, I believed his excuse.

I shimmied into the large sweatshirt and used the length of it to slide my sopping wet sleep shorts down my legs, dropping those in the backseat as well. The bag he'd given me had sweats in it, but they were huge on me. I pulled them up carefully and rolled the waistband several times to see my own feet.

Mon Dieu, the warm and dry clothes were incredible. I was still shivering and my teeth were still chattering, but both had slowed. Now, it was solely my heart racing and my mind a cascade of thoughts and memories.

"There are socks in there too. Put those on. There are shoes, but I grabbed whatever I could find on the way down, so there's a good chance they won't fit," Theo said, his voice pulling me back to the present.

Nodding, I dug back into the bag, finding the socks quickly and putting them on the icicles my feet had become. I almost cried right then and there for how good that cozy heat was. Now that my skin was warming, it brought painful prickles of circulation with the warmth. The needling sensation reminded me of

Gulliver's Travels, an old book from my childhood. I imagined myself tied down with hundreds of little arrows shot into my skin. The visual should have made me laugh, yet all it did was remind me that someone had tried to kill me. Had almost succeeded frankly, had it not been for Theo.

"*Merci*, Theo, thank you. I'd be dead in the water without you," I said, turning to face his profile. My throat still hurt, but this man had saved me, and I couldn't wait another moment to thank him. "Quite literally dead in the water."

He glanced over at me again then, with a soft smile on his face. "This is what we do. You made the right call," he assured me.

I suppose I had indeed made the right call, and just in time, it seemed.

We continued through the Normandy countryside, twisting and turning among the orchards, along the ocean, around ancient stone walls carving up the fields. Theo had the heater running full blast, and I kept my hands in front of the vents as I watched the familiar landscape speeding by in the moonlight. The painful reawakening of my hands had subsided, yet the disbelief in my current situation continued to grow and fester. Fester and flame more like it, I was so pissed at my brother. I held onto my anger tightly. It was far better than the heartbreak rising within me.

Of course, Adrien had found me. He was the only one who would know that I'd seek shelter in the area I felt most at home, closest to our familial roots. Our family's legacy was my life's work after all. Normandy was where our family had started—a British special forces Marine with COPP, nursed back to health in secret by a young French villager outside of Colleville-sur-Mer.

Our great-grandfather had been a British Marine with the Royal Special Forces on COPP, Combined Operations Pilotage Parties. Their group was sent ahead of beach landings in World War Two to conduct full surveys of the beaches to analyze and ensure that heavy vehicles would be able to advance across them. They'd been using new tech at the time, specialized miniature submarines known as X-craft, and they often surveyed the frigid waters under the cover of night.

Our great-grandfather had been successful in those reconnaissance missions, yet he'd also been deployed ahead of the vast invasion fleet for Operation Overload to help in guiding them in on that fateful June day. Although he'd made it safely ashore, he'd been badly injured in subsequent fighting and had to take refuge. Fortunately for him, fortunately for all of us who came later, a French family had taken him in and saved his life, hiding him in an old cellar they'd covered with dirt in their orchard to aid in the resistance.

Our great-grandfather had fallen in love with the daughter of the family, who was only two years younger than he was. Her father had been killed early on in the fighting, and the occupation of Nazi soldiers had long since depleted their resources, but her mother had refused to give up. They'd endured unimaginable hardships to survive the occupation, and saved the Brit at the risk of their own necks.

He'd been healthy enough to rejoin his company after Allied forces took back the region in the days following June 6, 1944, but he promised he'd come back for her, and he had. Claire and Thomas had married almost immediately and settled in the region, rebuilding her family's home and orchards. They'd had her grandfather, Hugo, precisely forty weeks after they got married and a baby girl eighteen months later. My *Tante* Marie Louise was the one who had left her trust to me, which had given me a fighting chance to try to save our family business and the madness that had apparently taken over Adrien.

That family business was the foundation of our history. Our great-grandfather had used his highly specialized training to start the family business after the war. Now, decades later, Richard Companies has expanded from underwater operations to multi-faceted safety and prevention devices. That solid foundation was mine to care for now—mine and Adrien's.

Thinking about what our family had survived to create and pass down to me typically filled me with a warm glow, as if my pride just shimmered through from my heart. Today, it felt like a weight, and for the millionth time, I wished I had parents to run to, a mom to snuggle into. A gentle hand on my head and a grounded, "It'll be okay," murmured against my hair.

Our parents, Olivier and Laura, had been killed in an airplane crash when we were eleven. They'd been on their way back to England from visiting family in America, leaving us to be raised by Hugo and Giselle, our French *Grand-père et Gigi*. It was long enough ago now that although I held the familiar flash of sadness over their loss, I craved a larger, more intense longing to have known them as people and not solely parents. Sometimes I just felt so damn alone.

Me, once a brokenhearted little girl, and my older brother, who was, years later, trying to kill me. My only surviving family member and he wanted me dead. Yep, maybe I was better off alone than with Adrien as my only surviving family. I felt like that little girl again, devastated and angry at the world, yet now I was definitely on my own, with no loving grandparents to take me in and love me.

Looking back, I wondered when Adrien had lost his mind. *Grand-père* Hugo had taken to teaching us both the family business, bringing us into every fold there was so that we'd both be ready to take the helm when the time came, together. The offices had become homes to us, the people there our extended family. I'd known and cared for many of them my entire life, some of them also multi-generationally. We'd celebrated together, grown together and when we lost our grandparents, we'd mourned together.

We'd lost our *Gigi* last January and then *Grand-père* Hugo on April 30. Both gone in three months' time. I hadn't thought my heart could take it, but they'd raised us to be resilient, and I'd had the family company and its legacy, our people to fight for.

Had Adrien been lost before their deaths? Or, was it only in the last few months?

In my heart, way down deep, I'd hoped that it would bring Adrien and me closer together again, similar to when we were kids. Sadly, it appeared to have the opposite effect. Over the course of the last year, I'd seen the changes almost daily. We were wealthy, ridiculously so, but it was never enough. Adrien seemed hellbent on pushing in every direction, acquiring smaller tech companies as he went. He was putting our longtime subcontractors out of business, firing long-term employees who were not only wonderful at their jobs, but who had helped build the success we enjoyed. Our company was a cold shell of what it once was, but the profits were through the roof. I knew that was not the legacy *Grand-père* and *Gigi* had wanted; it was nothing like what our parents would want to see. It was a hollow and hard crust of the legacy we'd been left. Chasing the dollar at the expense of the human was not something I could silently let us become. My heart ached for the boy Adrien had been, now unrecognizable.

"Shit, get down, Hensley." Theo's terse command startled me from my reverie. I'd been lost in thought, watching the dark miles zip past. "We have company, and they came up fast. Get down," Theo added.

I scooted myself lower in the passenger seat, going until the safety belt was up around my face. "Tell me how to help, Theo. Please." I was embarrassed I'd been daydreaming down memory lane when this beautiful stranger was trying to save my life.

"There's a gun in the glove box, can you grab that?" he asked me, his eyes on the rearview mirror and his hands tense on the wheel. He'd kept the speed steady, and we couldn't be far from the safe house based on what he'd told me earlier.

"Oui, yes, I'll grab it. Shouldn't we be trying to get away?" Panic was welling in my belly again. My body was still trapped in fight-or-flight, riding the rollercoaster of fear, relief, anger, anguish, plunging back down into fear.

"We are. If it isn't someone after us, it'll raise alarms if we take off speeding through the countryside at this hour and they'd call us in. If it is trouble, and Hensley, my gut says it's trouble, then we need to lose them," he replied.

"I can help you with that, I know this area like the back of my hands," I replied quickly as I opened the glove box and reached for the gun. I refused to be a victim in whatever this was, promising myself instantly that I would do whatever it took to survive and fight for myself, for my company, just like my ancestors had done. My hand closed around the cold metal as I saw the lights flashing across the interior of the car, held the weight of the weapon in my hands. "Theo!" I yelled.

"Hang on, we're going to take a hit!" he yelled back. I guess Theo's gut had been right after all.

FOUR

THEO

Damn, I'd been hoping for a clean getaway and for a few minutes, I thought we'd done it. Someone must have been paying close attention to the harbor area earlier, and more than one person . . . or that one person got lucky to see us drive away. My gut told me that it wasn't luck on this one, someone who knew what they were doing was after Hensley. My hands gripped the wheel harder, my knuckles turning white.

The car behind us had come up too fast to be coincidental, especially on this road at this time of night. I braced for the impact of the car behind us and tightened my grip on the steering wheel as I hit the gas of our car. I was hoping like hell the burst of speed mitigated the force of the incoming hit.

Our little car shot forward right as the car behind us came in for the kill, but that burst had worked. We absorbed the blow, but I had to work to keep our car on the road. If I hadn't been paying attention, there was no doubt in my mind that we'd be rolling in a metal box from that hit.

"Are you okay?" I called out to Hensley.

"I'm good. You?" I heard her voice and risked a glance down at her, caught between the floorboards and her seat.

"Good. Get back in the seat and tighten your seatbelt, but try to keep your head down as far as possible. Use the seat as a shield, but I don't want you caught on the floorboards without the help of the airbags if we wreck." My words were coming out rapid-fire, but she nodded along and did what I told her to do. She had the gun in her hands, which she pulled up onto her lap.

"We're about six miles from the safe house, but I don't want to get any closer than that unless we have to. We need to lose whoever this is before we lead them right to it," I told her. "Can you shoot?"

"I can shoot. I think. I've only done it a few times and not in years. Grand-père used to take me hunting once a year, but I never really liked it so he gave up."

For some reason, even in the danger chasing us, that brought the hint of my old smile almost all the way to the surface of my face, something I hadn't felt in a long time. I wanted to ask her why she hadn't taken to it, what it was about hunting that she didn't care for, but now was not the time and that wasn't who I was anymore. I tamped the curiosity down and refocused. We only had moments before the car behind us tried to run us off the road again.

"Where are we now?" she asked me.

"I circled around Bernières-sur-Mer and the house we have secured is between there and Courseulles-sur-Mer. I'm going to try to lose them in town," I replied. "Hang on."

I risked another glance and seeing her brace herself, jerked the wheel hard right down a sleepy little road leading into the village.

Fuck, the car behind us made the turn too. "I'm going to weave throughout town, see if we can lose them, but be ready to shoot, okay?"

"Okay." A sharp nod and she was ready.

We zigzagged throughout the small town, along low stone

walls and past ancient buildings. "Theo, this town isn't big enough to do this for much longer." Hensley's voice echoed my own thoughts.

"We're going to have to ditch this car to have a chance. Can you walk the last few miles into the safe house if we can get clear?" I didn't know Hensley, but she'd proven herself more than capable of surviving. This wasn't ideal at any point though, certainly not after what she'd already been through earlier in the night.

"Oui. Yes, I can do whatever we need to do," she assured me.

"Good. We need to do a few more turns and then turn the lights off and duck in wherever we can. When I turn again, I need you to take the wheel and be ready to steer like our lives depend on it. Can you do that?" Glancing over, I saw a quick jerk of a nod. That was enough for me. "Let's do this."

She shimmied over as I rolled my window down. Making sure she was good, I twisted around and shot toward the car behind us. They'd have to dodge the shots, which should buy us enough time to get some distance.

I turned back to scan the sleepy town around us, residents blissfully unaware of what was happening on their quiet, narrow streets. I assessed as quickly as I could on which turn to take next and seeing the alley I wanted, turned my head just in time. Bullets had started peppering our car, the back windshield now shattered across the back seat, the *thwap* of the bullets sounding like sharp rocks against the glass. Whoever was after us also had a silencer on their gun. Interesting.

"Now, Hensley!" I roared. I didn't dare look over and see if she was ready or listening, I put my hand on hers where she had clenched onto the steering wheel and jerked the wheel hard left again, sending our little car shooting down the alley.

Thankfully, Hensley hadn't hesitated. I reached backward, firing back at the car, which caused them to slow down. I yanked the wheel hard right and then another two quick turns back almost to a circle before I pulled the car to a hard stop and shut it off.

"Hensley, get out and get to the tree in front of us. I'll cover you in case they come around," I said. I'd pulled in between two older cars parked behind a home with towering old trees. We should be able to get away as long as the car from behind us didn't come back around in the next two minutes.

She eased out of the car, staying as low as possible and running to the tree I'd pointed to earlier. Seeing her make it safely, I grabbed the bag I'd stashed dry clothes in earlier and eased out of the driver's side, crouching along the car to watch.

Not seeing or hearing the car coming, I ran to the tree to join Hensley. "Made it out, but we need more distance," I whispered, drawing her close to my body with one arm so she could hear me, and because well, I needed to keep her safe.

She shifted against me, small and shaking, but her words came out strong and low. "I know this place, there's a bakery about eight blocks from here. The baker will be there preparing the day's bread. If we can get there, he'll call the police."

"Normally, I'd say that's exactly what we were going to do, but Hensley, we don't know who we're up against. I have a sneaking suspicion that whoever is after you is not an average criminal. Let Tad and Luke handle the police and Interpol while we get to the safe house. My job is you. Only you. Once we've gotten you to safety, we can work to solve this, and that means collaboration. For right now, Tad or Luke will already be on it."

Her head bobbed slightly, her eyes big and dark in her face. "Okay, Theo. I trust you."

Her words cracked a chunk of the stone loose that had been lodged around the vicinity of my heart. I hadn't expected trust from anyone outside of my team since that last mission in my Marine days. Their trust was something I still didn't deserve, no matter what they said, what our team doc said, or how many times I tried to forgive myself. No, trust was not something I deserved from her. Not from anyone.

It was dumb luck that I'd been in Paris and able to get to her that quickly when Tad called us in. Seb was on his way, but for the moment, it was only me and Hensley. I was the only thing standing between her and whoever was trying to kill her, and I took that responsibility seriously.

"Theo?" Her voice was strong but low and I realized we'd been standing there too long. It was still quiet, but we needed to move before that changed.

I took her hand and tucked her behind my own body, keeping the gun ready in my right hand, the bag from the car slung over my shoulder.

"Let's head toward the city center for now," I whispered.

"Theo. The baker . . . he keeps his bike and his wife's bike close by. Maybe we could ride those out?" she went on.

"Good call, maybe. Let's see how light it is when we get there. I don't want us to be sitting ducks, but I'd prefer not to crawl for miles across the French countryside, bikes might be our best bet around here," I replied.

We set off hand in hand, quietly running along the stone walls and darting among the quiet, dark homes. As intense as it had been in the car, with bullets flying at them, the escape through town was uneventful.

We'd been crouching, running, jumping over stone walls and hiding for about an hour and I knew she had to be exhausted. I kept active after retiring from the Marines, had to for Titan Group, and even I was feeling it. I imagined what it had been like during the dark days of World War Two, with resistance fighters crawling all over this place. I was so damn grateful for them, and that I'd been there last night to get to Hensley.

"We're close. I can smell it," she said to me, breaking through my thoughts.

I could smell it too, and my stomach grumbled in response. There was no better smell than that of baking baguettes along the French countryside. My mouth watered, and I quickly swallowed the saliva down before I embarrassed myself. I loved being in France, for the bread alone. And the butter?! Don't even get me started on the butter. I was lead through my stomach, and in that moment, I sent up another prayer of gratitude that she'd led us to a bakery of all places. Not that the moment called for shopping, which was a kick in the nuts.

It was still dark, but not for long. We'd need to get to the safe house soon or hunker for the day. I estimated that we were less than a mile away as the crow flies, or a few miles on bikes or in a car.

The sound of an engine springing to life jolted me again and I pulled her against myself, tucking against the rough stone wall of the shop. My arms tightened around her and I felt her heart beating wildly in her chest, flush to my own. Her eyes were on mine, round and worried. I brought my hand up along her neck, under her dried hair. "Put your arms around me," I commanded against her, low enough to not be heard by anyone else. Goose bumps broke along her skin at my tone, but I couldn't help it, we needed all the luck we could get and fast.

Fear brought her arms up quickly and I wrapped her more tightly against myself, my own fingers tightening around the gun I had hidden under her sweatshirt at her back.

"Be ready to run," I said. She nodded in response, yet never flinched from the cold steel at her lower back.

Tense moments wrapped around us, both of us held still and alert as I watched. I wanted her behind me, with my body between her and whatever was coming, but there hadn't been time.

"I've got you, Hensley. I've got you," I promised, catching myself by surprise. The vehemence that had slipped past my lips was new, but I didn't have the time to explore that in my own head, not now.

The car was almost on us now, but it never slowed. It continued on about its way, ignoring the couple wrapped in a lovers embrace.

"People are getting up and around, commuters to the city," I murmured against her ear.

Her body shivered against mine before she eased away from me. I was bereft suddenly, which was odd. Like something was missing, missing from myself that I hadn't even known before her curves had been notched against my chest.

I centered myself in what I knew and whispered again, "We need to get to the house."

I explained the choices, bike or stolen car, or walking through the plentiful apple orchards between the town and the home we were heading to. Without hesitation, she agreed with me that we should keep walking. It would be easier to hide, leave less of a trail than stolen bikes or a car, and it wasn't that far. With luck, we'd make it before daylight had completely exposed us.

FIVE

HENSLEY

I COULD SEE THE FIRST EDGES OF DAWN TRYING TO BREAK OVER THE dark waves in the distance as we made our way across a little gravel lane from the apple orchard we'd snuck through. The smell of salty ocean was on the wind and I knew we were almost safe, I could feel it.

The house was large and made of stone, with the orchards around three-quarters of it, the other quarter facing the ocean. We made our way behind the home and into an attached garage, a modern touch that was clearly added sometime in the last few years. These houses had character, they did not have modern amenities. . . typically. The garage held an SUV and before I even realized that I was doing it, I'd grabbed Theo's hand and pulled him back to make a run for it.

"Hensley?" He glanced back at me, his eyes questioning.

"Theo, there's someone here," I whispered, tugging on his hand again. Fight-or-flight, and I couldn't be sure which was about to happen. So much for that safety high I'd felt moments ago on the briny air.

I'd been assured that Titan Group was the best though, and so far, they seemed to be earning that reputation honestly. Thank goodness I'd happened to run into Tad all of those months ago and even knew about them. I shuddered to think about what would have become of myself if Theo hadn't fished me out of the Channel.

Theo turned to me then. "it's okay Hensley, that's ours too," he assured me.

"Let's get you settled in. I need to check back in with Luke and get an ETA on the rest of the team arriving. We're alone here though and while you shower and rest, I'll keep you safe. Are you good? *Bien*?" His voice was low in the large garage, the silence around us cocooning us in the darkness.

"*Oui*, yes," I replied, nodding at him. He tipped his chin back at me and gently pulled me back to his side.

"How do you know this is safe?" I couldn't help but ask.

"Mila and Wills are monitoring this property real time, around the clock, back in our DC headquarters. They also have perimeter alarms and cameras positioned pretty much every-where. If someone tried to access this property, we'd know. They also send the feeds to my phone and I've been monitoring it since I picked you up to ensure all was clear. Titan Group owns the home, but through some serious layers, going all the way back to a French family. There will be nothing to tie you to this place when whoever is after you is able to regroup and come searching." His last words were ominous and as he typed in a code on the door and led me through a dark entry way, he continued.

"If this is an act by your brother, he has the resources to ensure the job is done. They will keep coming, but they'll have to get through Titan Group. They'll have to get through me," he promised me quietly, his dark eyes solemn and yet also kind in the shadows of the home.

"Thank you. And, Theo?" He glanced back at me again when

I raised my voice in question. "I trust you. You've gotten me this far." I smiled at him.

He didn't reply to my words with anything other than a dip of his chin. He seemed uneasy with the compliment and I wondered more about Theo as a man. He'd saved me, and yet the mantle of hero didn't lay comfortably on his broad shoulders. He was both resolute in his responsibility, and simultaneously uncomfortable with praise regarding how well he did with it.

Meanwhile, I was an open book, having been completely transparent. I did trust him, completely. He was safe to me. He'd not only saved my life, he'd been calm and steady in doing it. I'd have to think more about that later. For now, I needed warmth and sleep, maybe not in that order.

We made our way farther inside, Theo re-arming the security system as we did so. He showed me around the home and then left me in a stunning bedroom, with windows overlooking the ocean on one wall and the orchards on another. I almost wept at the chance to grab a shower and some rest while he checked in with his team. The hot water was divine after the first stinging rush of warmth to my frigid skin and I stayed under the spray until my fingertips puckered and shriveled with it. I was drained, yet weirdly alive. I couldn't let my brain go to Adrien yet though, my heart wasn't ready.

But Theo? My brain certainly had gone there. He was easier to focus on. When choosing between trying to understand who my brother had become, a man willing to kill his own sister, or the handsome Theo who had plucked me from the ocean, my brain chose Theo. It was a pretty easy choice, really. He felt safe, familiar even. As if a part of myself had reconnected to the mainframe. Both expected and a relief, complete. That was likely the realization that I'd somehow survived the blast clutching on to my savior more than anything, yet I'd take it for now.

Theo was gorgeous, which hadn't hurt the appeal. I shivered

again under the spray of hot water, my body remembering being held against him, my heart racing against his muscular chest. The faint scent of saltwater clinging to the tan skin of his neck as I'd brought my arms up around him.

I'd be embarrassed to admit it to anyone, but I had barely registered the cold press of the gun against my back when we thought we may have been caught in that alley by the bakery. My heart pounded in fear first, and then after the danger had passed, it was an exhilarating thud of being held against him. Theo was solid muscle, and my body reacted the way any woman's would have, but it was his words that had most ensnared me.

"I've got you," he'd promised. His words had been murmured against the shell of my ear, the sensitive skin tingling with them, yet they'd reverberated throughout me. He had me. Was it the words or the actual promise that had caused the reaction within me? I wasn't sure yet. It had been a very long time since anyone had *had* me, kept me safe, made a promise to me. In my role, with the family background I had, people didn't tend to think about my safety, my well-being, they simply assumed I'd take care of myself. Appropriately, and yet even the most powerful and self-sufficient among us wanted to be cared for at certain points in life. I thought so anyway, I knew I did. I wanted to be both a boss lady and a passenger princess sometimes and yet, life had taught me the hard way that I only had myself to rely on.

And, I'd never met a man who had that underlying power, the drive to take care of me in the most primal of ways, to have me, have my back. Most men I dated or worked with were smooth finance types. Old money, polished, calculating. Considering of me in a way that made it clear they were interested in what I could do for them or their company, never in a way that indicated I was anything more than a pretty chess piece. That had all been fine with me, because I knew how to manage guys like that without them being any wiser to being managed.

I knew rationally that I was Theo's job right now, and that this hadn't been a first date with some adventure mixed in. This was a deadly puzzle, an escape I had barely made. The memory of my throat closing in from the smoke on my beloved boat, the flames licking at my ankles closed in on me swiftly. I dropped my forehead to the cool marble of the expansive shower wall, forcing myself to push air out of my lips, to fight through the terror the memories were bringing. I tried to think of happier times, yet my mind continued on to Theo again, being held in his arms, his eyes locked on mine. I held onto that image in my mind, his eyes steady on my own, his arms banded around my back. My breathing became deeper, more regulated, evened out. The image of him, affixed in my mind being the anchor of safety, the hamlet in the storm I'd needed to bring myself to center. I took another deep gulp of air, let the terror wash off my warmed body and watched it circle into the drain, mentally picturing it sinking away before turning the water off.

Stepping out through the glass door, I grabbed the fluffy towel on the counter, seeing myself in the mirror above the beautiful countertop. The bathroom was warm and stunning in a simple way, common for renovated homes along the Normandy coast. Warm marbles, brass fixtures, fresh soaps, plush towels, all the luxuries that I'd always been surrounded by, thanks to my family wealth. My return to this place, this home place where I was most rooted, had been unlike any other return, and yet I was at home. This was the place in the world where I most felt the love of my family, the legacy of my parents and grandparents.

Comforted in what that legacy was, and what it was not, no matter what Adrien tried, I re-dressed in Theo's sweats and sweatshirt. I even found some fuzzy socks for my poor feet, which Theo had left on the bed of the room he'd shown me to earlier, adjacent to the bathroom. He must have circled back while I was in the shower and left them, because they hadn't been there earlier. A smile tugged at the corners of my mouth,

Theo was certainly thoughtful in addition to being gorgeous. A delicious combo for any woman, I was sure.

I crossed the warm hardwood floors, across a thick wool rug, to the windows facing the ocean. Dawn had made its way across the waves, sending millions of sparkles across the water outside of my window. This was the land of wild waves, low stone hedges, apple trees, fresh butter, salty skin. This was where I felt most alive, most myself, most at home. I knew that I couldn't go to my actual family home here in this region, closer to Bayeux and the beach the Americans called Omaha Beach. I'd anchored farther away, closer to "Sword Beach," on purpose. I had hoped that putting a few towns, beaches and miles between my home and myself would be enough to stay hidden from Adrien, but he must have remembered the boat and guessed at where I would dock.

We'd hidden in and crept throughout the ancient village of Bernières-sur-Mer, an arrondissement of Caen, in the Calvados department of Normandy. I had spent time there growing up, the bakery one of my *Gigi's* favorites, the fresh tarte tatin a favorite of our family. Everyone made tarte tatin there, but the bakery in Bernières-sur-Mer made the best. There had also been a farmer down the road, closer to Courseulles-sur-Mer, who made the best Calvados, the apple liquor indigenous to the area. I loved this place. I loved everything about it, the history, the history of my family, the people, the air, it was part me of. The terroir that made me, like that of great wines throughout history. All of it. And now, it had become my hiding spot, apparently. I intended to be buried here, with my parents and grandparents someday, hopefully not soon, even if that could have easily been the outcome of the last twenty-four hours. My home could have been the last place I came to when I fled London. My family legacy could have began here and died here.

I hated that thought. I didn't want to lose another piece of myself to Adrien's madness and protecting what our parents, grandparents and great great-grandparents had built was too important. I wanted to survive this and be able to come home again safely, and not consider this area too painful. It seemed to me then, there was only one way to do that, and that was with the help of the man downstairs in this gorgeous hideaway. Theo.

With that thought, I made my way back down the stairs of the beautiful stone châteaux, searching for my somber hero.

SIX

THEO

I'D HEARD THE SHOWER SHUT OFF IN THE BATHROOM ON THE FLOOR above me while I caught up with Luke. I had the computer screen propped up on the marble kitchen countertop in front of me, his face as clear as if he was standing next to me. This place was insanely beautiful, and like everything Luke touched, top of the line. I ran my hands through my dark hair while Luke dialed in Seb. Luke had been my commanding officer in the Marines, and now he and Tad led Titan Group, where we all worked now. Luke was leading this op from our command center in DC, and Tad was already en route to London. He should be there or close by now.

Titan Group had been formed last year, when Tad had tapped into his family contacts to secure a partnership with the president, the CIA, the FBI, the police and Homeland Security. We were a private company that could handle the delicate areas that the alphabet soup could not, go where the president couldn't necessarily send people. We did protection for some, extraction for some, delicate spy work for others. We weren't mercenaries, but we were private contractors with practically unlimited resources thanks to Luke's prowess with numbers and smart investing back when we were all active duty.

We'd been Raiders, a special forces division of the Marines, something that I had wanted to be ever since I could remember. Tad was Luke's second-in-command, and I was the baby of the group. Frankly, I didn't know why they kept me as part of the team. Not after what I did, or rather, had failed to do on that last mission. But they had, and I wasn't going to fuck it up again, not for these guys. They, along with my family back home in Brooklyn, were everything to me.

We'd had a hell of a first year in business with Titan, with a hard launch of one of my teammate's and brother in arms rescuing Violet, an old friend of Luke's, after she stumbled into an international shit show of weapons being sold on the black market. Luke, Violet, and even Max had been injured in that fiasco, and no sooner had everyone healed, then Hazel, Violet's sister, also found herself in the middle of a clusterfuck of epic proportions.

Thankfully, Titan Group had not only worked to save Hazel, but Luke had also pulled his head out of his own ass and married Hazel. Finally. Those two had been in their own way long enough. I smiled at the memory of Luke proposing to Hazel for the first time, on his yacht, during the height of that clusterfuck.

She'd said yes, thankfully and unsurprisingly. She'd been stupidly gone for my brother from another mother too, both too deep into their own pain that it had taken all of us to wake those two up to their big kid feelings. Those Burke sisters had my "brothers" wrapped up tight, and those guys loved it. In that moment, something new flashed through my mind, my heart clenching painfully. What was that feeling?

Fuck, was it jealousy? Was I jealous of what Luke and Max had found? Jealous of Vi and Hazey's incredible love? I'd never felt even an ounce of jealousy before, ever. Even before, back when my claim to fame was being the ladies' man of the team,

I'd never met anyone who inspired a single ounce of jealousy. Jealousy meant possession and belonging, which fuck . . . I definitely did not deserve.

I was bone tired all of a sudden, a weariness that caught me off guard, sending thoughts of jealousy scattering. I was enraged on Hensley's behalf. Her own brother. The only family she had left in the world and he'd tried to kill her? Fuck! I wanted to fly to London, to that asshole's office and beat the shit out of him, slowly. Then, I'd let Hensley decide what should be done with his battered and broken body.

"Theo, my man, you look flushed, you good?" Luke answered the video call with the question, interrupting my daydreams of bloodlust.

"You are a grumpy Casanova today," Seb added, joining in from a third line.

These two, I rolled my eyes at them. These guys—my brothers in arms who had become actual brothers to me—were relentless. They were also supremely intelligent, highly trained warriors who could read me like a book. We were all trained to read people, but I was the youngest and, like the youngest in a group of brothers, they always knew what I was thinking. And of course, how to pick at whatever was bothering me. They'd also spent the last two years trying to tease me back into humor, but I'd yet to take the bait. No sir, no more laughter for me when the others were six feet under. I was getting angry again, good. As far as fuel to do better went, I'd found that self-loathing was high up there and I needed it. Without it, I didn't know how to keep going.

"I am grumpy. I mean, her own fucking brother is trying to kill her?" I asked rhetorically, the anger making me sharp. "Seriously, what the fuck is happening in the world when you're not safe from your own flesh and blood?" I asked again. It was also another rhetorical question, obviously, but damn, I was mad on her behalf. Where I came from, family was everything. My brain couldn't wrap around a man harming anyone, let alone their own sister. I loved my sisters more than anything. I'd kill for them every single day. Even when I kinda wanted to strangle them myself because older sisters were a pain in the ass sometimes.

"Theo, we get you. We're going to take care of it. Geez, man, you're off your game this morning. Where is our smooth, charming operator?" Seb asked me.

"He's pissed, and he's not smooth, not anymore. He had to fish Hensley out of the English Channel, give her mouth to mouth and hope she didn't freeze to death. And that is all *after* someone tried to blow her up and *before* someone tried to run her off the road and shot at her. Her own fucking brother. Did you miss that part?" I ranted at my buddies before I took a deep breath and tried to relax my shoulders. I was referring to myself in the third person, for crying out loud. I was clearly off my game; they were right. As usual.

"Theo, we know man. But you got her, she's alive, and I'm guessing she's warm now, or getting there. The rest we'll figure out and take care of. We got this. You got this, baby bro, deep breaths. You saved her, and I knew you would," Luke said, his deep voice commanding attention from across the Atlantic. I didn't miss the part where he tried to remind me of his trust. The fucker trusted too easily.

"Is she as hot in person as she is in her photos? How was the mouth to mouth?" Seb asked, the cheeky bastard.

"She was nearly blown up in her sleep, then nearly drowned, you asshole. Have some fucking manners . . ." I snapped before I realized that I was being baited. Seb's laughter cut me off.

"Chill, bro, just wanted to understand the dynamic as much as possible," Seb soothed.

"There's no dynamic, stop being a dick. She's had an awful night, and her life will probably get worse before it gets better," I said, resolving not to be baited again. Fuck! I needed some sleep soon.

"So that's a yes; she's hot. Hotties are your specialty, Theo, you'll be fine," Seb chuckled.

Luke's eyes were crinkling at the corners, but he kept his mouth shut, thank God. Allowing himself to love Hazel fully had mellowed Luke, settled him in a way and in that moment, I was extra grateful that he kept his mouth shut.

"Tell us what your text meant from the road," Luke commanded, and I did. I relayed how I saw her boat explode, fished her out, the getaway that wasn't clean after all, what I heard when they shot at us.

"I agree with you that whoever her brother hired has some capacity here, some reach, sounds like some expertise. I'll work on that stuff. You stay focused on her."

"Ya, Baby Theo, stay focused on Hensley. Seems a hardship," Seb drawled. I flipped him off on the video feed, and he laughed again.

"Listen, let's get some sleep and regroup once Seb is there. I'm guessing you haven't slept in too long. Mila and Wills have you covered for now security-wise, and Seb is in route. Seb, what's your ETA?" Luke refocused them.

"I'll be in by 0500 tomorrow. Who else is coming over?" Seb asked. "Will we see you and Hazey?"

Luke couldn't hide his smile, nor the love in his eyes when Hazel was mentioned. "No, not unless something comes up with this that takes more than a few weeks. She is doing a book signing down in Miami and we're heading back down. We'll head back to give the team here a break, if all goes to plan. Max and Vi are staying here with Mila and Wills. Max isn't quite ready to travel anywhere yet without Vi or baby Alex, and Mila is ready to pop. Wills won't leave her side and is making us all practice hospital routes every day, as if we're all amateurs," Luke laughed.

Anyone could tell that Luke loved his team, we were his family. Found family and literal family as his wife Hazel was Max's wife Violet's younger sister. Luke was officially an uncle to baby Alex, the first baby for our team, named after one of our lost teammates from that last mission in the Marines, and Max's literal brother. It was a tangled familial web, and we loved it like that, even if it broke my heart to see Max holding his son. How could it not break me to know that I was the reason Max was holding his son, without his brother Alex there to congratulate him? I'd caused that, Alex's death was on me, as were the others.

I understood that these guys wouldn't let me wither away quietly on my own, even when that was what I absolutely deserved. Titan Group was our business, but it was our family too. When Violet and then Hazel had been in trouble and needed us, it had been second nature to treat them like my sisters back home, the last little piece of who I used to be coming through. There was something about those ladies that made them family from the moment I had met them.

Business-wise, we were booming. Our wealth had allowed us to build whatever we wanted, and our connections respected how we did business. Sometimes, like now when I was bone tired, I simply couldn't fathom how my team let me stay as part of them. Forgiveness wasn't something I planned on giving myself, ever.

"Nate is with Tad in London following up on Hensley's brother, and Brian is heading your way, but he's not wheels up until early morning our time. He'll be about seven hours after you, Seb. You good until then?" Luke asked, his words jarring me out of my self-loathing momentarily.

"Ya man, all good," Seb replied. "Better go though if I want to stay on schedule. Get some rest, baby bro." He winked at us both and clicked off.

"Theo, I'm working with Interpol, and they're already heading to canvas town to see what they can find from whoever chased you. Great observation on the silencer. Now, get some rest and get warm. Take it easy, man. Call if you need help, but rest easy. We've got you and Hensley covered," Luke assured me and then clicked off as well.

I shut the laptop and leaned back on the stool I'd pulled up to the island, the kitchen quiet around me. I truly did need some rack time. I was getting disoriented and outrageously protective of my charge, that new sensation wiped me out. I worked to keep my brain centered on what I deserved and what I didn't. I didn't deserve moments of belonging with the gorgeous and smart Hensley, no matter how brief those moments were in my mind.

My eyes were gritty, and I rubbed them as I reached for the remote control for the TV. I'd go after that warm shower as soon as I saw the news coverage to see what they were reporting. I knew Wills and Mila had us covered, and I trusted that with my life, yet I had to check it before I got any sleep. I was surprised the chase and the bullets from earlier hadn't hit the news, but I suppose it had only been a few hours and maybe the villagers had slept through most of it.

I'd just clicked the TV on when I saw Hensley come around the corner into the living room. I sat up straighter. She'd showered and changed back into my sweats and a sweatshirt. Both were swallowing her smaller frame up, and I felt that rise of protectiveness again, along with a surge of pleasure at seeing her in my things. Shutting that thought down almost as fast as I had it, I tried to smile at her in a way that didn't make me seem a creepy fucker, but the motions were rusty.

"Are you okay?" I asked as I watched her sink into the couch. She folded her legs underneath herself and grabbed the blanket from the back of the couch, pulling it around her shoulders.

"For being on the run, having my boat blown to smithereens and then fished out of a frigid ocean, I guess okay," she replied. Her tone had been even, yet only the edge of her smile ticked up again. My God, the woman had grit.

My mouth twitched at the corners with the beginnings of a real smile, and the shattering of that rust falling away from my face. I'm sure I resembled the Tin Man, creaking at the laugh lines. "You forgot to mention the car chase, and the shots fired at you. And that we sadly, didn't get to eat at that bakery." This inexplicable need to put her at ease rattled around in my chest after the last words spilled out, a teasing note about the bread, when I hadn't even tried teasing anyone in a long time.

"Oh, I didn't forget those; don't worry about that. It's all very vivid in my mind. Focusing on that bakery is my saving grace right now, as are you. Thank you, Theo. I don't know what I would have done without you. I guess I'd be at the bottom of the English Channel by now. Adrien would have won." Her voice had died off in strength as she finished her words, the realization that she would likely be dead, by her own brother's hand, catching up to her.

"Hensley, it's okay, I've got you," I said, reaching a hand out to her inadvertently.

The words seemed to settle her, and she clutched onto my outstretched hand. It had been a reflexive gesture on my part to reach out, one I didn't remember ever having before, and again, I felt stilted in my movements.

"What do we do now?" she asked. A sheen of sheer determination had steeled across her eyes, yet I also saw the events of nearly drowning, and then creeping miles to safety, pulling at her.

"We should check the news stations and then we could head to bed. Separately. We could both head to our own beds." I snorted to myself. Even my internal thoughts were jumbled around her right now. So smooth, buddy, so smooth. I settled her closer to me from where our hands were joined, not quite ready to give up that which I did not deserve.

SEVEN

HENSLEY

"Now, we check the news to see what they're saying. Then, we get some sleep." His deep voice rumbled out. He was rumpled, and it dawned on me that he hadn't showered yet. He'd pulled me against his side, and the chill of his skin against my own warmth made me shiver.

"You must be freezing!" I couldn't believe that he'd been down here this entire time and hadn't yet gotten warm. I jumped up from the couch as gracefully as I could while all wrapped in baggy sweats and reached over to him to settle the blanket around his broad shoulders. He was slow with tiredness, and before I realized it, I had clucked at him like my *Gigi* used to do to me, and pulled the blanket more tightly around him. That seemed to snap him out of his trance, and he peered up right before I sat back down, a soft smile on his face, with a touch of something else. Confusion most likely. I'd acted before I had thought it through. He didn't need me smothering him and clucking around like a grandparent would.

"It's all good, Hensley, but thank you," he said, right as shivers coursed through his solid frame, belying his words.

"I need to check the news reports and see if they are saying anything, see if any of the people they catch on TV seem interesting. Whoever did this is likely back there, watching." He nodded toward the screen as he hit the volume. I had more questions about that, but it was clear he wanted to listen to the newscaster at that moment, so I turned toward the screen also and settled into the cozy couch. Theo hit the volume to crank it up and then reached over and clicked on another remote. The fireplace roared to life, a wash of heat whispered across my skin. I flashed him a smile of gratitude before refocusing on the news. This was the first time tonight that rush the heat of flames was a relief to me, not scary. Chills rattled me at that thought. Damn Adrien.

On the TV, French newscasters spoke rapid-fire about the explosion, detailing that a woman had been seen on the boat the previous evening. So far, my name hadn't been released, but it was a matter of time.

The news flashed to eyewitnesses, one saying that they had seen the woman earlier in the evening on the deck of the boat. The eyewitness cried then, lamenting the life lost.

The report switched back to the reporters, and I saw Theo's thumbs flying across his phone.

"Should we be doing anything right now?" I asked, curious as to who he was texting at this particular moment.

"Not really. We need to rest, retreat now to advance later. Seb is heading our way, as is Brian. We've got about twenty-four hours before Seb will get here, and there isn't much we can do right now anyway with everyone in transit. We're safe. Wills is manning the comms at home, Mila has taken over the cameras around the harbor and through Bernières-sur-Mer, and they'll log everyone in that area. Luke is connected with the local police and our partners at Interpol, so really, we need to focus on rest now." He rubbed at his eyes after he finished the report, the litany of names he rattled off long. Before I could ask, he continued.

"I'm going to go take a hot shower and then hit the rack. You should get some rest too. You've been through hell," he told me.

"I want to watch a bit more TV if that's okay. My brain is buzzing right now," I replied. I was somewhat fascinated by the news report about myself playing out across the screen.

"Of course, you know your own body best, but please promise me you'll get me if you need anything, and that you'll allow yourself to rest when you can." He stood and brought the blanket back to me. He handed it to me, smiled and then also handed me the TV remote. "You're safe here, Hensley. I'll be close if you need me."

"Thanks, Theo Rossi. Thanks for fishing me out of the Channel and bringing me here. Thanks for being an awesome getaway driver and for getting me here alive," I replied. I kept my tone light, as he'd shrugged off my gratitude earlier. I couldn't *not* say it again though; the man had come through.

"Just your normal workday at Titan Group." He laughed awkwardly, and I was reminded that this was his job. I'd been practically stalked and almost murdered, my gorgeous boat blown to bits, and he was simply doing his job. I was his job, as cozy as this felt in the moment, and as kind as his words were. I nodded at him and refocused on the TV, settling in to see what the news reports of my death were saying.

EIGHT

THEO

Making up my mind, I retreated to the bedroom I'd left my stuff in earlier and turned on the hot water in the adjacent bathroom. The space was quiet in its luxury, typical for anything Luke provisioned.

I needed to get some space, and to get warm. The guys weren't wrong with their teasing of me being a ladies' man, but those days felt like a lifetime ago.

In the before times, I'd never met a woman to challenge that, and I loved women. I had a brilliant mom, older sisters who were both incredibly smart, accomplished, and married. I was the youngest, the baby, the only boy, and the most spoiled kid in the family. I'd been raised as my dad's shadow, in a tight-knit Italian family in Brooklyn, with all the stereotypes that come along with it. Mostly, a huge family who were always in each other's business. I'd never dated anyone seriously, and I'd never had any intentions of changing that.

I'd joined the Marines as early as I could, following in my grandfather's footsteps, and now I had Titan Group. We'd gone all over the world in pursuit of the shit that kept my family, along with all other Americans back at home, safe. I didn't know the connection between Tad and Hensley, or what Hensley would do when we got her through this danger, but I couldn't be part of that.

For a moment there, I may have even had tiny stirrings of jealousy when I thought of Luke and Hazel, or Vi and Max. Even Wills and Mila could be pretty wrapped up in each other to the exclusion of all others, and they were always thinking about how to include others in their lives. My mind turned contemplative at those images of love, but I pushed them out as fast as I could. I wasn't the jealous type. Never had been, never would be. I had lost the right to those feelings two years ago in a hellscape of my own making.

I went through the motions of a hot shower, letting the heat release the knotted muscles in my corded neck and shoulders and the steam work through my jumbled thoughts. I stayed there with the hot water raining down until my fingertips were shriveled. I re-dressed in sweats and decided to check in on Hensley again before getting in bed. Retracing my steps to the living room, I found her there, curled up on the couch, wrapped in the blanket she'd tucked around me earlier. She was sound asleep. Who could blame her?

I turned around to head back to my room, yet something pulled at me again. She might wake up scared. We could have been tracked after all. Regardless of how I tried to rationalize it, I felt it in my belly. I wasn't leaving her side right now. Mind made up, I turned toward her again.

There was a basket of blankets by the fireplace, and I grabbed another one for myself and stretched out on the other couch in the space. The fire had worked to warm the space up, and snagging the remote from where she'd left it on the coffee table, I turned the volume down and watched the newscast. It was mostly repeating itself, but I watched until I couldn't keep my eyes open.

Hours later, I smelled the shift in the house before I saw it.

Hensley must be up; the aromas coming from the kitchen were heavenly, and I knew I hadn't slept long enough for Seb to be here yet.

I stopped by the bathroom to freshen up and then followed my nose to whatever she had cooking.

"*Bonjour*, Theo," she said as I walked into the kitchen. "Are you hungry?"

She expertly flipped the omelet she'd been working on and slid it onto a waiting plate. She'd already made a salad, and the tossed greens were dressed in a light vinaigrette. I loved that about France. The perfect omelet always had a fresh, herbaceous salad with it. Also, it typically had a crusty baguette, but it wasn't as if she could bop down into the village to grab one. Damn shame too, bread was my favorite food group and my stomach growled at what was laid out before me. She slid the plate in front of a stool at the kitchen counter, right next to her own. Thank goodness that, as usual, Luke had provisioned this house ahead of our arrival. Having an ungodly amount of money allowed him to keep safe houses all over the world, and to be able to have them fully operational at a moment's notice.

"This smells incredible, Hensley, thank you," I tossed her way as I beelined for the espresso machine and pushed a few buttons to see it whir to life. "Espresso?" I asked her.

"Yes please, I'd do another. Lord knows I need all the fortitude I can get right now," she replied.

"Tell me something about you. Not about what is happening. We'll get to that. Tell me something only about you." The words slipped out as I handed her the hot little cup. Obviously, I needed to know more about her for this mission, but telling myself it was all about the mission was lying to myself, a tiny bit.

"Hmmm, something not related to my attempted murder, okay. Let me think." Another tick upward of her lips. I watched her face for that little tick more and more. Not an outright smile, just the ticking upward of her soft lips.

"I love to snow ski, swim, eat great food, read mysteries, travel, you know . . . all the basic stuff," she said. "What about you? Who is Theo Rossi?"

"Turnabout is fair play, I suppose. I love all of the same things. I also love to dive, and I'm a mean chess player," I said, shoving another forkful in my mouth. I groaned; this woman could cook. Damn, I loved people who could cook. I took another drink of my espresso and cut myself off from telling her any more about myself.

"And what about your family? You know all about mine. Tell me about yours," she said between bites of her own.

"Oh, you know, also pretty basic. I'm the baby, the only boy, two older sisters. Big Italian family, lots of cousins in my business all the time. Aunts and uncles who ask inappropriate questions, parents who grill me anytime I'm home," I replied easily. My family was the easiest part of myself to talk about. God knows I had enough of them to keep me busy. I had cousins everywhere.

"And where is home?" she asked.

"Born and raised in Brooklyn, but I joined the Marines years ago and now call DC home. It's where we have our base," I said. I decided to tell her more about Titan Group, our team, Vi and Hazey. She asked more about my family, and I gave in and told her that my family all still called me 'Baby Theo,' much to her amusement.

We talked more about her hobbies, her work, where she wanted to travel to, where she'd been that she loved. It went unspoken that we wouldn't talk about the explosion or any of those things yet. I could tell she was grateful that we didn't have to dig into those areas right away, and it felt good to be able to give her these moments of normalcy, even if I was tracking potential threads to pull later. I couldn't help myself. I was grilling her, sure, yet I wanted to know for my own sake too, and that shit was disconcerting.

I knew my team too; they were working around the clock,

and my focus for the time being was Hensley. I genuinely wanted to know her more, curiosity about her life making me more talkative than I should have been. I needed to know her more, not only for the sake of my job, but for something niggling within me.

"Tell me more about you—what about you that isn't in your files?" I asked.

That got a laugh out of her. "Oh, there are many things about me that aren't on paper. I think so anyway. I hope! If my entire existence can be read in a file while you are on the move, I need to do some more living," she said, her features animated. She had a fair point there.

"Okay, tell me something I won't read." I wasn't even sure why I pressed. It was intimate and deeply personal, yet I couldn't help myself. My brain kept reminding me that I didn't get to care, and yet, I wanted to. The need to know every complication in her life was pushing me, the dissonance of wanting to know more and not wanting to know more warring within me. Curiosity won out.

She turned more fully to me then, took me in with a more serious study. "I'm restless. There is something missing in my life, and yet I worry that I'm not stewarding my family legacy as I should." She shrugged her shoulders then, stopping herself from saying more. Her shrug popped the bubble of intimacy created there at the kitchen counter. She jumped up from her stool and gathered both plates and headed toward the sink.

"I'll get those. You cooked, I clean. That's how it works," I said as I stood too.

"Okay, when did you say that Sebastian will get here?" she asked.

"Not until the wee hours tomorrow morning, sometime before 0500," I replied, already busy washing the dishes. "We have another handful of hours before we need to check in with the team, so we have some free time."

"If it's okay, I think I'll take another shower and then lie down. I woke up with a headache, and no matter what I do, I can't get warm," she said.

I should have thought about that. Of course, she had a headache.

"Of course. Get some more rest and some warmth. You're safe here, I promise you. Do you need anything for your head?"

She declined and headed up to her own room and adjacent shower. After she left the room, I turned back to finish the dishes and then wandered to the windows overlooking the ocean.

I loved the ocean. I could spend all day watching those waves and, as always, they allowed me to regroup. Hensley was something else. My response to her was immediate, and I allowed myself to think about her more without reminding myself I couldn't care. For a few moments, I'd allow myself the luxury of thinking about her.

I hated that she had a headache though, and I suspected that it was more than just a headache. She'd opened up and then withdrawn again. Rightfully so, I'd asked a deeply personal question, and she'd been brave to answer it honestly. What was it about this woman? I couldn't seem to stop myself from digging in with her. I wanted to know her, about her life, about her. The stuff I wouldn't read in a file.

Shit, that was enough of that. Luxury time over.

I re-checked the perimeter, stopping to gather a handful of apples from one of the trees in the orchard along the west of the property. Coming back into the house, I dumped them into a worn wooden bowl on the kitchen counter. Nothing beat fresh Normandy apples, except the bread-and butter-course.

I pulled up the video feeds and reviewed them all again before deciding to check on Hensley. Only when I got closer to the door of the room I'd shown her to earlier, I heard crying. Shit. I knocked softly, but there was no answer. I opened the door, poking my head through so I wouldn't scare her. I didn't even get a chance to say her name again before she cried out, in the throes of a nightmare.

I was across the floor and dipping into the cozy bed before my brain caught up with my body. Her pain called to me, to soothe, to protect. Pulling her against me, I ran my hands up and down her back, whispering to her as softly as I could.

"I've got you. It's okay. You're safe. No one will ever hurt you again. Shhhhh. I've got you," I repeated the mantra over and over again until she settled against me finally. She notched against me in her sleep, her face skimming my neck. Little puffs of her breath were hot on my skin and her arms snuggled into me, her tears drying on her pale cheeks. Something inside of me broke loose at that. This courageous woman, who had fled her own offices, her own family and stared down death, fit perfectly against me. Before I could talk myself out of it, I dropped a kiss to her downy head and closed my own eyes, feeling for the first time, utter peace. The blankets were soft and airy around us. She was pressed against my body, and I knew we were safe. It all felt too good, too perfect for a guy like me.

I forced myself to disentangle my arms from where they'd held her, but as I did so, she snuggled more deeply into me.

"*S'il vous plaît, restez,*" she whispered against my throat.

So, I did. I stayed.

NINE

THE SUNSHINE WAS WARM ON MY BODY, A TINKLING OF LAUGHTER floating to me on the salty breeze, bringing a small smile to my own face. I was happy, content, warm, cherished. I burrowed into my chair deeper, inhaling the scented air, with the strong arms of a man wrapping me more tightly to his hard chest. The trees were rustling overhead, their shade playing peekaboo with the sun across my heavy limbs. I was joyful, in that glorious way you are when you've played in the waves all day with someone you love and the salt water has dried against your skin and happiness wafts off you.

I tightened my arms around him and turned my face into his chest to press a kiss there. I nuzzled my nose along his warmth, my lips coasting up from his muscled pec to his neck, placing little kisses as I went. His face was scruffy, and he growled my name against my lips. I smiled and kissed him again before dragging the tip of my nose down his strong jaw. His hardness was pressed against my belly, and my core tightened in longing.

"Hensley, sweetheart, this is the best way to wake up, but um, if you keep that up I am going to embarrass myself." The man's rough voice rumbled across my sensitive skin, jarring me awake.

"Theo! *Mon Dieu, je regrette, merde alors.*" I sat up, his arms falling away from my body and my heart racing. Shit. That had been some dream. Wow.

Mortified, I risked a peek down at him. He was rumpled and sexy in the late afternoon sunlight breaking through the drapes, pillowy blankets rumpled around his lean hips, a sharp vee of muscle disappearing into the wrinkle of blankets. The scruff on his face needed shaving, his dark hair was sticking all over the place as if I'd been running my hands through it. His gorgeous, tanned chest was naked down to the waistband of a pair of gray sweatpants. I gulped. Holy Mother of God. I'd woken up to a deity in my bed. A man mere mortals would envy. I almost wished I could go back to sleep, to get back to that dream. He reached his arm up, his bicep bulging as he pushed my hair away from my face and lightly grasped my arm, as if to ground me.

"I'm sorry, Hensley. You were having a bad dream, and I couldn't leave you. Once you settled in, I tried to leave, but you asked me to stay, and well . . . I stayed." His eyes were contrite, earnest for me to understand. There was something else there too. I just couldn't put my finger on it.

"Nothing happened, I promise. I got hot and had to take off my shirt." He was nervous, anxious for it to be okay with me. He was taking all the responsibility when it had been me, all along. This handsome man was doing everything he could to put me at ease. Was there anything sexier than a man who faced responsibility directly? It hadn't even been his to face, and yet there he was, trying to shoulder that for me. *Mon Dieu*, that was sexy as hell. A flare of heat hit me hard.

"*Merci*, Theo. Thank you for being with me and not leaving." I met his eyes, determined to make light of the awkwardness I'd inadvertently created. "It was me, *vraiment*."

I laughed lightly then and gently smacked his tattooed chest, right above his heart. "Is this the Titan Group full-service package?" I joked, attempting to ease the tension I'd caused.

He laughed with me, and then a flash of distress crossed his handsome face. "This isn't a normal thing for me, Hensley. I'm sorry, but not that sorry. . ." He trailed off. "It was a hell of a great way to wake up."

He smiled at me then fully, and it transformed his already handsome face into something that would make the angels weep.

He tugged me back down and tucked me into his warm body. I'd known this man for slightly less than twenty-four hours but was content in his arms. I fit there perfectly, and he gently squeezed his arms around me in comfort for a few moments before he eased from the bed.

Studying me, I saw deep hurt in his beautiful eyes before they cleared into determination. Interesting.

"We better get around and start working on figuring out what's going on," he said, his voice still raspy with sleep. *Mon Dieu*, the man was sexy. And I'd been all over him! I waited for embarrassment to take over again, but before it could, he reached down from where he was now standing at the side of the bed and gently lifted my chin up with his larger hand.

"Hell of a way to wake up, Hensley, the best." The rough pads of his fingertips trailed along the smooth skin of my jaw, and he stepped back. "I'm going to my room to take a ridiculously cold shower and get dressed. Titan Group will have provisioned clothes for you, which will be in the dresser. Pick anything you want. It is all for you. Our team always plans well, so you should have great options."

With that, he silently left the room, the muscles in his toned back rippling as I watched him walk away, those gray pants sitting low on his hip bones. So freaking sexy. His muscles had muscles. I regretted waking up if it meant an end to what I'd been dreaming about and the start of sharing how we'd ended up in that bed together in the first place.

Deep down in my heart, I knew it was time, though. Time to sink into the tangle of my life and begin digging my way out, if there was a way out. I had let myself compartmentalize with the handsome Theo for long enough. He'd been good to me and it was easy with him, yet I knew this was his work. Sure, it may have gotten cozy there for a bit, but I knew Theo's type and knew that I was a file to him, one he would be glad to close once we got through whatever this was.

My reality was that I had only myself to depend on. Life had taught me that the hard way many, many times before, and I was exhausted from being slapped in the face with it. I may have been surrounded by luxury and until last year, loved by aging grandparents, but I also knew, deep within myself, that no one had lined up to be my person, the guy who would never let me down. My grandparents had it in each other, my parents had too, yet for me. . . I had only myself to truly rely on.

I steeled myself against the familiar flash of hurt that camped in the pit of my belly at the reminder and hopped in another quick shower to wake myself up more. At the rate I was showering, I'd run this house out of hot water if we stayed here too long, but it gave me the peace I'd been craving since going over the side of my boat. The peace that had been wrapped up in Theo, however fleeting it may have been.

TEN

THEO

I had to get out of that bed and out of that room before I lost my mind even more than I already had. Before I embarrassed myself or forgot for another moment that the serenity in her arms wasn't for me.

I was rock hard, my cock aching to stay in bed with the luscious Hensley. I forced myself into a frigid shower, trying to block all thoughts of her hair tangled around her gorgeous face, her lips puffy and skittering across my chest, up my neck, along my jaw. I cranked the water to the coldest setting I could and tried to picture anything at all that didn't entail dreaming about Hensley being in that shower with me. Talk about mission impossible.

After my second shower of the day and getting dressed in more than sweats, I made my way to the kitchen. I fired up the espresso machine for both of us again and waited for her to join me, which she did pretty quickly.

She'd chosen to wear simple black leggings and a loose T-shirt with a wide, scooped neckline. The T-shirt looked soft, and the fabric was clinging to the edges of her sexy shoulders. I saw a thin, tiny strap over her shoulder and realized I'd never been jealous of a bra before. I mentally shook myself and tried to refocus. This woman was undoing me and that couldn't happen.

"Another espresso?" I handed her a fresh cup.

"*Merci*, you are an angel," she replied, reaching out gratefully for the cup.

I took a drink from my own cup and walked to the large French doors overlooking the patio, gardens and ocean. "Sit with me? I want to lay out what we know. I'll dial in the team from there," I said, motioning my head toward the patio. The faster we could get through this, the faster Hensley was safe. I wanted her to be safe. I knew that also meant that she wouldn't need me after that, and for some reason a thud of discontent with the realization settled in my chest. There was that dissonance again, who she was intriguing me, beguiling me.

Thankfully, she wordlessly nodded in agreement on having this much-needed conversation and followed me out. The gardens here were spectacular, it was clear that Titan Group paid someone well to maintain the home. We took seats in the comfortable chairs on the patio, facing the beach and ocean. The property was steps away from Juno Beach, codenamed as such by the British for Operation Overlord. The tiny hamlet was Courseulles-sur-Mer, but to the outside world, it would likely forever be Juno Beach.

There had been chatter on the beaches of Normandy finally being named UNESCO World Heritage Sites earlier this summer and frankly, I didn't understand why they hadn't been already. Juno Beach alone had seen hundreds of Canadian casualties from the Ninth Brigade on D-Day. I'd read at one point roughly 30 percent of the landing craft at Juno had been destroyed by the already partially submerged obstacles the Germans had put up, making it incredibly difficult to reach the beach. I sent up a prayer for the men who did.

Most Americans were more familiar with Omaha Beach, as it had been the deadliest, with over 2,400 US casualties during the

Allied Invasion. Omaha Beach wasn't far from us now, as the beaches of Normandy weren't terribly far from one another, connected along the northern coast of idyllic French villages.

I'd participated in the seventy-fifth anniversary D-Day reenactment back in 2019 as a paratrooper, not far from where we were at that moment. It had been one of the greatest honors of my life. Very few Marines had participated in Operation Overlord as it was primarily an Army endeavor, so it was even more special that I'd been asked to participate in that reenactment. My team had been there to support me, some of them also participating. I'd worn my great-grandfather's Purple Heart, pinned to my shirt under my gear as I'd dropped onto the French countryside.

My great grandpa had been Italian American and had fought with his American brethren. He hadn't been on Omaha that day, but he'd fought in the war. He'd been a Marine too, stationed in the Pacific. He'd shared some stories of his brothers in arms with our family, but not too many. By most accounts, the Pacific Theater of World War Two was far more brutal, with some historians saying the death toll was double that of the European Theater. My grandfather had been one of the lucky ones and there wasn't a day that goes by that I'm not grateful for that.

I rubbed my chest where my heart was, the little purple heart inked there with the initials inside of it. My family had survived, and had been lucky to be Americans by then, as they'd had a home to come home to, which not many outside of the USA could say.

I took another drink of espresso. She'd been deep in thought too, sitting next to me and I hadn't wanted to jump all over her right away, but now it was almost time to refill both of our cups. It was time.

"One cup down. Want a refill and then we should talk?" I asked her, jumping to my feet to grab her cup. She nodded, standing up too, our cups clinking together as our bodies swayed closer to one another between the chairs we'd been sitting in.

"I'll get it Hen, sit down, enjoy the sunshine for a few more minutes before we have to dive into this." I smiled at her, the nickname spilling out without thought. It fit her and she seemed to pull an easiness from me naturally. Like the guy I was before it all went to shit was hiding in me somewhere, and she was teasing him back into the light. God, I sounded dumb, even to myself.

"Hen? You sound like my *Gigi*, she called me Hen all the time. To *mon Grand-père* I was Henny or *Le Petit Coquelicot*." She was happy at the memory, thankfully. The familiarity I had with her was comfortable, yet foreign and kind of boggy ground to step on.

"I like it," she said. Her eyes were steady on mine, a tentative light shining through those pretty chocolate-colored depths.

"Good, I like it too." Instinctively, I smiled back and then briefly raised my index finger to skim her jawline before dropping it softly. I cleared my throat and went back in for another round of espresso. I'd smiled more at her in the last day than I had in the previous two years. She was my own personal siren, luring me from the sea. But luring to what? Back to myself, or to more ruin for my brothers, their wives, our lives. . . like last time?

Pushing the question aside for now, I poured us both another cup and met her back outside, taking my seat again. This time, I pulled the chair around to face her and not the ocean. It was time for me to focus, and what I was about to learn could mean life or death.

"Okay, let's bring in the team. We try to have more than one of us hear the details firsthand. Even though we are trained for details, our brains can pick up on different pieces and threads to pull," I told her, in an effort to reassure her. She nodded understandingly as I dialed.

"Theo, Hensley, hi," Max's deep voice boomed across the stillness of the afternoon. "I've got Wills here and we're ready.

Glad you're okay Hensley." I glanced over to her and saw that uptick of her lips again.

"Hi, Hensley. Hey, Theo. Glad you're okay, Hensley. Sounded like you had a rough night. Glad our boy got to you in time." Wills's voice also came across the line.

"Thank you both. I'm glad he was there too." Her voice had taken in a tinge of quiet contemplativeness and she glanced at me then, nodding her head as if to say she was ready.

"Start at the beginning," I said, as reassuringly as I could. I had the sense this was going to be messy.

ELEVEN

HENSLEY

"Right, *d'accord*. Adrien is seven years older than I am, so we've never been particularly close, as maybe other siblings would be. Our family company, Richard Companies, has always been prosperous, but in the last year, Adrien comes across as possessed. Once *Grand-père* and *Gigi* passed away, the company transitioned to both Adrien and me. My work has always been in mergers and acquisitions, and the subsequent cultural integration. Specifically, identifying organizations who want to sell the technology they've built, working through humane acquisition, and then continuing our organizational culture and maintaining our 'employees first' approach through the mergers and changes in the market as we have grown." Seeing them following what I was saying, I went on.

"My grandparents believed, as do I, that a family company meant that you should take care of all employees, as you would take care of your own family. We are all in it together, interdependent and acting with respect and affection for the humans behind the decisions." I paused, thinking back over the last couple of years before continuing. "We've always been a 'rising tide lifts all boats' family until it was only Adrien and me left. Something changed for him, especially in the last ten months. His entire personality changed, and he pushed me out of every decision he could."

"He has been solely focused on acquisition. It seems to be the only thing he cares about. He's been buying up our subcontractors so that we can raise prices on the consumers, not giving a fig about my work, and our legacy, to only partner and bring on companies that we can absorb with our model, rooted in humanity. In the meantime, almost everyone who has been with our organization for any length of time has been let go for silly things, or given negligible severance and asked to resign. It's as if I've been mopping up a bloodbath for the last year. It's not what our grandparents wanted, and it's not the vision I hold, and I have 50 percent ownership of the company."

Shame, rage, hurt, disbelief—these washed over me as Theo watched me and waited for me to continue. He regarded me too patiently, those kind, soulful eyes on my face, as if he could see the myriad of emotions coursing through me. I continued, knowing the retelling was about to get worse.

"Things have been getting unbearably tense between Adrien and me over the course of the last couple of months due to this. He has also hired additional employees and surrounds himself with these new people who only report to him, for what, I don't know. They don't talk to others. They are all men, and they all wear dark suits with weapons hidden at their backs. They are his personal security detail, but that doesn't make sense. He's never used security like that before this last year."

Theo had been watching me, yet he stopped me there. "Wouldn't it be kind of normal to have security if you lead a multibillion-dollar company dealing in tech and safety measures?" he asked.

He was right, and I back-tracked. "Yes, kind of normal, but not to this level, and it isn't something we've ever relied on. Neither of us has ever used a security detail. I've always moved about freely, and maybe in hindsight, that's pretty dumb." I certainly felt dumb when I heard the stark, albeit unspoken facts in his question.

"It's not dumb at all, just surprising for a guy like me who is always thinking about that stuff. We'll circle back to that though, please, keep going," he said, rolling his hand in that international motion for continue. I mentally added, *check into full-time security* to my list of to-dos once this fiasco was resolved, because it was obvious that I had needed it after all. Who would have thought I needed it from my own damn brother?

"Adrien thinks he's been sending me on goose chases to keep me out of his hair, but I'm onto him. I've been paying close attention to everything going on, as this is my legacy too. I've been leading mergers, acquisitions and onboarding strategically for years, and only moving forward when all the conditions were appropriate. This is the legacy that *Grand-père* and *Gigi* protected and expanded, one that our great-grandparents built after World War Two in underwater safety prevention. Family was everything to our grandparents. It is everything to me. Taking care of the people around you, making sure that we *all* win, has always been our priority. It's never been about money, acquisitions, more, more, more, more."

This was the part that enraged me. How had Adrien veered so far from our family values? So far from the legacy entrusted to us by the people who had cared for us the most, the ones who had built the wealth we enjoyed? I would be damned if this legacy was crushed on my watch.

"Last week, Adrien was working later than normal. Most of the offices in London were dark, and he thought I was in our Lyon location, as that's where I prefer to work. I had come in earlier that day to try to talk some sense into him. In my mind, we were at a breaking point. I've done everything I can to reassure employees and try to make things right, but I've been in reaction mode. It was time for me to go on the offensive, and remind him that I'm an equal partner and that I lead that area.

I'd had enough." Equals, like our grandparents had intended, and respect for each other's roles in the organization.

"I decided it would be best to approach him after hours, because lately his goon squad is always surrounding him. Thankfully, you can get from anywhere in France to most places in the UK pretty fast with the TGV." I wasn't sure if he knew much about the TGV, the Train of Grande Vitesse, but it seemed he understood what I was saying.

"These men terrify me, and I have to think that's the entire point. Again, I know they're carrying weapons underneath their suit jackets, and I know many of them are former military from different countries, mercenaries or hired killers. I don't know which because they never speak to anyone but Adrien. It's obvious in how they move and the tattoos I've seen on their wrists and hands. I've heard them speak several Slavic languages, maybe even Greek, I don't know. I don't understand why he'd surround himself with armed guards if he wasn't into something he shouldn't be. I don't understand any of it—the new security that is clearly not from anywhere around us, why he needs it at all, why his focus shifted." At that point, I grimaced. "I also don't trust that he hasn't been having me followed. For the last few weeks, something has felt off in my gut. Every corner of Lyon, where I've been living, has a sense of bad energy recently."

I took another deep breath. I could hear my own voice getting higher, and my heart rate was climbing in my agitation. I couldn't believe this was my life right now, and that this was truly my story to tell. About my own brother, my own company.

"Two days ago, I approached Adrien's office. It was late on the nineteenth, maybe 10:45 p.m. As I got closer, I noticed that he wasn't alone. Because the lights were off in the offices around him, he didn't see me coming. Something in my gut made me stop. It made me pause. I don't know what it was. This is my brother, in an office I know like my own home. But I did stop, and I eavesdropped. I'm not proud of myself, but I think I overheard something that led to them trying to kill me."

Hot tears gathered in the corners of my eyes, and my throat grew tight. Saying the words out loud gave them such a weight, a realness that stunned me. I knew it to be true, and yet that weight was almost more than I could bear. Swallowing the knot of hurt lodged in my throat, I went on.

"My own brother tried to kill me. We aren't close, and I know we haven't been close for a long time, but to kill me?" I was shaking, my words incredulous to my own ears. "But it has to be him—there is no other explanation."

"Hensley, he can't hurt you now. I've got you, sweetheart. I'm here." Theo's deep voice vibrated across my skin, soothing the fire of disbelief and anger within me to a simmer.

He'd reached across the expanse between us and put his warm hand on my knee while he spoke, squeezing gently to reassure me, maybe to still the bouncing. The weight of his hand and the warmth anchored me to the moment, bringing me back from the edge of painful realities.

"Take all the time you need." His thumb rubbed circles on the inside of my knee, while his longer fingers remained still, offering comfort and that blessed warmth. I took another deep breath, closed my eyes and then inhaled deeply of the salty ocean air before slowly releasing it out.

"I overheard them talking about 'bombs right under their noses,' that night in the office. I heard the phrases 'make them pay attention' and 'won't see it coming until it's too late.'"

I opened my eyes again, waited for him to look at me, and said, "I heard them talking about 'civilian casualties.' They're going to kill people, Theo, I don't know where, how, or when. Or why."

Theo reached forward and gently hugged me. Tears I didn't know had fallen from my own eyes splashed on his neck.

"You did the right thing to get away, Hensley. I'm proud of you." He swept his arms down my back, waited for my stupid tears to subside, gave me another gentle squeeze and then sat back. When he did so that time, he gathered my hands in his, and kept his eyes trained on mine. His steadiness rooted me, bringing me into the present. I kept my focus on the hazel eyes in front of me, let them lure me, focused on the flecks of golden I saw there.

"I need you to tell us the rest. Do you need a break first?" he asked.

I shuddered, but my voice was resolute when I spoke. I refused to let this break me. Theo had given me the moment I needed, and now the best way to get through this was to keep pushing. I knew that. I had to keep going.

"No, I want to get through this. I can do this. I think I must've gasped, or hit something when I turned around to flee. Whatever noise they heard, I heard footsteps thundering behind me and shouting. I knew I'd never outrun that many of them, and I crouched down under a desk in one of the cubicles on the open floor and squeezed myself against the back wall of it while I pulled the chair in front of me to hide. I heard them rush by. It was quiet for a couple of minutes, but I stayed there, hoping nobody could hear me freaking out."

I was glad he held my hands in his own larger ones. His rough calluses and strength were holding me again to the present, where I was safe. Where he would help me. I continued.

"When the men chased after whatever they heard, they forgot to shut the office door. I heard Adrien pick up the phone and speak to someone. I don't know who was on the other end. Whatever the conversation was, I got snippets of him saying something about me, making sure they knew my location, and to 'Take care of it if it was a problem.' *It* being me, I think."

I gripped tightly onto Theo's hands and whispered, "I'm pretty sure I heard my own brother give the kill order for me."

TWELVE

THEO

I had to work incredibly hard not to flinch when Hensley finished her story. Normally, I could be detached while reviewing the details of the atrocities that we dealt with on a daily basis. Hell, I'd been a Marine for over a decade—a Raider to boot. I'd seen some awful things, things that I couldn't go back to in my own mind or I'd never recover. A sliver of memory floated by in my mind, threatening to take hold and drag me under. Alex telling Max to leave him in that inferno of a bombed safe house before he died in his brother's arms, all on our surveillance cams and comms as we'd tried to get there to help and couldn't. The woman that day by the coffee shop, how she'd held my attention. How my own stupid need to charm had cost me precious time, and the consequences had cost Alex his life.

I took my own deep breath. The shit memories always picked the worst times to rise in my mind, threatening to pull me under. I remembered what the team doc had said and tried to focus on replacing the ugliness trying to work its way back in with another, a happier time when Alex had called me Baby Theo after hearing my mom say it on speakerphone. Alex had always called me a Casanova too, just like Seb had called me.

I thought of little baby Alex, Max and Vi's sweet little guy back in DC, whom we all doted on as the adoring 'uncles' we were. That brought a smile to my face, and I dialed back into the present. I'd worked hard to put that shit behind me, but at the end of the day, it was forever there, part of me. I was the guy who was charmed into missing something that led to a team of guys being killed. I was that guy. Back home in DC, Doc hated it when I did that and I tried again to focus on what Hensley had said.

Hearing Hensley's story from her own lips filled me with abject rage on her behalf. I wanted to strangle her brother with my bare hands first and foremost and then take care of the rest. To hell with patience. I forced myself to calm down again, picking back up on the thread of her story.

This could also be bigger than we had originally talked about, and getting a handle on the scope was our first priority. Richard Companies owned dozens of companies. Figuring out what they were up to was going to take all of Titan Group's resources and then some.

One thing was certain; I was damn impressed with Hensley's strength. I pushed down the murderous rage that tried to steal over me again, hearing about how she'd had to hide from her own damn brother, the fear she must have had hiding on the floor of that cubicle. I hoped that when this mission wrapped, I'd have some one-on-one time with Adrien Richard. Brothers were supposed to protect sisters. That was our job.

"How did you get away?" I asked her, focusing on the present and the gorgeous woman in front of me.

"I waited under that desk until he left, and then for another hour just to be sure. By then, it was the middle of the night. Because I own part of the company, I also still have full access. I grew up playing in that office while my *Grand-père* worked, so I know every nook and cranny of that place, every single hallway and stairwell, every petty cash cache. We've had those offices since before I was born, and our grandparents lived solely in London the last few years. I was scared to use my cell phone or any of my cards, because I didn't want anyone to be able to track me. I probably watch too much TV for that to have been my first thought, but it was."

"Smart girl," I murmured, nodding at her. I made a mental note to tell her later that part of the services offered by Titan Group were absolutely chaotic digital wormholes Mila set up to discombobulate anyone searching. It wasn't a perfect system, as we'd learned early on in our work as Titan Group, but it helped, and we'd fortified since then.

"I snuck down to the janitorial area, and that's where I called Tad from. I met Tad in college. We'd been students at Oxford together years ago, and then I ran into him in New York at a fundraiser a few months ago. He told me that he was retired from active duty and about Titan Group. Little did I know how soon or how much I'd need that information."

"I told Tad the first thing I could think of when he asked if I could get to a safe location, and that was to meet me outside of Lion-sur-Mer. I told him about my boat, and that I was the only person who sailed it, or who even realized it was still seaworthy. Adrien had long ago forgotten about it, or so I thought." She shuddered again, pain wrenching her delicate features. Thank God Tad was a rich asshole even growing up, and had parents who sent him to Oxford.

"I chose this area because it's where our family got its start after the war, and before that my great-grandmother's family had lived here for generations, but I never expected in a million years that he would find me, or blow up my boat. I don't even know how he found me. But Theo, he's the only one who could have known to look for or even identify *Le Petit Coquelicot*. The boat is, was I guess, owned by a trust, it had to have been him." Her glossy eyes were practically pleading with me for answers, answers I didn't have, yet anyway.

"I've only used cash, and I followed Tad's instructions to the letter. *Je ne sais quoi.*"

"We'll figure it out, Hensley. You have Titan Group now. The important thing is that you did get away, and I have you now. Hensley, you are incredibly strong. You had practically saved yourself by the time I got to the harbor. If you'd been inside of that cabin, we wouldn't be having this conversation. Hell, if you hadn't hidden on the floor of the cubicle or if you had used your cards leaving London, we wouldn't be here now." My heart was thudding against my chest at those troubling thoughts. Shit, I barely knew Hensley, but I knew that I wanted more time with her, regardless of what I deserved in life. Thank God she hadn't been asleep in her cabin and that she was smart enough to act quickly.

Max piped in then from the video feed on my screen. "Do you remember having that creepy gut feeling in London between the call and the boat, like what you'd had in Lyon?" he asked.

"I don't. It was the first time in a month that I didn't feel it, so maybe someone *had* been following me before," she replied. "It was tricky getting out of the city. I waited outside of King's Cross until the last minute, then ran across the street to St. Pancras, bought a train ticket with cash to get to Dieppe, then came down to the boat in a private car, also cash," she answered.

Damn, Hensley was smart. "Good thinking to wait at King's Cross and then get into St. Pancras. Tell us more about the private car," he said.

"I randomly jumped into a ride share that had been pulling away from the Dieppe station, after they dropped their rider off. I flashed some cash and told him my phone had died so I couldn't get on the app. Once he saw the cash, he agreed. It was a ton of cash, and I spoke in French, which always helps here," she said.

"That alone could have triggered something," Max murmured from the screen. "Without knowing who and what we are dealing with, any of those points could have been the exposure point. We'll start digging," he said.

"And, Hensley, great job getting as far as you did. My hunch on this is that your brother, and whoever his team is, have tremendous access. With cameras everywhere now, you'd be shocked at how tracked you are as a normal citizen. Some countries are simply better at hiding it than others." Max grimaced.

"Why were you on the deck? How did you know to leave your cabin at that hour?" I asked softly, the tiniest niggle of a question burrowing under my skin. I hated to be digging deeply into this part, as I had the sense that the boat had also been very special to her, but I had to know, and I knew better than to trust blindly. My God, did I know better. So, I pushed a bit. After all, we had to talk details. In things like this, it was always the smallest of details between mission success or mission failure, between life and death.

"Whatever made me stop that night outside of Adrien's office, I suppose." She gave a Gallic shrug then, reminding me that although Hensley was half American and her dad was raised in England, she was also part French, and her French family roots were deep. That shrug was the universal symbol of the French woman, and it rolled off her shoulders naturally.

"I hadn't slept more than a few hours here and there, but something was off last night. I had gone ashore to get a few groceries to survive on and had that icky, terrible sense of being watched again from that moment on. Once no one came onto the boat or tried to grab me on the dock, I assumed that I must be paranoid. *Je ne sais quoi.* I let my defenses down, but I couldn't shake that prickling sensation, so I stayed awake."

She glanced down at our hands, still clasped together in her lap. Her eyebrows were knit in confusion, but she spoke clearly. "I don't know what the sound was—almost like a simple *thunk* and then crackling. I left my cabin and immediately understood that the boat was on fire. It was already filling with smoke and oppressive heat. I raced back into my cabin and grabbed the first thing I saw. I think it was a T-shirt, and I got it wet in the sink to cover my mouth before fleeing for the stairs. I remember now that I almost didn't make it up from the galley. I was incredibly lightheaded, and my lungs were burning. I don't remember much after getting topside, it all happened so quickly." Tears were again leaking from those dark depths. Her eyes resembled wide pools of melting chocolate, and the need to protect her, to be her safe space, swept through me again.

"I understand. Hensley, you are amazing. Staying alert and being able to get from a London skyscraper on a sailboat to the Normandy coast takes courage. You did that and I am so damn glad you made it. You're safe now," I assured her.

Before I could question myself further, I gathered her up in my arms, pulling her over to my chair. Perching her on my lap, I wrapped her up in an embrace. Her arms had gathered around me tightly, and she pressed her smaller frame as close to mine as she could get. Why that had been my natural reaction to her pain, I couldn't fathom. The only thing I knew for certain was that she needed a minute, and I needed to be wrapped around her, as if to protect her from whatever and whoever was after her. I'd sort the rest out in my head later.

"Guys, let us call you back. Hen needs a break for a minute," I said into the speakerphone. I didn't give Max and Wills a chance to respond, simply hitting the 'end' button. I knew they'd keep us safe no matter what. Right now, she needed me more than we needed to keep talking. For some reason, I also had a caveman brewing inside of me, one who was going to keep her as close to my body as was physically possible, as if to reassure myself that she was okay. She was there with me.

"I feel safest right here, Theo. I can't explain it, yet you seem to be my safe place these days," she whispered against my neck.

This woman. She'd been through hell and was still being brave. If I weren't careful, she could knock through my concrete-encased heart with that admission. She had certainly cracked it easily enough already.

I'd be completely gone for her before Seb arrived, and that couldn't happen. I'd made a promise to myself after Mosul. My life for theirs. It was only fair.

There was something about her that resonated within me though, another new sensation for me where she was concerned, someone who had never wanted to get to know anyone more deeply. For the first time in my life, I understood the instant and alarming connection Max had talked about. I'd been around plenty of women in my life, too many women most likely, and that made me feel cheap in that moment.

Before grasping at Hensley's hair under the water, my vow to trade my life for theirs had never wavered, and I certainly had never felt a connection to another person like this. I pushed that thought away, content to hold her in my arms for now. That had to be enough. This moment. Nothing more than that.

After her body relaxed in mine some time later, I hugged her to myself and then stood, gently easing her from my lap. "Let's see what the chatter is about your boat. There's bound to be news, and sometimes, the news crews pick up important stuff on their video feeds."

Hensley nodded at me and quietly padded back inside, following me out of the sunshine and into the living area of the charming home. I gently pushed her into a corner of the expansive couch and then settled in right beside her, bringing the blanket from earlier over us both. Kicking my feet up onto the coffee table between us and the fireplace, I clicked on the TV and found the news station from earlier, which was still covering the explosion. I also shot a text off to the team to let them know that she was okay, and that we'd reconnect later. I knew without a doubt they'd keep us safe for now.

The news was everywhere, as it had been earlier. The coast of France was dotted with little towns and villages along the rocky shores. News like that would consume all of them, terror brought to their homes across to tightly knit communities, pulling focus from what had been the jubilant preparations for the upcoming Paris Olympics.

The reporters had spoken of a woman on board the sailboat earlier, when we'd watched it almost immediately after the explosion, but the tone had changed. Now, they were focusing on the search transitioning to attempting recovery for the woman believed to be on the boat. No body had been found, and people were getting antsy.

The need to protect her grew within me. I wanted to keep her here, go completely off-grid from everyone, even my team, and learn everything there was to know about Hensley Richard.

I shifted back slightly and glanced over at Hensley, waiting for her to turn toward me so I could meet her eyes. She must have sensed that I wanted to talk, as I found her eyes already watching me.

"Hensley, I need to be straight with you. I can't quite keep my hands off you, and that isn't normal. Not for me, not for Titan Group. And yet, I can't be who you need either. I'm damaged goods." I pulled her to my chest and rested my forehead against hers. "I need you to know that I don't normally act this way with our clients. That this, this is, you are incredible." I was tongue-tied, for the first time in my life. A flush flamed across my neck and crawled up my cheeks again. Fuck, I was not smooth at all, not with her. "The guys give me a hard time about being a Lothario, but I haven't been that guy in a long time, and I never will be again."

She pulled her hands out from where she'd been curled up under the blanket and brought them to my chest, resting them over my heart. "Theo, I know. I mean yes, the timing is terrible as my emotions are on a roller coaster right now, but being here with you—that is the only thing that feels right. You don't feel like damaged goods to me. You feel like strength and kindness, which I need." She caught that luscious lower lip of hers in her teeth when she finished talking, and I wanted to kiss any sting that caused them away. "Please, Theo, tell me I'm not alone in this connection."

Alone? Hell no, I was right there in that crazy whirlpool of emotions with her, regardless of what I told myself about deserving it. I lowered my head closer to hers, let my lips barely graze hers, let my words vibrate against her. "You are never going to be alone in this Hen. I'm here, right here with you. Tell me to stop though, because I can't stop myself unless you tell me to. Tell me and I'll back off. You're in control here," I said, my voice painfully low in my chest. I couldn't tell if I thought the words, or said them. A part of me hoped I had only thought them, because I should never give in to this need that had built for her.

She closed the whisper of distance between us, claiming my lips. I must have said the words out loud, I guess. I let her lead completely. I needed to know she was okay with what was happening between us. I wasn't even sure what that was yet, but I hoped that she was experiencing what I was. She explored my lips with her own, nibbling and then claiming my mouth. My pulse was racing, Hensley tasted sweet on my tongue, and I wanted more. Regardless of having only met her a day before, or my vow to trade my life, a vow I could never break. The word 'claim' beat throughout me. That caveman was back, and he was in charge.

She shifted her legs from underneath herself, turning to throw one of her legs over my other knee, straddling me to bring herself closer to my body. Framing her face with my hands, I angled my kiss deeper, my tongue sweeping into her hot mouth. Her hands were roaming across my chest, and she wiggled in my lap, bringing her sweet, soft curves closer to my own hardness, settling into the crux of my lap, fitting perfectly.

THIRTEEN

HENSLEY

THEO TOOK HIS TIME EXPLORING MY MOUTH, LEARNING THE contours and taste. His thumbs were skimming along my jaw and tangling in my hair to hold me more closely to him, angling his mouth more into mine, his tongue sweeping along my own. I shifted against him even more, desperate to get as close to him as possible, my core hot, desperate to be held tightly to his length, with only our clothes separating us. I ached, and the cure to all the achiness was right there, right there for me to take.

Theo was a wall of muscle, putting off a level of heat that drew me in as if I were a moth to his flame. His chest was broad and hard against my own, completely protecting me within his embrace. I skated my hands across his muscled chest, tracing his heart beating wildly under my palm. I stroked my hands outward to his shoulders and down to his biceps. I followed the dips and valleys of his muscles, reveling in the solidness of his strength. He eased back slightly and nibbled my bottom lip as I did so, then nuzzled his nose along my jaw up to my ear. His tongue lightly traced the sensitive shell there, and I shuddered into his arms. My aching breasts scraped across his chest, and I felt how hard he was against me again, that puzzle piece notching against me. He ever so gently tugged my earlobe between his teeth, worrying it just slightly before rolling it between his soft lips. Mon Dieu. The man was molten sin.

My core was melting from the need to be against him, desperate to grind more deeply into him, to be filled with him. I wanted to take his soft T-shirt off and trace the muscled grooves on his chest with my tongue—a thought that caught me off guard. I was more eager to get to know Theo than I'd ever been before with any other man. My own brother had tried to kill me twenty-four hours earlier, and the only thing I wanted to do was feel Theo everywhere I could get him. I'd practically come on to him in my sleep, and now here I am rubbing myself against his gorgeous body every time he offers an ounce of comfort.

Theo must have clocked my body tense with that internal diatribe.

He breathed into my ear. "Hen, sweetheart, you are perfection."

He eased back slightly, enough to meet my eyes, those golden flecks pinned on me. His eyes were dark pools of lust, and I watched as he steeled himself to tone it down. He trailed the pads of his fingertips back down my jaw, kissing me again softly when he reached my lips.

I leaned back into him, dropped another kiss to his lips and then inched back and stood before we got caught up again. Losing myself in him was amazing, and yet I barely knew him, I reminded myself. He stood with me and then brought my body against his again.

"Gonna have to make myself let you go again, but I need one more minute." His voice rumbled across me, my own smile hitching up at the corners. Apparently, he was as discombobulated as I was. That was good, I think.

The thrill of this incredible man needing one more moment to collect himself before he could physically let me go almost had me pushing him back down to the couch. It took everything within me to live in that moment and allow myself to step back when he dropped his hands from me. This type of magnetism was completely foreign to me and yet I was deeply drawn to it. Like the waves crashing outside, I wanted to roll over him, become one wild moment together. And yet, he'd stood back, putting some distance between us. He was right to do it, but I was bereft without his heat.

The coldness at the loss of his hands on my body caused a shudder to rack through me, as if the piece of myself that had finally clicked into place was loose again and it had enjoyed being whole. I shivered, a coldness seeping throughout my warm limbs as he led me back to the kitchen. By tacit unspoken agreement, we both took a metaphorical step back.

We decided to make a late dinner. The house had been provisioned for every possible need, which Theo assured me was part of Luke's touch. That explained the groceries I'd found earlier.

I lost track of my own worries in his stories of his adventures and his teammates. I caught myself physically clutching my chest when he told me how Titan Group had formed and the first two "cases" they'd had to save both Violet and Hazel. It was obvious that he loved them all, and that they loved him. It shone in his eyes in a way that was completely intoxicating.

I'd even read some of Hazel's work on cultural foods and the histories they passed down, not realizing the connection. Her work was truly wonderful, about lost cultural foods and events bringing people together. I'd had no idea that Hazel was with Luke and that Luke and Tad were the founders of Titan Group. Such a small world. Thank goodness I had decided to go over to New York for that fundraiser a few months ago. That reconnection to Tad had saved my life.

"And of course, Wills and Mila had to be dramatic too, but at least they were both okay. They were obvious, Hensley. We had all been waiting for him to make a move." His laughter rang out, keeping my mood light when it otherwise would have been all-consuming in grief, confusion and anger. He told me about

Mila's special shortbread, how insanely protective Wills had been since Mila had shared her pregnancy news, how little baby Alex was always being carried around, how Blitz constantly slept in the middle of the melee. I loved dogs, and that detail made me laugh.

We shared more stories while we ate, me of my family before it seemed to all go haywire. How the boat had been gifted from Thomas to Claire, the original Little Poppy. They'd left it to *Tante* Marie Louise, and she'd left it to me in her trust. I had painstakingly cared for it for years, off and on, with the little free time I had while building my own professional career. The boat was a connection to the love story that launched our family, something tangible that I could imagine each of my parents, grandparents and great-grandparents sailing in together. When I was super stressed, as I was now, I entertained myself with visions of all of us together, as if they'd all lived long, healthy lives. As if we'd had the huge family of my dreams and done family things together.

We'd long finished a fresh tarte tatin that I'd whipped up for dessert from the apples he'd brought in earlier when the mood of our conversation turned back toward the more somber parts of our respective lives. We'd taken our dessert back into the living room, cozy by the fireplace, to talk more comfortably.

Theo told me some about the last mission the team had been on for the Raiders, how it had all gone wrong. He spoke of how they'd lost three of their brothers, including Max's actual brother Alex. He skimmed over chunks of the details, yet I could practically smell the pain on him. I could tell this was a huge part of who he was today, and yet I couldn't pry. The walls he'd erected around this were evident, and I respected that. He had a right to that privacy, and I was only a passing ship for him. The thought made me sad again, reminding me that I was only ever a passing ship for most people. Just out here alone on the dark ocean of life, I guess. His next words shook me out of my melancholy, thankfully.

He told me about coming home on that leave and how Violet had breathed life and hope back into their buddy Max. I really wanted to meet them based on what Theo shared. I wanted to meet Blitz. I had always wanted a dog, but had never made the time. I have no idea why. I also wanted to meet the new baby Alex and snuggle him. My deepest wish, within the recesses of my soul, was to have a large family of my own. Three kids at least so that they had each other to grow up with, two dogs, maybe a cat? A husband who was my person, through and through. Cousins, aunts and uncles over for holidays and regular days, sharing in their joy. That thought took me right back to my own sibling.

What was Adrien thinking? I couldn't believe my older brother had come to this. My only living family wanted me dead. Being money-hungry was one thing, but a murderer? And of his own sister? That was a new level of darkness, of evil, that I couldn't fathom.

"Theo, I simply can't wrap my brain around Adrien's actions. He's always been super greedy, but to murder a family member, his only living family member at that, is a new dimension of insanity, right?" I asked him. Something about this darkness wasn't sitting right inside of me. Had I grown up next to it and not noticed it in him? I felt like an idiot if that was the case, and it didn't ring true to who I knew Adrien to be before the last year. "Adrien and I weren't close because of our age gap, but we were siblings. We had an easy camaraderie. We talked often at one time, we were raised together. We love each other. I love him. He loves me. I mean, I know he loved me at one time. He's my brother. So, has he lost his mind? Is this a new level of derangement?"

Theo had been sitting in a large armchair near the couch I was on, and I noticed that when I asked him the question about Adrien's potential insanity, he mulled it over before answering. He considered my question before responding, which made me realize he was always listening to me. This sexy man next to me was also a great listener, which was a rare occurrence lately in the men around me.

The guys I'd known until then were more likely to tell me what they thought was happening rather than listen to me, even when it was about something I was an expert in. It was annoying and off-putting, but not Theo. Sexy Theo listened, making him even sexier.

"I think you're on to something, Hen. Let's call in and talk about this with Luke. Tad is either still in London or on his way here as we speak, but Luke is kind of 'command central' for us with the others right now, he'll dig into this," he replied, nodding toward me.

I watched as Theo joined me on the couch, opened a laptop that had been on the coffee table in front of my comfy spot and initiated a video call. Moments later, an extremely handsome man's face came onto their screen. Were these guys also secretly models? *Merde Alors.*

"Theo, you good, man?" the smiling face asked.

"Good, Luke. Thanks, man. Meet Hensley. Hen, this is Luke." Theo turned the screen toward me as he joined me on the couch.

I raised my hand in an awkward, shortened wave. "Hi, nice to meet you. Wait, not great to meet you, but also thank you." An awkward laugh rambled out with that greeting. I was apparently slightly struck dumb by how handsome the men of Titan Group were. Together, these guys packed a punch.

"Hi Hen, nice to meet you. I'm Luke. Tad gave me an overview, and we are amassing quite a dossier on you, obviously. While I wish we were meeting under different circumstances, it is still a pleasure to meet you. My wife has asked me to tell you that she is enormously impressed with how you've saved yourself thus far." He smiled again. The handsome man was charming, and also clearly besotted with his Hazel.

"Tell her thanks. I'm still in shock, I think. Also, I love her work. We made a tarte tatin earlier from an old family recipe I used to make with my *Gigi* when we would be here," I answered, the memory streaking through my heart. "Hazel's work always reminds me that part of my family lives on in the recipes I like to make when I have time."

"I'll tell her, thank you for sharing that. She's always right, and I'm glad that is true for you. For me, it's my mom's brownies." His eyes were kind, and a sadness was there, but he was smiling too. I knew then, without knowing the specifics, that Luke also understood the pain of losing a parent. How the earth was never the same again without them.

He continued on, "With her book out soon, and Vi's young adult mystery currently in editing, it's an exciting time for all of us. But that's not why you guys called me, I know. Your shock is to be expected. We'll figure it all out though. Theo is solid, and the rest of the team will be there soon. You also have ground support here in DC from me, Max, and our lovely ladies. Mila and Wills are here too and round out the team, anchoring our tech. Trust me when I tell you that you will be stunned by their nerdiness," Luke said.

"I heard that, Luke-a-licious." A curvaceous blonde with the face of a cherub rolled into the video screen on a large leather-looking chair. She was cradling an enormous baby bump, her hands idly rubbing her stomach as she talked.

"Hiya, Hen! Nice to meet you, Mila here, at your service. Here's the deal though, I've had to dig deep into your cyber footprint, so I'm apologizing now if I say something out loud that I shouldn't. Pregnancy brain has melded with my cyber stalking too much, I don't remember what I should know and what I shouldn't know. You know?" Mila's lips were moving crazy fast that I had to work to keep up with what she was saying. "And he calls us nerds, but as a term of endearment, you know?"

"And seriously, your apartment in Lyon is amazing," she rushed on. "Honey"—she turned to Wills—"I want to go to Lyon. Home of the *bouchons* and *quenelles*."

"You got it sweetness, let's wait until after the baby though okay?" Wills answered without missing a beat.

"Also, your vacation board on your Pinterest about the Oregon coast is doing it for me. It's amazing there too, you'll love it."

"Thank you," was all I managed before Theo laughed at my side.

"Mila, sweetheart, let Hen breathe," he said.

"I think she'd love Cannon Beach too though Theo, in case we want to bring everything back stateside," Mila replied, a smile on her beautiful face. "Hen, watch *The Goonies* as soon as you can, seriously, you'll want to see that place even more after that. And Theo, I miss you already."

Laughter bubbled up in my throat. I had needed this lightness, the happiness of a friendly face. Mila was warm and joyful, I couldn't wait to meet her in person someday. Wow, the thought took root in my mind as if it was a given. Like I might just survive this and get to meet these people who were helping me. I sure hoped so. I realized then that one of the things I was seeking in life was time. It was a luxury, and those of us who never had it with the people we should have are always wishing for more of it. More time.

In my case, time to learn another person, a man who could be my husband, to create the family I was desperate to have. Time to rebuild my company, to solidify the legacy I was clutching at protecting. Time to get Adrien help, maybe? I didn't know, but the thought deepened my resolve to see whatever this was through.

Theo was talking to Luke about my concerns of fratricide being the next level of insanity. Adrien was greedy, but was he also insane? I couldn't fathom he had that within him, even as my throat was still tender from the smoke. I tried to set the question aside internally and focus on the conversation playing out on the video screen.

"I think you might be on to something here Hen, it's a valid question to ask if Adrien metaphorically made that leap. I mean, he could have meant that he wanted 'it' or you, taken care of in a completely different way. We need to explore it to be as clear as possible on the scope we are dealing with." Luke was responding to what Theo had verbally laid out. Theo was nodding his head, a smile sent my direction now and then.

"If this wasn't the work of Adrien, then we explore the who portion of the scope, the players. That's always the thread that unravels Hensley, great thinking on starting there," he said.

"Let me connect in Doc and see what she says. She's the one with the psych background in behaviors. We have her on retainer Hensley, she's part of the team, although not full time. I promise she's good and we'll keep you safe while working to figure this out. My boy Theo has you and Seb should be there soon," Luke continued.

"I trust Theo. I trust you all, thanks Luke. Thanks Mila. I don't know if this is a thread or not, maybe I'm being delusional about my own brother," I replied, feeling a sliver more broken than earlier. Was I that wrong about Adrien? Could he possibly have done this? I couldn't help the flutter of hope that someone else was responsible for what had happened to me, even if my brain was trying to shut that flutter down.

"We got ya Henny!" Mila cheerfully added. Her brightness coming through the screen across the miles of ocean separating us all. "If you change your mind on Oregon, I got ya there too." She laughed as she waved. "Toodles Theo!" Mila blew him a kiss and rolled herself back out of view from the camera.

"Honestly, the happier she gets, the closer to the due date she gets, the more absurd her word choice gets and the faster she talks. I'm going to talk about that with Doc too. Maybe let Wills know if he should be worried," Luke added, laugh lines deepening on his handsome face.

"I heard that Luke-a-licious! I'm telling Hazel to withhold the good stuff from you if you keep it up." They heard Mila's light voice from wherever she had rolled to.

"You wouldn't dare. And she wouldn't listen, she loves the good stuff," Luke replied confidently, a knowing smirk on his face. "Speaking of good stuff, I need to go find my bride Theo, Hen. You're good. Seb will be there soon okay. We're monitoring real time, as always, so rest easy." Theo nodded at Luke's words as he clicked off the line.

"Are they always like that?" I asked, gob smacked at how fast that had all gone down.

"Always. It's light, laughter, lots of lust-filled glances when the wives are in the rooms, definitely some inappropriate touching that no one tries to hide. Honestly, being home with them all is amazing." Theo pursed his lips and shook his head in the affirmative. "I love those assholes." He laughed.

His laughter was contagious and took me by surprise. I hadn't heard him laugh before this moment, and it suited him in a beautiful way that made me lighter to even see. I couldn't help but laugh with him, the love and general enjoyment of his people shining through his words. These people were all transparent in their affection, they were unabashed in their bonds and it made me long for that connection. People that never made you wonder about their love, or question a motive, they were simply there for you. No matter what. Family in a different form, one you chose, and equally binding and meaningful.

I missed what had been of my family desperately in that moment, a loneliness that dried up my laughter quickly. A surge of jealousy was caught in my throat and although I loved the lightness his family brought to him, I couldn't help but wish I had something similar. Here I was, on the run from my own, the tiny little thread I'd been holding onto for so long.

Theo must have again sensed the chaos coursing through my head because his laughter died out too and he regarded me quietly. He didn't push for information, he didn't ask what was bothering me, he calmly waited for me to talk if I wanted to.

He patted the space immediately next to him on the couch and I scooted in closer, laying my head on the side of his strong shoulder instinctively. He was solid, concrete. A beacon in the dark night, the light I needed to see by more clearly. We sat together quietly while I worked through the fear threatening to overtake me.

There was something about Theo that made me comfortable in my own skin. I could be myself fully, feel what I needed to feel, and he'd still be there, anchoring me to realness and light, and laughter. To safety sure, but also to exploration. I wanted to set aside the turmoil of the last year and remember who I had been before losing my grandparents, watching our company culture crumble, before my brother became a monster for all intents and purposes.

Who was I before all of that? I'd been independent, self-assured, someone who was comfortable in the role I was born to play, someone who was filled with hope for the future. I was happier, far less jaded and scared that when the chips fell, I'd be alone.

I'd wanted a big family, a playful love, but a dependable love. A man who made me laugh, yet also could shoulder the hard stuff and I thought maybe was out there, even though my dating life had been pretty boring. At least there had been dates though, this last year had taken its toll. That damn thread I was clutching onto to keep it all together had become a noose.

My mind skittered back to Theo. What kind of guy was he? He certainly checked many of those boxes I'd inadvertently lined up. More than anyone I'd ever met in the environs of board rooms, the realness of him being a genuine tie binding me to him. And yet, these were extreme circumstances, which was bound to amp everything up. Time. There it was again, the wish for time to know more.

"Hen, whatever you need. I'm here. We've got you." His deep voice rumbled across me, his large hand soothingly rubbing my thigh next to his. That rumble had shaken me from my reverie, igniting something inside of me that I'd thought long buried. Real lust. Fire. Deep within me. For him. I remembered the strength of him against me from earlier and I decided to pull on those binding ties of him. Live a little, remind myself that I had survived Adrien's attack. I needed to feel alive.

"I'm okay Theo. I will be okay that is. You are giving me exactly what I need. Right now, I just need you. Please." I shifted my body to climb fully onto his lap, facing him with my back to the dormant fireplace and TV screen, the coffee table littered with computer screens and phones. I sat back slightly on his broad thighs and brought my hands to rest on his chest, bringing my eyes to his, those deep pools drawing me in. I was reclaiming some power, as a woman, and I was starting now.

FOURTEEN

THEO

"Are we safe here Theo?" she asked me, her voice low and her eyes were intense on my own. Something had happened inside that beautiful head of hers, that was for sure.

"We're safe Hen. If anyone comes close, we'll know in time to do something about it. Are you okay?" I asked her. I was curious as to what had led her to my lap, and frankly, she felt too good there for me to ask too many questions for fear she'd move again.

I wasn't sure what had been going through her head, but if I had to guess, she'd run the gamut of emotions in the time we'd spent quietly snuggled against each other on that couch. Now, there was a streak of impishness in her eyes that made me take notice. This was a woman who was confident in her skin. A woman who knew what she wanted and took it. Whatever it was that had led her to her current position, my dick had immediately taken notice and I willed myself to calm down.

I wouldn't rush her. I wouldn't press her. Hell, I didn't even know if this was a good idea. I also wasn't sure I could deny her anything. Perched on my thighs as she was, trust shining in her eyes, lust seeping out of her pores, her hands stroking my chest . . . I would deny her nothing, proving I hadn't learned my lesson in the last two years. I was spellbound.

"Theo," was all she said. One word. My name. One word I'd heard my entire life, likely more than any other word in the English language. One word was all it took, and I broke. My own misgivings at what I knew I deserved and what I definitely didn't were on the back burner so fast, I should have been ashamed, if I could feel anything but stark need for the woman in my arms.

I straight up devoured her. My hands had immediately gone to her waist, anchoring her to me, my own need for her palpable. My mouth was ravenous on hers, tongues tangling, lips colliding. My blood was lightening through my veins, pulsing for her, streaking throughout me.

She leaned back lightly, and I used my hands to tug her soft T-shirt up and over her head, exposing her delicate collarbone and rounded breasts to my hungry gaze. She was covered only with a layer of fabric from that damn bra that had been teasing me all day. It had to go.

I leaned in and nibbled along the path of that strap, adding little licks and the tiniest bites as I went. I brushed the back of my fingers along her arm as I nudged the strap down her shoulder with my nose. I returned to where the strap had been and kissed the imaginary line down toward her breasts. My fucking mouth watered. It had been so long, and she was perfect. She had pert, round breasts, and I gripped the fabric with my teeth as gently as I could, nudging it down. She gasped and arched into me, pressing all of that luscious mouth more fully into my face. So responsive, my little Hen. It only made me want more. If I thought I was mesmerized before, having her in my mouth made me feral.

Her fingertips were dug in to my biceps, her smaller hands not quite big enough to fully wrap around them and it fanned the flames consuming me. She held me to her, her little whimpers as I worked my lips and tongue along the now lowered bra to the other strap. I repeated my motions until she was completely bare before me, the very tops of her glistening from my mouth. I was painfully hard and needed to be inside of her, immediately. It may very well kill me to stand up now, but I had to know.

"Hen. Be sure," I growled. I was savage, there was no blood left in my brain. I'd never been this raw before. In the before times, I was a smooth charmer and yet there I was. Insatiable. Desperate. Hard as a rock and jagged in my hunger for my little Hen.

Instead of answering me, she leaned back enough to gather the fabric of the bra sitting lower around her waist and pull it up, over her head, and off. Her hands came up to cradle my face.

"Theo." That damn word again. Commanding all types of things. My siren.

I leaned in ever so slowly and nuzzled her, making sure to keep my lips closed, reverent, under her breast. She shivered, goosebumps breaking along her gorgeous skin. I repeated the motion, the next time opening my lips ever so slightly to drag my tongue along with my lips. Her skin pebbled immediately and I flattened my tongue, swiping it along her rosy nipple, bringing it into my mouth and rolling it around in the heat there.

She squirmed in my lap, her core burning against my leg. I knew that if I could feel her skin, it would burn me in the best way. I needed it, her skin against my own, her wetness. I trailed a hand down her waist to her waistband and tugged. Without words, she shifted and kicked free of her leggings, her eyes never leaving mine.

She perched on my lap, beautifully naked and confident. I absolutely could not look away from her. Someone could have been storming the beaches, breaching the house, it wouldn't have mattered. She was indeed my siren.

"Hen," I whispered, hearing the desperation for more bleeding into my own voice.

"Theo." Her one word command.

I dropped my lips back to her neck, right to the center where her pulse fluttered against the ivory of her skin. I tried to be gentle as I kissed a path downward to drag across to her breasts, to not take this too fast. I wanted to taste her, to savor her. I laved her nipple with the very tip of my tongue and she shuddered, pressing those gorgeous breasts more fully into my mouth. I smiled against her skin. My mouth was full of her and her heat was scorching against my thigh. Taking it slowly with her to savor her was both the easiest thing I had ever done and the toughest, I wanted inside of her heat more than I had ever wanted anything before in my life.

Oh, my wicked little siren liked that. I dropped a hand back down to her upper thigh, dragging it upward toward her core while my tongue licked at her breasts. Her skin was cool, but my mouth was hot and she moaned as I trailed my fingertips up. I ran my finger along her heat, giving her the lightest touch while I kissed her more firmly. She went wild in my arms, loving the teasing at her wetness, the nibbling along her incredibly sensitive breasts.

Hen was mewling against me, little chants of 'yes,' and more 'Theo' coming faster and faster. I leaned back and blew a puff of breath against her hardened nipple before switching back to her other breast.

I opened my mouth around her nipple again and sucked, just as I pushed my finger inside of her wet heat fully and firmly, pressing along that little bud of nerves. Doing both in tandem, mirroring what I wished my aching cock was doing with my finger. She was drenched for me, and tight.

"Hennnnnn . . ." I breathed out her name, curling my finger backward enough to tease that little bud of nerves nestled deep inside of her. I pressed against it firmly, then straightened it out, pumping into her surely.

"Theo. Please. Theo!" She was frantic against me, lost in sensation. I continued to lave at her breasts, my finger buried within her. I rocked against her, desperate to be closer to her heat. Her fingers were tight in my hair, clutching me to herself, her fingernails lightly digging into my own skin.

I added another finger to her wetness, coating them in her and pressing more deeply against her. My mouth was getting rougher against her as she began to shake against me. I knew she was close, I could feel every quiver of her, sense that she was lost to everything, anything but me. My savageness was back. I wanted to mark her as mine. Mine. Theo's. The thought pushed me on and I pressed my thumb more deeply against her little bundle of nerves as I gently bit down on her collarbone. That was all it took. With a gasp of "Theo," she came against me. She shook, her body had been strung so tightly and was sent flying so high, she slumped against me as her orgasm waned, her lips finding mine as she came back into herself.

I brought my other hand up against her back and held her to me, willing my cock to settle down and my racing heart to slow. I had just shifted her on my lap, dragging her bare skin along my muscular thigh, when the alarm on my phone pinged. Shit.

FIFTEEN

HENSLEY

I HEARD THE PING, BUT COULDN'T BRING MYSELF TO WORRY TOO much. Mainly, because my body was mimicking a heavy cloud, if that was a thing, and also because Theo didn't seem worried and I knew he'd heard it too. I knew this because I saw a flash in his eyes that was pure regret and pain. Over what, I hoped was not what had just happened between us.

For my part, I was heavy with satiated endorphins, yet lighter with joy. I wanted to get Theo out of his pants and keep exploring whatever that euphoria was, chasing that connection when he gently grasped me around the waist and shifted me back from where I really wanted to sit. When he shifted me back, I almost came again. I was so sensitive after what he had just done to my body, and him dragging the bare, exposed skin of my legs along his sweat-clad muscular thigh heightened every-thing. I stretched back into him without even meaning to. My body wanted what my brain was slow to understand wasn't going to happen.

"Henny, baby, the alarm was a courtesy. Seb is here." He huffed out a quiet 'fuck,' as he held me to him though. His lips were in my hair and his hands had reached over to find my shirt. I wasn't going anywhere until I had to. If he wasn't rushed, I wasn't leaving his lap. I had no idea what had overcome me, and yet it was the only modicum of control I had in a long time.

He gently pulled my shirt down over my head and then leaned over to grab my leggings from where he'd tossed them earlier, helping me into them. I should freak out. I was also typically modest, practically prudish, and yet, I couldn't get myself to move with any amount of urgency at all. Zero urgency. Zilch.

My limbs were languid, and I felt more comfortable in my own skin than I had in ages. Who knew that a great, no . . . fantastic . . . orgasm, would make me feel so invincible.

"Hensley." He waited for me to look up into those deep, dark eyes. I smiled at him, feeling only a teensy bit embarrassed that I was being no help in taking care of myself. Didn't I always take care of myself? Good grief, what had this man done to me?

"Theo," I replied when I finally made eye contact.

He laughed and pulled me against his hard chest again, where I felt his laughter ripple through my own languid limbs. "Hen, you kill me. It is taking everything I have to not lay you down and show you how crazy you make me. Right here. Right now. Mission be damned. Seb be damned. The entire world be damned but you, me and your gorgeous body that was made for mine, all laid out on that coffee table."

That popped the bubble of embarrassment I had started to feel and before I even realized it, I was laughing with him. Regaining the boldness and my own typical control freak nature, I leaned back and peeked up at him with a tentative question. "But later yeah?" I asked him before I could chicken out.

"Later. Yeah. He's here early, the fucker." He mumble-laughed the last part under his breath.

He helped me stand and then stood next to me, adjusting himself before he gave Seb an eye full. As his hand grazed himself, my mouth watered the tiniest bit. I had never been this turned on by anyone in my life before. Theo was not the smooth corporate type I was used to being with. He was. . .Theo. Different, in the sexiest of ways.

"You go. I'll meet Seb in the kitchen where he is sure to be raiding the leftovers." He grinned over at me.

"Won't he wonder what kept you?" I asked.

"Nah, he knows, or rather, he guessed. You'll see. He knows before the person knows what they are doing. Whatever he thinks, he'll wait for me to come to him because he knows we are safe. The alarm ding was his way of telling me to hurry up, that we have work to do. Someone is out there searching for you and I need to figure it out," Theo replied, his grin dimming with his words.

Embarrassment was creeping back up within me again at how brazen I had been, but I couldn't seem to find the energy for those negative emotions with Theo after he'd so thoroughly worked my body into a beautiful frenzy. I briefly wondered if shifting my need for control could be that easy in other parts of my life, maybe I could learn something from this. Or maybe whatever this moment was, it wasn't real. That thought made the wash of shame sting a little more on my cheeks. What had I been thinking?

"Hen. Wait. I have to say this to you before we leave this bubble." His hand had reached for me again and then he seemed to change his mind, bending his arm instead to cusp the back of his own neck.

"This isn't normal for me. I want you to know that. I need you to know that this is different. Well, I'm different. I'm not who I was, I. . . I guess I don't know who I am anymore," he said, his eyes solemn now and his tone firm. "You're different for me. I can't explain it, but what I do know is that I really don't deserve anything good in this life more than what I already have. And well, shit, I probably shouldn't have let myself get carried away, but I couldn't help it. I'm sorry."

The fact that he was sorry about what had happened between us made that wash of shame spread across my entire being, my neck was flaming with it. See world? This! This is what it meant to give up control. Pain. I plastered the best smile I could muster on my face and shook my head.

"I think I know what you are trying to say Theo. It's okay, really." I gave a true Gallic shrug and left to go to my room, which was all I could think to do in that moment. I needed some distance to get my brain working again. I needed to think about anything other than "later" with Theo that we had joked about moments before. Mon Dieu, had it only been moments before? For someone who loved control and order, the wildness of the last hour had really been amazing, and yet now the fall from that mountaintop left me battered and broken, laying at the bottom. Clueless even.

And sadly, my rational problem-solving brain was also trying to take back over and consume all of my thoughts. Either my own brother had reached a level of insanity to try to kill me, or this was much larger than any of us could guess at, which meant I was even more clueless.

I finally had the courage to go back downstairs less than an hour later, put back together and dressed in another set of leggings and a soft sweatshirt. Whoever had provisioned these clothes was an angel because everything fit perfectly, there were endless options, and everything was incredibly stylish. It was as if I'd been on a shopping spree for myself too, as they were all items I would have picked out if I had chosen it all, except for one small problem. These were my favorite type of clothes, and I kind of wished I had some of my typical business wear to hide behind.

My *Gigi* had always described fashion as a form of armor, clothing that gave the impression the wearer wanted it to give. For me, I had two personas I typically relied upon. The first, the business person and philanthropist, the identity I had spent most of my life wearing proudly. Pencil skirts, silk blouses, sheath dresses and formal gowns, that was the uniform of my life. The armor I wore into the daily battle of the role I was born to play. I loved those clothes, loved how they made me feel about myself, and especially loved that men always underestimated me when I was wearing that armor.

The second clothing persona was more my real self, the woman and not the heiress, the actual person versus the public figure. That woman loved the soft leggings and scoop shirts that hung off her shoulders. I rarely enjoyed those things when outside of my home spaces, yet when I was in my private domain, it was all I wore. These clothes were the sliver of the girl I used to be, not the woman who was holding together a multi-billion-dollar empire. Right now? I wanted to be the woman who had the armor.

The stark realization that I hadn't even considered needing that before now, even after Theo fished me out of the ocean, was terrifying. Theo could be dangerous to me in ways no one else was, or ever had been.

SIXTEEN

THEO

WELL, SHIT, MY RAGING HARD-ON WASN'T GOING ANYWHERE, EVEN after remembering that I had absolutely no business taking anything from Hensley, certainly not her gasps of pleasure or bare skin against my mouth.

I tried counting to twenty. I tried reciting the alphabet in other languages. I tried thinking about the time I accidentally walked in on my parents making out when I was a teenager. Awful, terrible images and yet nothing worked. Shit. For the last two years, I had been plagued with self-loathing and regret, and the one time I needed to call that shit up to move forward and I couldn't? What was happening to me? For fuck's sake.

I quickly shot Seb a text before making my way to the bedroom and bathroom I had claimed as my own.

Theo: 20 minutes.

Seb: Poor girl.

Theo: Eye Roll Emoji

Maybe I'd be better off taking care of it, taking the edge off, so to speak. She was seriously gorgeous and after being tangled up in her warmth, having my mouth and hands on her, I didn't think my dick was going to settle down until I took care of it. Apparently, that part of my body would now be making all the decisions. Great, that was sure to work out well.

I laid my phone on the travertine bench in the walk-in shower, knowing we were safe and that Seb would wait, but this was still an operation and I needed to be accessible.

Giving in to the body part making my decisions in the last hour, I quickly lathered some of the almond soap into my hand and reached down, my fingers wrapping around my cock. I closed my eyes and dropped my forehead to the stone shower wall, firmly pulling along my own length. The suds made me slippery, and the hot water all around me was incredible, surrounding me in warmth. I allowed my mind to remember her skin against me. How she'd moved, how her gasps sounded in my ears, that wet heat drenching my hand. My own hand picked up speed around myself, firmer and faster as I dreamed of what it would have been like to pull her back down to my chest, to roll her underneath me. I pictured her hair spread out around her and her breasts glistening from my mouth, laid out in a feast on that damn coffee table. I'd have teased her more first, dragging my lips along her jaw, whispering the filthy things in her ear I wanted to do to her as my cock teased her hot entrance with just the tip. I had seen that anticipation drove Hen wild. My cock swelled in my hand, growing harder and what I had seen in Hen.

Fuck, I was so close already. I pumped faster, my muscles bunching in my shoulders, my abs rippling with exertion. I flashed back to dropping my lips to her rosy nipples and popping one into my mouth again, laving my tongue along the sensitive bud while I trailed one finger down her belly, pushing inside of her wet heat and teasing that other sensitive bud at the same time. This time, I'd make gentle circles first, stretch it out even longer. I'd suck and lick at her breasts, making her crazy before I pulled back. I pictured those rosy nipples, wet from my mouth, and squeezed myself harder. I dreamed that I would blow a tiny blast of breath onto those nipples and watch them harden further. I'd lick again and then nibble ever so gently as I worked her up with my hand, my thumb pressed against her clit. The memories were crashing into me now, intertwined with my own fantasies of what I wanted to come next. I could still taste the faint salt from her skin on my tongue, feel the smooth texture of the underside of her breast, the plumpness of it in my mouth.

Right there, fuuuuuuuck. I pumped myself again, remembering her coming on my hand while I watched her. Her gorgeous skin had been glowing, and this time, instead of the ping of my cell phone, only the sound of our breathing and her whimpers would prevail. I'd push into her, watching myself disappear into her. I'd drown myself inside of her, be fully engulfed in her. My hips rocked, my own hand tight around my cock, and I came hard with that picture in my mind. Ropes of my own release splattered against the tile wall, washing away in the hot water.

My breathing was harsh in my own ears. Good Lord, this was yet another first for me. I didn't think I'd ever come that fast, and I wasn't even inside of her, had never been, should never be.

With that reminder, I rinsed off and stayed under the hot spray longer, willing it to be enough to take the edge off and bring me back to my vow. A life for a life. My life for those I caused to lose theirs.

I clamped my hand around the faucet with the heartache fresh now and got out to dry off and get dressed. I glanced at my profile in the mirror as I dried, seeing the purple heart inked on my chest. I'd originally gotten it after completing the requirements to earn the USMC Raider "Dagger" insignia. I had wanted to honor my great-grandfather who had been wounded in World

War Two but returned home alive. I'd finally felt like I'd earned it. Earning that dagger insignia was tough to do, but instead of having that inked on my body, I'd gone for something else. The purple heart I now wore. The one that I had absolutely lost the right to wear.

I'd added initials to it after that last mission in Mosul when I'd lost track of the informant and missed critical information, information that could have saved three of my team member's lives. I wanted to have to see those initials and that Purple Heart that they had earned every day of my remaining life, to see those letters in that heart and remember that I had cost those men their lives, cost my brothers.

Of course, Alex would have told me to stop being such a crybaby. I knew that, and yet I couldn't let myself forget how stupid I had been. How in the blink of an eye, I'd been charmed into missing what I had been sent to watch for. I caught my own eyes in the reflection, grimacing at the man before me. Who was I now?

With that impossible question in my mind, I got dressed and made my way back to the kitchen, knowing Seb would have a stupid-ass grin on his face. Ah, fuck it. Worth it, even if it couldn't happen again.

I had no sooner rounded the corner than I heard her laughter, along with Seb's.

"Theo man, good to see you." Seb stood as he spoke and came around the corner of the kitchen counter to give me a bear hug, slapping my back as he stepped away and sat back down.

"Seb, I see you've officially met Hen. Hensley, I mean." I was tongue-tied, my deluge of chaotic emotions rendering me dumb. I saw the flare of surprise in Seb's eyes at my behavior and braced myself for the teasing or questioning. Shockingly, it didn't come. Rather, Seb's eyes took on a more assessing light, something that kind of scared me more than the teasing. The thing about Seb was that he saw everything. You never wanted to have Seb staring you down; he'd walk away with secrets you didn't know you had, weren't even ready to admit to yourself. It felt like he was working his voodoo magic on me already, so I shuffled around and picked up his now empty plate and took it back to the sink to wash it.

"I have." He nodded toward Hensley. "I wish it were under different circumstances though, Hensley. I've heard great things about your philanthropic work."

Hensley's face, which had a gorgeous flush to it, thank you very much, took on a deeper hue at Seb's words. "Thank you, Sebastian. I only do what I should be doing in the communities I am fortunate to be part of," she demurred.

"Nah, you do what you should with what you have, but that isn't as common as it should be. You've got your hands full being a boss ass bitch and still find time—its impressive. Also, call me Seb, please," he replied.

She laughed at him. "Seb it is, thank you. Is a boss ass bitch a good thing?" she asked.

"Indeed, it is. Means you're doing it and doing it well. I saw it on *Ted Lasso*, and anything on that show is worth remembering," Seb assured her. I was glad he was here. Not only was he another person to protect Hen, Seb could put anyone at ease.

He was early, and I remarked as such. He went on to regale us with his trip back through Paris, and what it had been like in preparation for the Olympic Games. I knew Seb's path, yet I realized that he hadn't shared that with Hensley and neither had I.

"Hensley, Seb has been by your apartment in Lyon." I gestured with a lift of my chin toward Seb. "He checked for anything external and set up some cameras before heading back up to Paris and then here."

"Oh really, did you see anything?" she asked, curious now.

"Nothing, but I did set up some cameras of my own. If anyone breaks into your space, we'll know. I didn't go inside, as my plan was always to set up backups at this stage, which I did, and then join Theo and you here," he replied.

I turned back to Hensley to elaborate. "When we got your

call, I came to you with your chosen safe word, Tad and Nate went to London and Seb went down to Lyon. The team in DC is monitoring all of your companies, houses, friends, etc. Seb and I had been in Paris ahead of the Olympics because the US has a vested interest in it being as safe as possible. We were on reconnaissance, but not on an active case. We always move as quickly as possible, yet this one was cutting it close, for me anyway." I felt the words as I said them, rolled them around in my mind after they left my lips. It had been close, too close. I'd come within a current push of the ocean from never finding her, never knowing her. That pissed me off.

She'd been chatting with Seb about those backup plans when I tuned back in. "Wait, I want to circle back to the last couple of weeks. Were you at your Paris office before you went to London to see Adrien?" I asked.

"No, I've been at my home in Lyon." Her eyes lit with excitement after she said the words. "That's it, Theo! I have been tracking all the things that don't add up with Adrien and our company for months, and all of my notes are in my apartment in Lyon. I didn't think anything of it until you asked about my life before the call from London, but maybe there's something in there? I stopped in Paris only for a morning before catching the Eurostar over to London. I don't know how I didn't think of that before," she said, excited now to consider that maybe she had more answers than she had realized.

"Well, to be fair, you did overhear your brother give an order to kill you, flee from the city that's a second home to you, sneak across the Channel and down the coast of another country, and then were blown up on a boat. We'll give you a pass this one time for not thinking of it in the first twenty-four to thirty-six hours," I deadpanned.

"I guess this means I'm heading back to Lyon sooner than I expected," Seb added, laughing.

Seb was right; we needed to head to Lyon and see what Hensley had recorded, but we needed to be careful about it. I fired off a quick text to our team with a head's up, and they went into planning mode.

We'd moved the conversation back to the living room and hours later, in the middle of the night, Hensley fell asleep amid the more logistical planning we were working through.

We'd decided to lay low for another twenty-four hours and then drive to Lyon. Seb had a car too, and we decided that we'd leave his in the garage and take the SUV, as it hadn't been out and about recently, hence no one should be watching for it. The drive would take us seven and a half hours on a normal trip, but we had to add some redundancy to ensure safety, so it was shaping up to be a long night once we decamped from the Normandy coast. The drive would still be safer than being pinned on a train, or exposing other civilians in case anything happened. That settled, Seb glanced over at me.

"I'm going to head to bed, man. I need rack time, and so do you if we are leaving tomorrow night," Seb said, standing. I'd been watching Hensley sleep before turning back to him and realizing what he was saying. Damn, caught in the act.

"And, Theo, we'll keep her safe." He squeezed my shoulder as he walked past me for the stairs. Seb had let me off the hook by not saying anything, but that squeeze was a reassurance. How these guys could have possibly forgiven me for Mosul, I will never know. I couldn't say anything, so I just nodded at his retreating back.

This thing between Hensley and me was growing; it was warming; it was consuming. I was scared, for the first time in my life, for someone I felt responsible for who wasn't a fellow Marine, a brother. No, not responsible for in the sense that I had to keep her safe, responsible for in the way I *had* to keep her safe. I had to for myself, for her, for us. Us? If anything happened to her now, I didn't see how I could forgive myself. I couldn't forgive myself for a multitude of sins already. I couldn't add her to that list.

And wasn't that the biggest kick in the gut? I'd never been

scared of keeping anyone safe before, but maybe I should have been. I'd failed my own damn team, my brothers, once before, in a deadly way.

Hensley was light and joy, and she needed me, needed all of us. She needed me to be at my best. I doubled down on my internal fortitude as best as I could, and with that thought, gently picked her up and carried her to her bedroom. I laid her down on the bed and as she stirred, I shushed her and wrapped her up in the warm blankets surrounding her. Then, I did one of the hardest things I'd ever done. I left her in her bed, alone.

SEVENTEEN

HENSLEY

THE ROOM WAS COLDER WHEN I WOKE UP, ALONE IN THE BED I HAD shared a nap in with Theo the afternoon before. Disappointment echoed in my chest before I could talk myself into being glad. Theo was an elite operator, with danger behind every corner, and clearly, he was working through some heartbreak of his own. His life was independent and fluid. I craved structure and stability.

His life was back in the US, with the family he'd created at Titan Group and his actual family in Brooklyn. Mine, on the other hand, had always been in France or London. I'd spent time in America growing up and occasionally for work, yet not the same as if my mom had lived long enough to raise me. No, my home was here. My life was messier than it had ever been, the control I loved fading more and more every single day.

Here I was, worried my own brother had tried to kill me *and* worried that it had been someone else. If it had been someone else, that meant we knew nothing about what was happening, and holding those two terrifying thoughts at the same time practically overwhelmed me. I was damn tired of feeling like life was swirling around me, spinning me every which way. I'd been holding on so tightly to the legacy I believed in and yet doing so alone was exhausting. I could picture a rope in my hands, and my hands grasping it as tightly as I could, while the rope slid further and further out of my hands, burning and tearing at my skin as it went. On the other side of the rope, my heritage. The family, the lessons, the company, even myself.

Grappling with the rope made it almost impossible to be myself ever again, to be who I was before the deaths of my grandparents had thrown Adrien into overdrive. Before my own life was tossed into a spiral of playing clean up and catch up, all while trying to move through the fluidity of grief yet again.

Resolving that it was 100 percent a good thing that Theo hadn't slept in here with me, I got out of bed to face the day. My heart hurt, and a knot of tears threatened in my throat, but I pushed the sensation down. Theo was a good guy, a great guy, but he wasn't my guy. I wasn't going to be the one to mess with his life when mine was falling apart.

With that mantra resounding throughout my internal dialogue, I took a hot shower and headed toward the kitchen. When I'd fallen asleep, in the living room and not my bed, they'd been talking about timing. I was eager to hear the final plan this morning and see how I could help. I reminded myself that I was actually pretty damn smart, a 'boss ass bitch' as Seb had said. I kind of loved that.

"Bonjour," I greeted them as I rounded the corner. "Ah, bonjour Seb. Just you this morning? Theo sleeping in?" I asked, curiosity making me frown.

"Bonjour Hensley. Nah, Theo is taking a leisurely bike ride into the village to see if he hears anything of use to us, or of any threats," Seb replied.

"A bike ride?" I asked. That was the last thing I had expected to hear.

"Yep, spandex suit and helmet to match. He looks like an Italian tourist cycling his little heart out along the coast. He needed some activity and fresh air, as I am sure you do as well," Seb replied.

I did, I really did. I'd been cooped up in that house for a day and a half, not my typical way of being in the world. I also tried to hide the hurt that flared at the idea that Theo had left me here with Seb, that he needed to get away. Did he need to get away from me? He was right, and yet it still stung.

Turning, I noticed that the sky was a dark gray, the ocean frothing along the darker sand of the coast outside their windows. That called to me.

"Seb, if you think it is safe enough, I'd love even a walk on the beach before the storm hits. Anything to get some fresh air," I said.

"You got it. We're covered here. Let me just shoot a text to our team, and then we can head out the patio doors. I'll be close by, and I need you to stay tight to right in front of the house, but you can at least get some saltwater therapy. Vitamin sea and all that," he said as he stood.

"That would be wonderful, thank you, Seb," I replied softly.

"Hensley, I told Theo to go. He's Italian and fluent, so he can pass for a likable tourist more easily than I can as an American, even if I do know some French. I told him to go and clear his head while he was at it. He didn't want to leave you and I did promise him I'd die before I let anyone else in this house," Seb said, the most serious I had seen this jovial man be. "For what it's worth, the hurt I saw in your eyes might be justified, and that's not my business, but he didn't leave to get away from you. He left to keep you safe," he said. "The more we know, the safer you are."

I didn't trust myself to reply, and I simply nodded at him, as if I understood. As if that was perfectly clear when really, nothing was clear to me at all right now. Nothing made sense anymore. The control and resolve I had earlier were now slipping out of my grasp. I clenched my hands around the imagery in my mind, unwilling to lose the control I had fought for this morning. I needed to get outside before I broke.

Seb was tapping out a quick text before he turned toward the patio doors.

"A walk on the beach it is. We're all set," he said as he re-pocketed his phone, guiding me outside.

EIGHTEEN

THEO

I FOUND HER ANKLE-DEEP IN THE ANGRY WAVES BEHIND THE HOUSE. I'd nodded to Seb, sending my buddy back inside and making my own way to her. I needed to debrief him about what I saw in town. I'd taken some photos and sent those off to the team, yet it would take some time to track those, and from the looks of it, she was spiraling slightly. I felt kind of spun out myself.

"I'm not going to have to fish you out again, am I?" I tried for laughter, but it died in my throat when she turned to me, sadness heavy in her eyes.

Wordless, I made my way into the water and gathered her in my arms. I wrapped her against myself and simply held tight to her as the water swirled around us, cold raindrops beginning to land on us both. I'd give her the strength she needed right now, and that was all it could be.

From what I knew of Hensley, I was honored to be able to give her strength. She'd been strong for too long and had clearly reached a breaking point if the silent sobs against my chest were any indication. I sincerely hoped that I hadn't fucked with her head last night when I had lost my mind.

The rain was falling more steadily as the wind began whipping at Hensley's dark hair. I tightened the band of my arms around her again briefly and then kissed the edge of her ear gently. "Let's get you back inside, Hen, please." I had to let this woman go. She was not mine to keep, only to protect.

She nodded against my chest, then squeezed me tightly to herself before releasing me quickly and stepping back. It happened so fast, I almost missed it, but I had been paying attention to her. It was hard not to; she kind of consumed me most of the time. It was a goodbye squeeze, which I respected and needed myself, even though I hated it.

She still hadn't said a word, and yet her eyes were clearer. More determined. She dipped her chin again at me, stepped back toward the house, but held out her hand in my direction. A peace offering. Solidarity or reassurance, I wasn't sure, but I took her hand and started back for the house.

We made it about eight feet before the thunder boomed across the beach and a torrent of rain hit. We'd almost made it all of the way back, yet weren't quite inside and were drenched in moments. Seb held the door open for us as lightning streaked across the sky and the splitting sound of thunder rocked us again.

Seb was laughing at us as we made our way inside. He'd grabbed a few towels and handed one to Hensley first, and then me.

"The storms here come up quick, just like back home," Seb said.

"They do. Growing up, I always loved our time here, but the voracity of the storms scared me when they would blow in over the water like that. There's something about it here when that happens—the wildness of it, or, I don't know, the power in it . . ." She trailed off as she continued to dry her hair with the towel she'd placed between her hands. "I like control and order. The fierceness of it scared me then." She finished her sentence quieter, as if the realization was hitting her as she spoke. If I had to guess, I'd say that the all-encompassing power of the storm made her feel small and out of control; something that combined with her background would be terrifying.

"Sometimes it rains so much that the ocean and the sky become one, and even though I can appreciate how beautiful it can be, I'm grateful to only experience it from the shore. I'd hate to be out on the water when one of those blew in. I'd be toast." She took a beat and then firmed her shoulders.

"Guys, they blew up my boat. They may not have killed me as they intended to, but I loved that boat. It was part of who I am, a remnant of the family we once were, the life we once had. Now I'm pissed. Let's get these assholes, even if the asshole in question is my own damn brother."

Seb let out a whispered, "That's boss ass bitch Hen," after she finished, and I felt myself smiling at her. This woman was a warrior. And that . . . that was so fucking sexy.

We decided to take a quick break to each change into dry clothes, grab some coffee and then reconvene back in the living room to talk about our plans again, check in with the team, and monitor any local news sources for news of the explosion.

I was back downstairs before Hen so we went ahead and dialed in the team, bringing them up on the laptop monitor that Seb had set up. We were being regaled with little baby Alex cooing at us when Hensley joined us.

"Is that the newest member of your elite team? Recruiting starts earlier than I expected." She laughed and sat down next to Seb.

"He's actually the CEO. Tad wasn't getting it done, and Luke is worthless now that Hazel has a moment to relax after writing her book and getting it out in the world," I replied.

She laughed with him and Seb while a voice boomed out, "He'd fire you assholes first. He's a genius already."

That had them all laughing. Before too long, faces began

populating on the screen from across the world, some of them not in their DC headquarters. Lastly, Luke and Hazel had joined them, with Luke immediately sweeping baby Alex up into a snuggle.

"Hazelnut, we need some of these, pretty please?" Luke asked while the ladies introduced themselves.

I heard Hazel laugh. "Soon, Luke-a-licious, soon. Let me love on my nephew, please you big baby hog," she chided him, completely joking. It was an ongoing, playful fight among them all, who got to hold Alex next.

I had always laughed it off, okay with passing the little dude to the next pair of waiting hands, scared to hold on to him too long for fear I'd spill my guts to a newborn. 'Sorry I got your namesake killed, my dude. What can I say? A beautiful woman sidetracked me, and I lost our informant. Yep, your good old Uncle Alex went down, your dad tried to die with him, and our two others did, but hey, most of them are here now. Best I could do.' Yeah, no. Best to pass the baby along, cooing appropriately for three seconds, hoping no one paid too close attention to how I couldn't stand to hold him in my arms. My gut tightened at those thoughts, the breath robbed from my lungs as pain swept through me.

Hensley must have sensed something shift in me because through my fog, I saw her small hand on my knee, then felt the gentle squeeze. I allowed myself one singular moment of her comfort, and before I could make it awkward, she'd already removed her hand. Maybe she sensed the darkness seeping out of my pores, likely singed her hand where she had squeezed me.

"*D'accord?*" she asked me quietly, so as not to draw attention to either of us.

"*Bien, bien. Merci,*" I assured her, my lips automatically switching to the French she had uttered to me. I didn't know if she had switched languages to protect my wandering thoughts from the scrutiny of my team, or if it was instinct on her part.

She likely knew most of the team spoke multiple languages, but I thought that she was trying to protect me to a degree, which filled my heart with another new sensation, a surge of wonder. I realized that I liked it, whatever had driven her. My daydreams were interrupted by Tad's voice, being the last to join the video call.

"Hey, Hensley! If you wanted to reconnect, we could have thought of a better way!" Tad greeted her first, then his brothers in arms. "Assholes. Pleasure is all mine, obviously."

More greetings were exchanged as Hensley replied with a quiet *'bonjour'* and a murmur of thanks to Tad for sending me to her just in time. She was talking with Tad and the others, but her eyes kept coming back to mine.

I needed to snap out of it before they all asked me what was wrong. What would I tell them? Probably something like I'd confess to baby Alex. Cool, cool.

That would go over well, I was sure. Max might kill me, which was definitely what I deserved. With a mental eye roll at myself, I refocused on the conversation at hand. Tad was telling the others about Hensley's London office, that Nate was still keeping an eye on for any movement, and that he was due to report back any moment.

The conversation shifted to me and I updated them on what I had seen in town earlier on my tourist-looking mission. Briefly, wondered if I should have told Hensley privately what I saw before now, yet there hadn't really been time and besides, I wouldn't have worried about preparing anyone else. With that reminder to myself, I debriefed them all.

"There are guys searching for her. All men, none of them French from what I could tell. They are showing her photo to people and asking specific questions, claiming she's 'missing.'"

"That's good though, right?" she asked.

"No, I don't think so. The only people who would know to look inside this town would be the guys shooting at us that night. Otherwise, they'd still be searching closer to where the boat went down."

I ripped off the Band-Aid of the truth as quickly as I could, spelling it out clearly. No, we were closer to exposure than any of us would like to be.

"What else?" Luke asked.

"No sign of Adrien anywhere here in London, nothing. No sightings since the night of Hensley's call in the office or at his place in Kensington," Tad replied.

"No sign online either," Wills reported. "We haven't picked him up on anything, which is also weird. The lack of a hit in today's modern society of traffic cams, phones, security cameras, etc. makes it more interesting to *not* see someone."

"I was worried about that," Seb added. "So, what do we do here?"

"I think it's time to take a gander inside Adrien's place. We were hoping for a better report, and I try not to break and enter, you know, as a promise I made to my dad when we took this business live," Tad said.

"Hmm, he did authorize us to work adjacent to the lines. Can we consider this adjacent?" Seb asked.

"I left the definition unclear on purpose, and I can deal with him. It's time. We need more information, and that is the quickest, easiest place at the moment," Tad replied.

"It wouldn't be breaking and entering if I gave you all the code, right?" Hensley's voice spoke up. "If he hasn't changed it, I know it. I can tell you how to override his security systems. He lives in the house my parents had there. I can get you in."

"Hot diggity dog, Hen, yeah, that does make it cleaner," Tad said.

Hensley went on to walk Tad through the system, where to find an errant open window, and other security measures we would never have known about. Tad and Nate would have figured it out perfectly fine, but it was sure as shit easier this way.

"We'll breach tonight and see what we can find," Tad said.

"But back to here, stay the course for now?" Seb asked.

"I think so. You're covered there, and we don't want to react and get flushed out when we don't need to be," Luke added. I glanced up then at the faces of my team, spread out on the screens and sitting in front of me. I had to know, to double-check. With Hensley's safety, I had to.

"You're sure we're covered here?" I asked.

"That depends. How good was your Italian accent today in town? Any chance you were followed?" Seb asked. It was exactly the thing I needed to hear. My team had this, we were good.

"It was good. I replied as any Italian cyclist would." Smiling now, I also had to defend my birthright.

"You know my mom would kick all of your asses for even laughing at his dumb question about my accent. And Seb? She'd destroy you, you know it!" The moment of levity was exactly what we all needed. That was Seb though; he always knew what to say and when to say it.

"Ya, Baby Theo, I know." He leaned over and ruffled my hair as everyone laughed. I snuck a glance over at Hensley as I leaned out of the way. She was smiling, which made me more relaxed too.

"Okay, Adrien's place tonight in person for the London crew, lying low for you guys there, Theo and Seb, monitors here rolling for Wills and Mila, and Max and I will be rotating. Copy?" Luke made eye contact with each of us as he spoke.

Versions of 'copy' resounded on the call as we each acknowledged our orders and clicked off the line.

"So now what?" Hensley asked.

"Now, we lie low, talk through what you can remember specifically about the guys surrounding Adrien, talk about what he could be up to, nap, watch our own backs and well, talk some more," I replied.

Seb slapped his knees and stood. "I'm going to go check our perimeter and then dry off. You guys good here?"

"Yeah, all good. Be safe," I replied, not bothering to look up. I needed to talk to Hensley and wouldn't mind a few minutes of privacy to do it, even if I had the cameras pulled up and could watch Seb get drenched while I did it.

"Copy," he said again as he walked toward the patio door. He glanced back at me, nodded his head toward Hensley and tapped his watch. Of course. Leave it to Seb to tell me to talk with her and do it efficiently. I tilted my head toward the door he should walk through. *I know, bro, I know.*

As soon as he was through the door, I pulled up the security cameras on my phone and watched him make his way to the stone fence line. Talking to her as I did so, I played it on the larger screen of the computer in front of us.

"Hensley, we should talk about last night. I owe you an apology."

"No, Theo, you don't." She waited until I made eye contact to continue. "You really don't. It's I who owe you an apology. I came on to you, I called you guys for help, and you're just doing your job. I get it."

It was the out I thought I needed. The out I had to have. The reality is that as drawn to her as I was, and I was like a moth to a fucking flame, nothing could come of it. I wouldn't allow it. Not after the promise I'd made and, hell, I'd known her for zero seconds. Whatever this was, it had to pass. I knew that. I knew all of that, and yet, something still welled inside of me at her words. A denial still formed on my tongue, yet she cut me off, thankfully.

"I like to know what's coming, Theo. I like stability, I crave control, and this? This is completely out of control. That's the only reason I have to explain why I was so brazen with you last night. I mean, I barely know you." Hearing my own thoughts echoed back at me stung, even though they were my own damn thoughts.

"So listen, can we please not talk about this ever again? I need to focus on my life, figure out what is happening and then take control of whatever disaster has bloomed. I need to get a handle on this. Okay? *D'accord*?" she asked me.

"*Oui*." I nodded back at her, any words I could say stuck in my throat. "*D'accord*, okay."

She stood as I glanced back at the screen, watching Seb make his rounds.

"I'm going to take another hot shower to warm up while Seb is out." She hadn't made eye contact again after her speech, and at some level, I understood. I didn't love the churning inside of me and had nothing to say that would make any of this less awkward.

"Sounds good," I said, but she'd already left the room. I turned back to the monitors, watching Seb and trying my damndest not to feel like something was lost here in the last ten minutes. She needed control. I was the opposite of that. I loved those damn storms that whipped up and raged around me, inside of me. I welcomed them, but she was terrified of them. She was polished and posh. I was a smarter than average Marine. Former Marine. Former because we'd all gotten out after I had colossally failed everyone and gotten three of our guys killed. Oh yeah, that.

She would survive this and go on to do great things, live the life she deserved. I, on the other hand, did not deserve anything all that great. No matter what the team doc had said, I still couldn't come to grips with my role in how it all went down. I would never be able to. I had tried, I'd listened to the doc, I just couldn't let her words in fully. Sure, I had my moments of not being a total recluse now, especially since Hazey and Vi had come along, but I didn't deserve what they did. I wasn't going to have the happy ending they were enjoying. One, I had made a promise on the sand that night as I'd watched my brothers die, and two, I carried the secret of it with me, not man enough to talk about it with Max.

I couldn't lose him too. I sure as hell hadn't earned a place in his life these days, yet I'd die without it. Max was one of my brothers, too. I couldn't lose them, not when they were all I had.

She'd been right to walk away. Explosive chemistry aside, we were night and day, and a guy like me could only pretend to be worthy of the dream for so long.

NINETEEN

HENSLEY

I worked hard to push thoughts of Theo from my mind. He was incredible, and comfortable in a way that had completely floored me. I'd lost my head last night, caught up in him. Using him, I think, even though the idea of that left a sour taste in my mouth. I hadn't meant to, and I was drawn to him, but was that because of who he was or because he had seemed so safe?

For as long as I could remember, well. . .since the night my grandparents had come into my room and told me that my parents' plane had gone down, I had needed to be in control of my emotions. Call it a reaction to the trauma, call it an only-girl thing, whatever you call it, I needed it. I was well known for my control in the company, and with others I worked with. It was one of the things that made me most effective in my role. I was controlled and kind, which made my job of mergers and acquisitions much smoother.

What it didn't do for me was keep me warm at night. I knew that I only dated certain guys for a reason, because again, I knew I could control them. But last night? Last night with Theo, I had been over my head. Drowning in his very maleness. His lips, those hands, the surety of his movements and how he had commanded my body. I had given him control so easily, and that scared the hell out of me. It was completely out of character, and my heart couldn't take it right now. Right now, I needed my vaunted control more than ever.

I had this trick that my grand-mère had taught me when I was young, right after losing my parents and feeling like my whole world was over. It had kept me going this far, so I closed my eyes and started to count. Starting at ten and working my way backward, I gave myself the count to mentally spiral, to worry, to freak out, to panic, to regret walking away from Theo downstairs, to regret not asking him to hold me.

Three, two, one. Done. I took a deep breath and arched my back, dropped my shoulders and pictured the giant one in my head dissolving. There, freakout complete. Now, a shower and then down to the business of finding my asshole brother and getting him help. Or locked up. I didn't care which at that moment. My empathy was buried along the bottom of the ocean floor at Juno Beach.

Doing just that, I made my way back downstairs to find Seb heating up something that smelled delicious on the stove. And holy shit, was that fresh bread baking?

I asked him as much as my stomach rumbled.

"Yep. Luke and his provisioning team are the best. Doesn't matter where we are, how much time he has, he makes it all happen. I found it in the freezer with instructions, along with the vegetable stew." He stirred the pot as he spoke. "I didn't even know you could freeze bread."

"I hadn't thought about it, but why not? I guess we could get arrested here in France for that though. It's literally against the law to sell bad bread," I told him.

"*Vraiment?*" He smirked at me. The man was also seriously handsome. Dirty blond hair, blue eyes, he looked like an older surfer type. Objectively, everyone on Tad and Luke's team was gorgeous. Must be in the water in America.

His switch to French passed me by at first, mentally trapped as I was in trying not to picture Theo under me last night, his hard thighs holding me steady. Dang, there he was creeping back into my thoughts again and again.

"Parlez-vous Francais?" I asked him if he spoke French.

He'd asked me, "truly" about the bread, confirming what I'd said about it being against the law to sell bad bread.

"Oui, but I prefer English if that's okay with you," he replied.

"Of course, glad to know you speak it though. How many languages do you speak?" I asked. My experience with American men was limited to business relationships, and they had simply expected to do business in English.

"We're required to have mastery of four languages for MARSOC, the Marine Special Forces," he replied.

"Oh really?" That genuinely intrigued me and I wondered which languages Theo spoke. Italian, French and what else.

"German, Spanish and Arabic, both Iraqi and Levantine dialects," Seb said, reading my mind. "He speaks six languages. Baby Theo isn't just a pretty face and big muscles." He laughed.

"That's incredible. I had no idea you guys were required to speak so many languages for your job. I guess I never thought about it, but I never would have assumed that level of mastery," I told him.

"Most people don't realize that, or what it takes to make it in special forces, but I've always thought that's okay. I don't want people to have to worry that we can't do it. We can do hard things, you know?" Seb asked. I got the sense he was asking rhetorically, so I waited.

Sure enough, he spoke again. "Theo has had a hard couple of years, but he's one of the best guys I've ever known. His story isn't mine to tell, and well, we are working but who am I to judge the timing? Be patient with him okay?" He had poured the soup into three bowls and he turned to me then, his stare more intense than I'd seen from him this far.

"It's not like that." I wasn't sure what to say, but I didn't want Seb to have the wrong idea. "Really, he saved me, he's been great. No patience needed," I assured him.

"Okay Hensley, I'm hearing you but for what it's worth, I haven't seen this Theo in two years and here we are, two days after he fishes you out of the water, and there are glimmers of the guy he used to be coming back to us. So, no pressure certainly, but I wanted you to know. I think you did that. I'll drop it for now, but please remember that you might need to be patient with him at some point. What can I say, us guys are pretty dumb when it comes to women, even when we speak six languages." He winked at me and turned back to the oven to pull the bread out, leaving me speechless.

Glimmers of who he was? What exactly had happened two years ago? I started to ask and then caught myself, he'd already told me it wasn't his story to tell and frankly, I needed to control my own curiosity about Theo.

It didn't help matters when Theo sauntered in, bare chested, gray sweatpants slung low on his hips, that deep vee of muscles flexing as he walked. His hair was still wet and my eyes followed one single drop from the ends of his strands, down onto his shoulder, then sliding down his pec. I swallowed sharply and turned away, busying myself with grabbing spoons for all of us as the guys talked about what Seb had found to heat up.

No sooner had that first slurp of soup hit my tongue than Theo's phone rang. I saw "Mila" on the screen as he pushed the speakerphone button to accept the call.

"Hey, Mila, you're on speaker with all three of us," he said.

"Good, hi Hen! How are you guys holding up?"

A tiny smile grew at her words, she was such a joyful person and her energy vibrated across the Atlantic. She was one of those people who made you smile before you even realized it. The idea of getting to know her more after this was over started to bubble up in my mind and even though I knew that to be a small likelihood, I couldn't stop the tiny kernel of hope that I would have time for that from welling up.

"All good here," Theo quipped. Seb said something too, the easy camaraderie among the three flowing while I ate another bite of soup.

"Awesome sauce!" Mila's enthusiasm was expected at this point, yet what I didn't expect was that she also then immediately launched into business mode. It was an impressive switch, and I was again struck by how smart these people were and how lucky I was that I had called Tad when I did.

"We are picking up an increase in chatter there, which we expected ahead of the Olympics, yet one phrase keeps coming up: *Liberte*," Mila said.

"'*Liberte, egalie, fraternite,*' a motto of France. It means liberty, egality and fraternity. It's the motto of the French Republic, dating back to the Revolution in the 1700s," I shared.

I'm sure they all knew that, yet I continued on just in case, "It means exactly what you'd expect it to. Solidarity, togetherness, equality of people, freedoms from tyranny. It's one of those patriotic sayings a culture has, a rally cry of sorts. You can see it on buildings all across France."

"I take it you're hearing this more than you'd expect? I would imagine that right now, it's a pretty popular thing to say, with so many people coming in for the Olympics in Paris," Seb said.

"Exactly. At first it didn't hit my internal radar, yet when I stepped back, got some altitude from it and reviewed it from a larger perspective, I realized only that word, *liberty*, from the three in the motto is used increasingly. And, only in pockets of geographical areas, one of which was London. I think it is a code of some sort," Mila said.

"The motto rose to popularity in the 1790s, leading into the French Revolution. It was a rally cry and became institutionalized in the 1800s. If someone is using it as code, it means they've weaponized a very powerful part of our culture." The thought struck me as incomprehensible, yet something was niggling at my memory. A rush of queasiness rose in my throat, burning there as I forced a swallow down.

"I've seen this word, I've heard it recently too, more than the other two words. I just didn't pick up on it because I see those words everywhere. *Mon Dieu*, had Adrien been working on our project named *Liberte* again?" Thoughts were blurring through my memory, trying to remember specifics, trying to remember the context I've heard liberty lately. I heard the others voices low in the background of the buzz inside of me, yet I couldn't focus. It hit me, I knew which project that should have been, yet it had closed three years ago, why was Adrien in it now?

"I. . ." I started, but stopped. What if I was wrong on this? Doubt spiraled through me, mixing with disbelief. It didn't make any sense, but why else would he be back in that project?

Coughing slightly to clear my throat, I glanced up as the words flying around me died down. Two sets of expectant eyes were watching me, curious. The phone with Mila on the line laying on the counter, waiting. The clacking on a keyboard was Mila working in the background while she waited for me to talk.

"Project Liberty was the name of the buyout of a company in Lyon that we did three years ago. The project is closed, there is nothing that still should have been coming up for Adrien, yet it's the most logical answer."

"Tell us more about the project, how it came online, anything you can think of." Theo commanded, all business mode now. My chin dropped to my chest in an effort to nod, but my motions were jerky. I forced myself to push air out and then breathe it back in to slow down the memories. We were on to something, I could taste it, yet I had to get through as many details as possible, not knowing which detail might help us.

"I first visited Lyon when I went with my Grand-père Hugo to visit a smaller technology company he was buying, Liberty Devices. That family wanted to retire and had no one in the upcoming generations who wanted to work there. They'd been successful and didn't have to work, so they reached out to

Grand-père to strike a deal and sail off into the sunset with their money."

"How long ago was that? Do you still own that company?" Theo asked at the same time Seb asked, "What do you mean by tech company?"

"It was a little over three years ago and yes we still own it. They manufactured, we now manufacture, a scanning technology for explosives. Like a CT scan, but instead of using it on people, the devices are typically used in train stations, airports, some larger venues in the UK and France. We aren't in the States yet, but that was part of the expansion plan when we bought them. Grand-père saw an opportunity to bring more aspects of the safety industry under one umbrella. Our base expertise is underwater sonar, exploration, recovery. From there, we expanded into maritime safety at ports. Our company expanded with using the same operational formulas, combining with new tech as it came online, to protect more places, like airports."

"And no one from that family would have defined it as a hostile takeover?" Seb asked, glancing my way.

"Not that I'm aware of and I was on-site for the entirety of their transition. I fell in love with the city of Lyon, and decided to move there to help integrate them into Richard Companies, which went well. We've bought many smaller organizations over the years for the technology they created, and integration and transition planning are my department. I lead Mergers & Acquisitions, but our formula is about more than EBITDA and SDE." Noticing that both Theo and Seb had gone from nodding along to furrowed brows, I retraced my steps. Ah, okay. "Earnings Before Interest Taxes, Depreciation, and Amortization and Seller's Discretionary Earnings. Those are just two parts of the M & A formula. Traditionally at our company, merging one organization into another takes intricate planning, communication and levels of care. This has ironically been the point of issue between me and Adrien lately. In the last ten months, he's been on an acquisition bender, with zero strategy laid out. Not only does that undermine my actual position in my own company, it de-legitimizes the value I've brought in adding more to our M & A formula." Heat was creeping up my neck thinking about it. Anger did that to me and I was reminded again that in this mess of my brother's making, I'd been losing control over this for far longer than I realized.

That made the heat spreading across my skin bloom even more, but I continued, "In turn, it will cost us more if we stray from the cultural integration part of my formula, and long term, those people won't be as invested as they should be. Then, we'll suffer higher turnover, all things that cost us money and most importantly, isn't who we are to the people."

"But you said it went well, right?" Seb asked.

"It did, and it was wrapped over a year ago, or it should have been. Liberty Devices was a well-oiled machine when we bought it. They didn't need to sell, they wanted to."

"And there hasn't been any issues since then?" Mila asked from the speaker.

"None. It went smoothly. I've stayed in Lyon because I love it, yet operations there are mostly manufacturing. The administration aspects are all in Paris so that the French employees didn't have to move far, with a main presence in Richard Companies headquarters in London," I said. "I called Tad from the London office."

"Have you heard the word 'liberty' lately from Adrien?" Theo's voice was low, contemplative. The furrow was back in his brow.

"Yes. We don't call the company Liberty Devices any longer, yet I have noticed that he's used the word and I've seen notes on his desk with the word on them, I just didn't think anything of it. I feel pretty dumb right now, why didn't I think about how that shouldn't be coming up any more?" The crux of the matter for me is that I really did feel incredibly stupid. What-ever was happening with Adrien had happened right under my nose and for someone who prides themselves on knowing other humans well, reading people, and knowing the business, I should have caught on somewhere. The shame of not doing so was brewing a toxic cocktail inside of me, with anger as its base.

The guys had been silent around me, waiting to see if I'd continue, but I was tapped out. The realization that I hadn't had any control for months was sitting heavily on my chest, pushing me down. I could hear the clacking of Mila's keyboard on the speakerphone still, yet it was as if we were all caught up in what to say next.

"I'm sorry I didn't think of this until now, truly," I added.

"Hey, you didn't catch it because you live it every day. It's normal, don't beat yourself up about it." Theo's soft-spoken words broke the spell around us all and although I didn't believe him, I appreciated his attempt to absolve me of missing something that could be life and death. It would have been life and death, my own! Sitting here with Theo and Seb, it was easy to forget that I had almost burned to death, trapped on my beautiful boat just a few days ago. I could have drowned. I would have drowned, had it not been for Theo's excellent timing. I definitely wouldn't have made it out of the water and away from the shoreline without him either. It seemed the heroics were stacking up and at the bottom, my life.

I knew I owed him and frankly, it cut deeply that I'd let myself be in that situation to begin with. How could I have been this blind to my own surroundings? I could blame Adrien, and I did, yet I took full responsibility too. My own naivety had comforted me, blinding me to what was really happening, and I'd almost paid with my life.

"Hensley, I agree with Theo, you are overly close to all of this. Being that close, we miss things. I didn't think about it at first either, I simply have the benefit of amazing tech and the ability to step back and map word usage, patterns and geographic hits all at the same time. I mean, Uncle Sam pays us very well to put these types of things together, don't beat yourself up." It was the most solemn I'd heard Mila, and frankly, I missed the joy. She too was giving me a pass, one I still wasn't sure I could accept.

"Let me see what I can dig into now, knowing what we know about Liberty. We're deep into Adrien's accounts and hopefully, we can catch a break soon. This may be nothing, yet we don't know if we don't explore it," Mila added.

"I think it is something. I don't know why and I don't even trust myself fully right now, yet I think you found something important." My words were for Mila, yet Theo caught my eyes, his own steady. He gave me a nod too, an *umph* of agreement.

"Copy. Bye boys, bye Hensley. And seriously, don't stress on this stuff, I'm like a lab with a peanut butter bone on this stuff. I'll find the links. Toodles!" With the last flash of her orneriness, the line went silent.

"She's absolutely right, she is like a dog with a bone. She'll find it. Let's finish up some lunch and then we can talk more about any other companies you've worked through the acquisition on. We might be right about Liberty, yet there could be other paths from the word liberty that I want to talk through," Seb said.

"Agreed. You mentioned the word started as part of the French Republic rally cry in the 1790s. Tell us more about the historical usage and we can go from there," Theo added.

Shifting gears mentally, I devoted myself to anything that would help get me, my company, and what was left of my company back on track. Sifting through my primary school history lessons, I told them everything I knew about the French Revolution, the days of guillotines and Robespierre.

TWENTY

THEO

I thought I knew French history. Turns out, I hadn't known as much as I thought I did. Story of my life. We were still talking about liberty, egality and fraternity hours later, late into the day when the team from DC called us again on the laptop I had set up our first night here.

"Bonsoir guys, find anything?" Seb, being closest to the computer, had pushed the accept button and greeted them. They must have found something, everyone was on the call from various locations. Greetings were brief, something was definitely going down.

"Hey guys, I just got an alert from the cyber alarms I set up," Wills cut through immediately. "Babe, pull up the news feeds please," he said to Mila.

Within moments, we could all see the reports that the boat which exploded in the harbor off the idyllic coast of France belonged to Hensley Richard, of the global empire that was Richard Companies. Mila had pulled up an English-speaking broadcast in addition to several French-speaking stations.

Witnesses were being interviewed claiming to have seen a

woman board the boat earlier in the evening and many feared the philanthropist and business leader to be killed in the explosion.

As more images of the wreckage interspersed with old videos of Hensley at different events flashed across the screen, the London-based reporter's voice interrupted, "I'm told we have a Richard Companies spokesperson on the line now, one moment and we'll move to our on-site reporter Lana Taylor."

My gaze locked on Hensley, watchful in how this would impact her when I should have been scanning the background of the people at the scene. She'd been determined to tell us as much as possible all afternoon, but I could tell she was still conflicted on missing the signs within her company and from her brother.

"Lana, tell us what you know." The video feed had switched to a petite redhead standing along the shoreline where emergency crews still worked in the background.

"Yes, Lana Taylor here with Ken Seimers, Richard Companies vice president and spokesperson." The camera panned out to include a man joining Lana at the microphone. He was well-dressed, in his sixties, with tanned skin and smooth blond hair. He was polished, with the right tinge of grave concern, and I knew his face, had just seen it this morning.

Hensley's face had gone completely white as Ken spoke into Lana's microphone. "That is not our VP, nor our spokesperson." Her words were whispered, as if she was in disbelief, and something in the tone caused the hairs on the back of my neck to stand up at attention.

"It is with deep regret that I share the impossible news that we presume Miss Richard set this explosion herself. We've done our best to hide the deterioration of our beloved colleague's mental state, and yet our intention in doing so was misplaced. We know now that underestimating her was both dangerous and naïve, and now Adrien Richard has likely paid the price. Coming on here today is a plea from me to Hensley wherever she is hiding. Hensley, please come out, tell us what you've done to Adrien. Was he on the boat? Have you buried him elsewhere? Please Hensley, for the honor of your grandparents and their legacy, come forward and tell us where he is so that we can lay him to rest properly." Ken's voice had been strong, perfectly pitched. He stared hard into the camera as Lana gathered herself to reply, shock evident on her impish features.

"Sir, are you saying that Hensley Richard did this? The noted philanthropist, revered business leader, and society darling . . . is a murderer? Are you saying she's killed Adrien Richard, her own brother?" Lana stuck the microphone back to Ken's lips.

"We believe so Miss Taylor, sadly. Hensley Richard is out there somewhere and she should be considered dangerous. We need her found to get her the care she needs and peace for her brother. To help with that, we are offering a one million pound reward as to her whereabouts. We have set up a tip line to report any sightings and information . . ." His voice trailed as he nodded back to Lana and the London reporter's voice came across the video.

"We're loading that from the studio now Mr. Seimers," she said as the number began to roll across the bottom of the screen in a ticker.

"Okay, listeners, you've heard it here first on UK Broadcasting Central, Hensley Richard is a danger to herself and others. Call 0800-269-2653 immediately. . ." she repeated the number and lamented over how such a tragic story was unfolding for one of the most beloved figures in both the UK and France.

"Hensley, are you okay?" Tad said into the quiet that had descended upon all of us as the newscaster continued to verbally dismantle the credibility Hensley had built her life creating.

Hensley's darkened eyes flashed to mine and what I saw there made my heart stutter in my chest. Fear. Abject fear. And yet, now I wasn't sure I could trust it, trust her. Shit, fear welled within me too, had I been conned? Again?

"I've never seen that man in my life. Never. I promise you, he is not our spokesperson, he is not a VP, I don't know who he is." Her words were softly spoken and yet firm in their conviction, but now something else was churning within me. Anger of my own. Was I being played again? Was another beautiful woman fucking with my team, and was I the weak link, again?

"You have to believe me, please. I have never seen his face before." Hensley was speaking to everyone, but her eyes were on mine alone. A desperate plea, one I didn't believe for one second.

"You may not have Hensley, but I have," I said, ice racing along my veins, doubt making me cold.

TWENTY-ONE

HENSLEY

THEO'S WORDS WERE AKIN TO A BOMB DROPPING IN THE LIVING room of the beautiful old home, popping the bubble of safety and raining reality coldly down on our heads.

"He's one of the guys that I saw earlier this morning in town." Theo's elaboration did nothing to slow the spiral I was feeling deeply within my core. Thoughts and words were jumbled in my mouth, rendering me completely speechless. That fortitude and unshakable control I was known for and loved, now completely obliterated. What in the world was happening?!

"Shit guys, that asshole just put a bounty on her head. Now everyone is searching for her," Seb said. "It's brilliant of him, now they've turned two countries filled with people who are hunting for her, and that one million pound reward."

"For that kind of money, there will be Americans making the trip over to find her. That's way over a million dollars in reward money," Wills added.

There were grumblings around me about the wrinkle of complication that brought out, but when I moved my lips again, the first thing that came out surprised even me.

"You believe me? Just like that?" I asked.

"Of course we do Hen!" Mila assured her as the others nodded and added a version of yes. I glanced back up into Theo's handsome face, seeking him through the reassuring faces. His was not reassuring, nor was there a smile there. His eyes were calculating now, cold, assessing.

"Like Mila said, of course we believe you. Why wouldn't we?" He asked me. The emphasis he placed on the last words were not lost on me. Did he seriously think I could have done this? He was the one who pulled me out of the water, saved my damn life. My life! Why would I do this? My brother! Physical pain cramped my heart in that moment, I didn't know which way was up, which way was down, nor how to get out of the death spiral I found myself in.

"Adrien is missing now too? Is he okay?" Confusion was making me slow, but what if Adrien was really missing, or worse, dead?

"He's either in hiding, in on this to lure you out, or . . ." Theo kept staring at me, that questioning glint in his eyes. Was I the only one who noticed that his entire demeanor had changed?

"Or the situation escalated quickly and we need to consider that he's a victim too," Seb finished Theo's sentence, yet I got the sense that wasn't how Theo had wanted to finish it.

"Hensley, this could mean that he is in over his head, to your earlier question of the levels of insanity he may have reached," Max said from the screen of the laptop.

I wrapped my arms around myself as they all started talking at once. Theories whizzing around, ideas shifting and then dropped, shared and then discounted. And every single time I looked up, Theo was watching me like a hawk.

A new wave of fear curdled within me. If Adrien wasn't the bad guy, who was? Who was Ken Seimers and how could he be speaking as a VP of my own damn company? Exactly how powerful of a person was this that they were dealing with? I was scared, so damn scared, and so alone. We were privately held.

We had a small board of directors, and I trusted those people with everything we had. There is no way we had a VP that I didn't even know about.

Thank goodness I'd called Tad back in London. I'd be dead more than once over the course of the last forty-eight hours without them. But why was Theo examining me like that? We'd formed a connection, but maybe that was the danger? I clearly didn't have one single clue as to what was going on in my own life so what did I know. I wondered if Titan Group could help me solve this. These men and women were the best of the best, and their resources had to outmatch those of whoever was after me, right? If we could just get to Lyon, I knew I had to have some type of proof there that I hadn't done this.

Hope lit within me that this wasn't my brother's doing after all, and yet he was the only one who would know how to find me, the only one who would know the significance of the area, of the sailboat I'd been on. Damn it! I was overly conflicted right now. What if he was hurt in this? Or worse, dead? The thought that somewhere, Adrien had needed me and I'd failed him cut like a knife.

"We stay the course," she heard Tad say. "You guys head to Lyon and see what you can find in your notes Hensley. The only path through this is forward and we need to get as much data as possible to make sound decisions. We've got photos from this morning from Theo and will stay on tracking those leads. But now, you need to lay as low as possible from everyone. No one can see Hensley's face or you'll be tracked like a reality show."

"I agree," Luke added as the others nodded. That settled it then, I was heading back to my townhome in Lyon, which I was eager to do, even if there was a bounty on my head. I had tons of notes detailing what I'd observed, names and accents, anything I could think of to notate, I'd done so before impetuously heading to London to talk some sense into my brother once and for all. I had to have something in there that exonerated me and hopefully, found my brother. If he was alive, that is.

"Nate and I will break into the offices here and see what we can access. I hate to do that, but it's time. We need to move into offense on this, guys," Tad said.

"Again, I agree. We'll keep digging into Adrien's life here and I'll connect with our friends in the French authorities, it's time to give them an update," Luke added. "And we need to know everything about Liberty Devices. I don't like that the tech they created is to scan for explosives, we've had a boat blown up, and too many unknowns."

"Agreed, it's all too coincidental. Start there, then see where this Ken Seimers came from and what his background is. Hen says he's not who he says he is, and he's made a pretty big play to do what he just did," Seb said from next to me, a still deathly quiet Theo watching me.

"Check Adrien's new acquisitions," I said, my voice soft at first and then gathering conviction. "It has to be something regarding the acquisitions he started in the last six to seven months, that's when his patterns changed." I knew it, felt it in my gut. Something was there.

"Follow the money," a few voices said at the same time. I focused on the screen, seeing the faces of these people I had met that were willing to do so much for me, then glanced to Seb and to Theo.

"Yes, follow the money. The new money," I added, praying for something that would both exonerate me, and maybe, just maybe, prove my brother wasn't a monster.

"Guys, be careful. We've got a bounty on Hensley now and they know they're likely to flush us out with this, and they know we are in the area. Time's up. Take care of her, yourselves, and get your asses safely to Lyon," Luke ordered.

"Copy that," Seb said, Theo still watching me. A shiver raced up my back, sending goosebumps along my arms. That stare was menacing. Confusion curdled inside of me at the assessment in his normally kind eyes.

We made plans to disconnect and prepare to leave for Lyon at nightfall, counting on the darkness to shield me as much as possible.

Everyone had their jobs to do, and they'd do them well and ask for help when necessary. That's what it meant to work on a high functioning team. You did your role and were transparent when you needed help. You relied on others to do the same, and you worked together for a shared vision. It was all so easy, as long as human egos didn't gum up the works. But these guys weren't like that, they were brothers by choice. They'd been thrown together and forged in blood, courtesy of Uncle Sam, but there was no going back. They'd always operate as a team, and I was overcome with gratitude that they were on my side in this mess, even if Theo had gone dark on me. I was hurt, deeply hurt by his withdrawal, the lingering unspoken accusations. I thought we had something last night and then this morning, he sensed I needed a hug when I was at my lowest standing there in the surf. Lowest. Pfft. Now perhaps, I was lower. I hoped this was my lowest, I wasn't sure how much more I could take. The one stalwart I had in this crazy situation was now inspecting me as if I was under a freaking microscope.

I needed to get back to my desk and for the first time in my life, I was ready to leave this part of the world. I had this prickling sensation that we were on borrowed time here as it was with Ken in the village earlier. *Merde!* That meant he'd been extremely close to Theo too and the idea that he was putting his life between the bad guys and me again practically knocked the wind from my lungs. The storm had gathered strength outside of our beautiful stone home, raging and angry. It matched the tempest inside of me then, mirroring the chaos within my head.

With not much else to do, I set about packing some food for us for the road. The guys were loading weapons and checking maps while I did that. I packed as much as I could, filled a few travel coffee mugs with fresh espresso and threw some of the wonderfully soft clothes from my appointed room into a bag. Perhaps that would help me blend in. If anyone had studied me, they were likely hunting for the professional and public-facing version I gave to the world, not realizing that I didn't always look like that. Snagging a ball cap style hat from the closet that read 'Chiefs,' I added it to my head, looking very American in the mirror staring back at myself.

Ready to go, I waited for the guys to grab their clothes and close up the house from the kitchen, overlooking the patio and the ocean across the expanse of yard. I loved this place, and I made a vow that I'd be back some day, alive and healthy, not tracked as if I was a crazed killer. The storm had metaphorically dragged me inside of the depths, and I would do whatever I could to climb back to safety.

"Let's roll," I heard Seb call out as he headed toward the garage. I turned to head that way and found Theo in the doorway, watching me. Wary, intense. His eyes never left me, but the softness, the gentleness, the laughter from before was gone. Wordlessly, I got in the waiting car.

With that, we left the stone house along the churning waves of the Atlantic, headed east for Lyon, yet deeper into the storm.

TWENTY-TWO

THEO

SEB TOOK THE FIRST LEG OF THE DRIVE. WE DECIDED THAT WE'D
both sit up front and keep Hensley in the backseat so she could
lay down and hide when necessary. I wouldn't typically let
someone I wasn't sure I could trust get behind me, but I knew
she didn't have any weapons. I'd checked, not willing to leave
that to chance. Thankfully, she had no idea that I had conspicu-
ously patted her down in those skin tight yoga pants. Glancing
touches as I helped her into the car, loaded the bags, even took
the offered coffee from her hands. Nope, I wasn't trusting her
without checking, but having my hands on her, even for a
moment had done a number on my head. I wanted to trust her,
this woman who had shared so much of herself with me in such
a short time. Yearning to be able to believe her churned in my
gut, yet I didn't even trust myself to know at this point. The
dissonance was back, as was the lack of trust I had in myself to
discern which way was up and which was down.

It was early evening, that melding hour of twilight when it
wasn't quite dark and wasn't quite light. I'd have preferred to

wait to leave until it was darker, but we needed as many hours as possible and the twilight departure time allowed us a sliver of hope to blend in. With the storm, there was likely to be less traffic too, which made it tougher to blend.

My thoughts were a mess. I was a mess. I fixed my gaze on the countryside and tried to make sense of the turmoil rolling through me. I'd always loved this time of day, caught between the intensity of the sunlight and the cloak of a dark night. I was a night owl too, I was more comfortable in darkness these days. It kind of matched my anguish at the moment. Caught in between. I wanted to trust Hensley, this woman who had ensnared me, yet I didn't even trust myself any more.

The last two years had been a hell of my own making, even when there were lighter moments, like after the guys had saved Vi and Hazey, or when we'd found Wills and Mila after they'd been taken. I felt like I'd snuck out into the daylight a bit and laughed with Hazey last summer, but the darkness kept dragging me down. What kind of man was I that I had made a vow two damn years ago, and I had already wished for more when Hensley climbed on to my lap last night. Shit, had it just been last night?

She came across as genuine and rationally, I knew that she hadn't blown herself up, I'd seen her thrown from the damn boat. But, old wounds scarred deep. I'd let a woman sidetrack me before, at the coffee shop in Mosul that day, the day I should have been following Max's informant. Had I not been sidetracked, I would have seen the informant being tailed by someone else, someone truly evil. Someone who had tortured our informant for the information they'd shared and then used that intel to ambush us.

That damn mission had been fubar from the beginning. Fucked up beyond all recognition, indeed. Two of our fourteen man MARSOC crew had been sick with food poisoning, but we'd decided to go anyway, thinking we were fine. It should have been an easy recon night, not the disaster that awaited us.

Three of our team had been killed. Alex, Max's little brother, and two navy corpsmen who were newer to the team. I hadn't known Sam and Luis long, but fuck, their deaths were on me too.

Alex, I'd known forever. We'd met early on in the Individual Training Course, ITC, required for special forces in the Marines. I'd known Max since school and naturally, Alex fit right in. We'd been tight because we were the youngest.

It should have gone down so differently, would have been different, if the informant hadn't been picked up and tortured . . . on my watch. The shame of it was my darkest secret. Only Luke, Tad, Seb, and me knew that it was the informant who gave us up. I'd seen the post-op report and debriefed with both of them after we knew Max was going to make it. Max still didn't know what had happened. He hadn't been ready and then Violet had burst into his life and he'd left that horror behind him, with the help of the team doctor. Max would never forgive me if he knew, and I would never want him to. I couldn't tell him now, it had been too long. Living with what I caused and now, not telling Max the whole story, was my own personal hell. Flirting, being taken in by a pretty face, I had been the death of his brother and two others. Now, was history repeating itself? Hensley was gorgeous, distracting, had almost come on to me. I hadn't pushed her away, being lured in by her, intoxicated by her. I wanted her, and if I'm honest with myself, I still do. But now, now I can't go there. She could be lying and I'll be damned if I fall for that again.

Hardening my heart against Hensley and the woman I had thought she was, I forced myself back to the here and now, scanning the road behind us.

Twilight was a time caught between the worlds, maybe there was something to that. I had that type of tension stirring within myself, a dissonance in where I was. Who I was. I couldn't be taken for a fool again, my team, my brothers, depended on me.

The first four hours of the drive were uneventful. Seb did

most of the talking, asking Hensley about Adrien, who Ken could be, anything else to pass the time. We'd mapped a route down to Lyon that avoided Paris, where security and masses of people would be tight. It added time to the drive, yet taking the lesser roads and going through the smaller towns and villages along the way was far safer, particularly with such a large public bounty on Hensley's head.

We'd only left Bourges moments before the satellite phone rang. The inside of the car was tense, waiting for the proverbial shoe to drop so when it rang, all three of us flinched to varying degrees. Relieved it was Luke calling in, I accepted the call over the speakers in the SUV.

"Checking in, guys. We have some intel on Ken Seimers and it isn't great. Ken Seimers is a billionaire recluse. He made his fortune from an inheritance built in oil and gas and is tough to pin down," Luke's deep voice boomed across the quieter expanse of the car.

"Something is weird. Why would an oil billionaire be the VP of someone else's company, unless there is fuckery afoot," Seb said. "By tough to pin down, what do you mean?" he went on.

"As usual, you sniffed something out alarmingly quickly Sebby," Luke replied. "Ken Seimers hasn't been seen in years. He was known for being ruthless in business and at growing his fortune, and yet he left the public eye about twelve years ago to get married and raise a family out of the limelight, on the island of Corsica."

"So, he's back? Coming back in hot?" I asked.

"I've never met Ken, I swear," Hensley added.

"I don't doubt you for one minute Hensley," Seb reassured her, but continued. "Why is he popping up now, and in a new industry? It doesn't make sense, especially without you having any prior knowledge of him."

It didn't make sense, unless she was lying. Cramps sharpened in my stomach.

"Did you check with our old pal Anton? If anyone has a

pulse on oil and gas over the last few decades, it's him," Seb added. We'd tracked Anton last year, thinking he was a master-mind to gain control of oil and gas resources in the Gulf, but we'd had the wrong guy. Thankfully, having the wrong guy hadn't gotten us all killed and in that insanity, Luke had finally admitted he loved Hazel, and that he could keep her as reason-ably safe as a human could for another human. I was glad he'd pulled his head out of his ass, I loved Hazel like a sister now too.

"My brilliant Hazelnut recommended the same thing, so we'll get on that. Fucker owes us," Luke replied.

That made both Seb and me chuckle and I caught myself right before I let Hensley in on the secret. If she was playing us, the less information she had, the better.

"The other thing is that Adrien still hasn't been located, likely since shortly after leaving the office that night Hensley was hiding and waiting him out to flee," Luke added. "Any advice on where to search for him Hensley? We can't ignore that he could still be on the run or chasing you."

"He has a house in the Lake District, his primary is a flat in London, he could be in the States hiding out in Colorado . . ." She trailed off, and I was reminded that Hensley Richard was rich as fuck. I hadn't considered that yet and frankly, I didn't care. I was also rich AF, thanks to Luke's head for numbers and pooled investments. I hadn't been raised with any money to speak of, had never really thought much about money, which in hindsight, I realized was a true luxury itself. To not think about money as a kid was a privilege, and that just grew as you aged. I was an ass for not realizing that sooner.

I'd tried to lure my family out of Brooklyn, down to DC, or to buy them houses wherever they wanted, but they wouldn't hear of it. I had a few properties myself, yet not like Hensley had. I was happy to be in DC most of the time, close to the other guys, and now, their wives. I was home where they were, and that worked for me. Not much to tie me down. Thinking about that reminded me of how I'd come to be in Paris in the first place, as

Seb and I had been the team members easy to send. Thinking about Paris, I interrupted Seb and Luke as they were talking about the drive and which road they were still planning to take into Lyon.

"Does Adrien have a Paris apartment?" I asked.

"*Oui, naturelment,*" Hensley replied. Naturally.

"Adrien won't be in the States, you'd have picked him up on comms by now. My money is in Paris or London. He'd want to be close to the last place he knew his sister was, regardless of the battle of good or evil," I said.

"Agreed, good one, Baby Theo," Seb added, reaching over to ruffle my thick hair before I could swat his hand away.

"We'll send Tad and Nate there after they clear the London place," Luke said. "Also, sensing a clusterfuck on the horizon, I sent Brian ahead of you, straight to Lyon, versus into Normandy."

"I wondered when he was going to show up, thought maybe he was out of vacay or something," Seb laughed.

"Brian loves vacations Hensley, he's a glutton for a beach trip," Seb added for her benefit.

"He is, but for now, he's on the clock. He lands in the next hour and will make contact with you via this number. He'll operate separately unless we need to bring you all together," Luke said. "For now, we keep digging into Ken from here. And, guys, not gonna lie, there is some heat on this with Interpol, but Tad is smoothing that over via his dad. We know Hensley is being set up, and we're working through that now."

"I swear you guys, I have no idea who this Ken person is or why he is doing this. I don't even know how he has been able to say he works for us, I am confused. You believe me right?" she asked, her voice barely above a whisper.

Damn, catching her dark eyes in the rearview mirror after that raspy question was a kick in the gut. She'd managed to save herself from attempted murder twice, and now she was being framed for the same crime. If she was innocent, which I still couldn't accept fully, she'd have to be scared. I bit my tongue hard enough for the metallic taste of blood to fill my mouth. I couldn't be the one to reassure her, not when I wasn't sure myself what to believe. Luke spoke before my thoughts could spiral any more than they already had.

"Of course we believe you, Hensley. We know what this is, but that brings me to the specifics of the bad news. Ken isn't alone. They have some team behind him and they are really churning out the news that Hensley is dangerous and depressed, a lethal combination. They've pegged her for either kidnapping or killing her brother and people are frothing at the mouth to bring down someone who is so sick as to kill their own brother," Luke said.

"Is this the gaslighting you keep telling me about?" Seb asked. "Do the bad things and then accuse the person who did them to of doing them? Straight fuckery."

"Something like that Sebby, but hey, we are handling it. This is what Tad excels at, you know that. For now, we only trust each other, and we operate as we know how to in order to keep Hensley safe. We stay the course."

"Copy," we both replied. We made plans to reconnect later, hopefully once safely in Lyon. Trust no one outside of my team, check. No need to worry about that. I wondered if both Luke and Seb were also curious as to how deep in this our pretty Hensley's neck was.

"We have about three more hours now, if we can get there as planned. Tell us about Lyon, Hensley. What do we need to know?" I spoke once we'd hung up, my eyes finding hers in the rearview mirror. I saw sleepiness creeping in on the edges of those chocolate eyes and I knew she was due for some rest. Good, tired and untrained people talked more. I'd keep her gorgeous ass awake and learn what we needed to learn.

"Right. *D'accord.*" She squared her shoulders slightly. She had fire within her, I'd give her that.

"Lyon has two rivers running through Her, and the center of

town is the Vieux Lyon, old Lyon, the original part of the city. That's where I live, in a renovated space, built originally in medieval times. The area was the first registered as a French Conservation area and has hundreds of these homes clustered in tightly, many like mine, with the original courtyard and repaired terracotta tiled roofs. Locals also joke there is a third river, that of Beaujolais, and the food. Cou, the food. It is one of the greatest food cities in the entire world." Her voice had taken on a reverent tone, it was obvious that she loved where she lived. "And of course the wines, such as the Beaujolais, are incredible."

"There are tons of restaurants and shops tucked into every nook and cranny, the old cobblestones are worn and yet in great condition. Oh! This might be important, Vieux Lyon is filled with hidden passage ways. They were originally used by the silk workers in the city and are called Traboules. Notably, they were key in helping the resistance fighters evade capture by the Nazis in World War Two," she said.

"How well do you know the Traboules?" Seb asked.

"As well as I know the area we just left, like my own hands. I often wander about when I have free time, and they are one of my favorite haunts. Those and the Roman amphitheater ruins. I take the Funicular up Fourvière Hill and then wander back down. Walking and eating in Lyon are my only hobbies outside of work, reading, and the occasional snow skiing holiday. It might be odd to say that out loud, as walking and eating might be unusual for an American to think of as hobbies, but in France, in Lyon, they are the life."

"I think it sounds incredible, not unusual at all." Seb smiled at her in the rearview mirror.

"Why live there when you can live anywhere? Especially if you love the area we just left," Seb beat me to the question burning on my tongue.

"Lyon is magical, you'll see. She's alive, energetic, warm, steeped in tradition, yet young at heart. I can't describe it to you with mere words, but you'll see. Or rather, you would if we were there under normal circumstances," she continued.

She was being genuine in her love of the city, I could at least tell that. Even in the darkness shrouding the car, I could see her eyes sparkling. It was sexy as hell, and I needed to get a grip on myself. We sure as fuck had better be close to Lyon.

TWENTY-THREE

HENSLEY

Shockingly, we made it to Lyon without some crazy car chase or shootout. The relief I felt was equal to the disbelief if I'm honest with myself. The entire last week of my life was surreal, I'd kind of expected it to play out like a movie. I had been sure we'd encounter trouble on the road, yet it was uneventful. Tense even, yet no one had chased us or shot at us yet. Whatever was going on inside Theo's gorgeous head was making it awkward for all three of us, even though Seb had the grace not to mention it. Was he wrestling with guilt over our intimacy? For how emotionally honest we'd been with each other? He'd shared a great deal of himself with me, telling me some about that last mission, being dependably there for me when I'd needed him, and yet now, that man was gone. In his place, a cold stranger. He'd been polite, yet cold. There was a distance to him that I hadn't experienced earlier, even after we'd let reality prevail over misplaced hormones. He had never before been cold, yet now that unwavering stare of his was downright glacial.

For as long as I lived, I would never understand men. Clearly, I was not as great at reading people as I thought I was. My present situation was proof enough of that. The emotional toll I felt relative to Theo right now was proof enough for me that I should stay out of situations that I can't control more. I have enough bullshit on my plate thanks to Adrien.

Sadness rolled over me. Adrien had brought so much bullshit into my life, yet he was my brother, my only living relative. Hope that he was okay was dimming in my heart, yet I was trying to ignore the reality there.

Coming into Lyon in the wee hours of the morning, I was exhausted, and I hadn't even driven. The last week catching up with me. The guys had taken turns and, perhaps shamefully, I'd slept. I'd fallen asleep with their low voices in the front seat and awoke to the same. It had been fitful sleep, yet more than either of them had gotten. Grittiness in my eyes was making me blink, the watery drops escaping faster than I could wipe them away. It was a clear sign that I was overtired, and yet it appeared as if I was crying. I didn't care anymore. I'd never felt so alone, and I was essentially trapped with someone who was distancing themselves from me after being a rock to cling to, all for me to save my own future.

It was worth it to me. My family legacy was everything, and yet, it still hurt. I sat up straighter and stretched, my muscles protesting as I did.

"Good morning back there, Hensley," Seb greeted me. He was polite and still the same kind guy who had interrupted Theo and me back in Normandy. Had it been years ago? Sure seemed like it.

"Bonjour Seb. Are we heading straight for my home?" I asked.

"No, our first item of business is to get to a safe house, yet it's close to your place. Luke and the team will have it all provisioned like the home we just left. We'll get some rest, do a little recon and then make a final plan to go to your place and see what we can find. And food, I could use some food," Seb replied.

"You could always use some food." Theo's gravely morning

voice scraped against my skin as he talked, the timbre warm, and I briefly wished he'd been talking to me before Seb's laughter shut that down inside of me. That's for the best. Their banter about the best things to eat in France faded into the background as I took in the surrounding scenery.

The rest of the way into the "safe house," as they called it, was also uneventful, but beautiful. I loved Lyon, this city where I had made my home like so many before me. Lyon was often overlooked by many on the global stage for the larger Paris, and yet Lyon was it for me. Of course, I loved Paris, yet Lyon had a magical quality that I couldn't explain with words. I hadn't been dramatic when I had told the guys that earlier in our journey here.

Lyon was both bright and welcoming, and ancient and warm. The rivers were lavender ribbons in the pre-dawn light as we crossed them, curling and cutting through the city. The sun was barely hitting the tips of the homes stacked on the hillside along the old Roman amphitheater, standing taller and stalwart over the newer parts of the city. We were close to my own home, maybe less than a few blocks. I guess they would want to be close; that made sense. I tried to relax as the car climbed over the stone roads, turning sharply among the oldest part of town.

The streets were narrow here, the turns tight and climbing or descending, depending on where you were heading. Newcomers struggled with knowing which was which in this part of town, and I remembered again that Titan Group really was the best as I watched Seb navigate our car through the maze like a pro. I myself would never have seen the garage door open just in time and just enough for us to dart in before closing again. It was like being snatched off the street by someone covering your eyes. One moment we were snaking up the hillside and the next, we were parked in a dark space, the guys' voices still calm and controlled. This must be the safe house.

"Hensley, stay close to me. Theo will be ahead of us clearing the house as we go through. The team has made sure it is safe, yet we always check. We're ready to head in. Okay?" Seb's voice pierced through the darkness in front of me.

"Okay, I'm ready." I gathered my little bag in one hand and pulled the handle of the door to step out into the small garage we were parked in. My eyes were adjusting, and I could make out the exposed stone walls of the space. It was well cared for, with a heavy door Theo was now standing at, typing in a code. He glanced back at me as if sensing my eyes on him. His eyes held a weariness, maybe even a flash of longing, but it was gone before I could be sure, and Seb's strong fingers had settled on my elbow to keep me close.

We made our way in without incident, quietly and surely. The guys had the townhome cleared quickly, and moments later I was in a room by myself to shower and rest. I assumed they were taking turns doing so, yet I wasn't privy to the details. It was almost like I'd been sent to my room, but I didn't have the energy to care. The room was as beautiful as everything else Titan Group had provisioned, and the bed too inviting. I wanted to shower, let the hot water wash over me, yet I didn't have it in me.

I lay down, the fluffy blankets enveloping me. Pushing my provisioned tennis shoes off, I curled up under those blankets and folded my arms under the pillow, bringing it in tight. Tears streaked down my face, leaking out of my eyes almost of their own accord. I was tired, darkly heavy with the weight of all that had happened, the press of loneliness, the stark reality that I could be the only one left. I'd failed them, all of them. Their laughter gone, the love cold in their graves.

The apologies to my family were on repeat in my mind, the sharpness of the failure closing in on me, tightening my throat. I'd let them all down, let *us* all down. Adrien was either a murderer, or had maybe even been murdered himself, and some random person I'd never heard of was speaking on behalf of our company. The company my great-grandparents had survived a literal war and hellscape to create. Shame was hot within me, leaving me broken and begging for forgiveness from the ghosts of all those I had loved.

My dreams weren't kind to me either. It was a relief to wake up, to finally escape what my own mind had trapped me within, and to rub the sleep from my eyes. It didn't feel like I'd had any real rest at all, and yet I was still groggy getting out of the stupidly comfortable bed and making my way to the adjacent bathroom. The hot water hit was a jolt, slapping me fully awake in a way that I needed, but still stung. *Grand-mère Gigi's* voice floated through my head, telling me to take a hot shower, eat something and everything would be better. Was she right about that at this moment? It felt as if all was lost, and yet her voice brought a smile to my face. The single kindness it brought along with it comforted me.

She was probably right too. She usually was. Was I forgiven? Was it my own subconscious cutting me some slack or was she really telling me to move along? Knowing her as I did, it was easy to picture her smiling at me, her hand held out.

Her voice cut through me again. 'You control how this goes for you. Only you. You hold our love, our trust, our legacy. What will you do with it, dear girl?'

What would I do with it? Did I control how this went for me and for our family legacy? Emboldened by her voice within me, I pushed the brass handle on the wall of the shower down to turn off the water and met my own eyes in the mirror across from the shower. My 'dad's eyes,' my grandparents used to say. My dad's eyes, my mom's face, my grandparents' love of life, my great-grandparents' strength. They were with me if I let them be.

I joined Theo downstairs in the kitchen. He had been sitting at a worn oak table in the small breakfast nook, the wide windows showcasing Lyon. The view there took my breath away momentarily, and a gasp escaped my lips before I could pull it back. A rush of emotion swept over me. There, this was Lyon. Magic.

The picture windows had perfectly captured the view that

these building were so profoundly proud of, the city below sparkling in the sunlight, the sparkles caught and shimmering across the river below, the cobblestones warm, people moving about on foot, bicycles and tiny cars. Bright red flowers adorned the railings along parts of the river walk, and large trees offered a respite of shade. Vibrant, rich riots of color and people, an energy that had been asleep when we'd gotten in earlier today. Glancing at the clock, I saw that it was late afternoon. Damn, I had slept most of the day.

"Bonjour."

The word was tentative coming out of my own lips, as if words were rusty and our thread to each other was tenuous. Which Theo was I going to get today? The man who had pulled me from the English Channel frozen and afraid, who had shielded me from gunshots pinging off rearview mirrors, the man who had shared so much of his pain with me? The guy who had felt like the first safe place in my life that was just for me? The man who had lit need deeply within my body, coaxed plea-sure from within my core? Or the cold operator that had taken over in the last twenty-four hours? Confusing, confounding and frankly, a guy that pissed me off. That thought didn't make me tentative any longer, and I rolled my shoulders back.

I was Hensley Richard, a deeply capable and independent human being who was going to focus on fixing the mess that had become my life and claw my family legacy back, even if it killed me. Even if I did it with a broken heart and regret for what could have been. Those moments with Theo in Normandy were gone, and what I needed now was to fight for me, for my family, not to be worried about this man. I owed my family legacy that much.

I filled a cup of espresso from the machine on the marble countertops in the open kitchen, my back to him and that stun-ning view of Lyon. He had replied with a morning greeting, and I was going to hit this head-on. Setting the small porcelain cup on its saucer, I carried both over to the breakfast nook and sat down.

He was watching me, those hazel eyes steady and bright, yet quiet. He had a MacBook open in front of him, and his own saucer with cup.

"Did you sleep?" I asked him, bringing the warm cup to my lips and drinking. Ah, sweet nectar. Yes, this is what I was going to do. Straightforward and controlled, this was me.

"I did, thank you for asking. Seb took first watch and just went down around midday, so I had more hours than I needed. How did you sleep?" His question and the general openness in his tone surprised me, as it was different from the coldness from last night.

"I did. The bed was amazing, and the hot shower restorative. And it's good to see the city laid out in front of me. It reminds me that I have so much to lose in this, and I am committed to figuring it all out and reclaiming what is mine." I stared at him while I spoke, daring him to question anything I said. *Bring it, Hot Theo, bring it.* I was spoiling for a fight, apparently.

"What is yours, Hensley?" His quiet question pricked at the heart of the matter. It held tension and tenderness as he awaited my answer.

I took another fortifying drink and, instead of returning the cup to its saucer, I held it in my hands. I took a beat, letting the warmth of the white porcelain cup seep into my hands, imagining it filling me with more courage.

"Richard Companies is mine. The Richard family legacy is mine. Mine to steward, mine to protect and mine to carry forward. The people who work there, the families who depend on us—they are mine. Adrien? My imbecile brother, who may have tried to kill me? Still mine. This Ken person? He can be mine too if we need him to be, mine to find, mine to expose. I don't know who that man is, but I will damn sure find out. I will fix this mess of mine, Theo. I hope that I can trust you to help me, and I'm not sure what's happening with us, but I will take care of what is mine, what is my family's."

TWENTY-FOUR

THEO

GRATEFUL THAT I HAD SPENT THE LAST HOUR ON THE PHONE WITH the team doc, I met Hensley's chocolate eyes. They flashed with fire and fierceness, and it was so damn sexy. How I could have doubted her, thought her capable of blowing up her own boat and setting this shitshow in motion, was beyond me.

The starkness of that thought hit me between the eyes. Fuck, I had really thought she could do this for a while, yet she'd shown me who she was. And who she wasn't. She wasn't a killer; she was a warrior, and a victim herself.

Shame hit me again, and yet I pushed it down. Dealing with my own trust issues was the hurdle before me, the reason I had called the team doc, even though it was seven hours earlier stateside. Doc was an early riser though, and she'd answered on the first ring, as always.

Mental health was something our team had always focused on, and never more so than after that last mission. As elite operators, we were expected to be at our best at all times, and that meant eating right, working out, understanding our bodies and their limits and how to push them, and keeping our minds as sharp as we could. We worked with our team doc almost as much as we worked out. For one, a person could see the physical results in the muscles gracing our bodies; for the other, the unseen, you could depend on to keep you safe while in our care.

For me, trust was a funny word. I trusted Seb, Luke, Tad, Max, or any of the others with my life. I trusted Hazel, and Violet, and my family with my heart. Mostly. What was left of my heart, anyway. I trusted Blitz, Max's black lab, to snuggle into me on cold nights back in DC when I was with them. I trusted Seb to read a person, Luke to have plans for his plans, Tad to take care of any red tape Titan Group faced with ease, and Doc. I trusted her implicitly to set me straight, even when I thought she was wrong at first. She wasn't wrong. She made me uncomfortable as fuck, but she wasn't wrong.

She had taken great pleasure in my call this morning, telling me that she had been expecting me to call at some point about 'this trust thing.' We'd talked about trust and my own cynicism of the idea, my lack of trust in myself post-Mosul. Real trust, the kind that I had in my team these days, was unshakable. How anyone else could be unshakable when I didn't count on myself to be, was the issue.

Doc and I had been working through this mess of mine since returning from Mosul. I trusted them, yet could no longer fathom how they trusted me. Not after what I had cost them with my inattentive flirting with that woman in the market.

And yet, here I was again, with another beautiful woman. And this woman? Far more beautiful, far more dangerous to me and maybe my team, one who was already much more deeply ingrained in my own being. A woman who notched within my jagged spaces perfectly, or so it seemed. Hell, not a woman, Hensley. Labeling her simply "a woman" in my mind was part of the crux, as the doc had pointed out. She wasn't just "a woman," and I'd used that label in the last twenty-four hours to distance myself from her, from Hensley, the person.

I'd been wrestling with the facts as they were emerging, and with knowing who Hensley was in my experience with her. I'd found that in life, the "facts" sometimes emerged from others in a different way than I was experiencing them. My experience with Hensley was where I could place my trust, according to the doc. Hensley had shown me who she was, who she wasn't, and those pieces of her were genuine.

Believing in my own read of her meant forgiving myself for not seeing the danger in that woman in Mosul the day of the attack. Fuuuuuck. That was deep.

"Don't you think it's time you got some altitude on this, Theo?" Doc had asked.

"Altitude? What do you mean?" Baffled, per usual, I'd asked her.

"Let's say that Luke was in the market that day watching. Luke was approached by a person, a beautiful woman, let's say. That woman was charming and talkative in an environment where women weren't allowed to always be that. She was an anomaly, one Luke was kind to. Are you with me?" Doc asked.

"Yes, I think so." Shit, Doc was on to something here, and I could tell I wouldn't like it.

"Luke is kind to this random woman who is clearly trying to engage with him, maybe even sidetrack him. Okay?" she continued, and I nodded dumbly to the screen she was on, picturing that day in the market, only this time I saw Luke as myself, and the woman who was being practically needy.

"She tricked me. She was sent to sidetrack me, and it worked," I said. I knew this; we all could have guessed this, although no one has ever seen that woman again. A separate team had been sent to clean up the chaos we were in that night and in the aftermath, yet no one had ever found her or the guilty party.

"Theo, Luke tried to move past this woman in the market. He was kind, because he is human and a kind person, but he still tried to maneuver around her. Didn't he?" Doc's voice had gone low, yet the proverbial steel bar slapping me against the hard head.

"Didn't *you*, Theo? *You* tried to move past the woman multiple times, and multiple times she interfered, but you still moved around her. You, a highly trained operative, moved around the woman as fast as you could. She weaponized her charm, yet you didn't fall for it. You didn't linger any longer than anyone else on your team would have. Did you?" She let the question hang in the quiet space of the kitchen perched among the stones overlooking the city of Lyon.

"No, I didn't linger. I kept trying to move around her," I finally answered, an unclenching around my heart, from my head, making my words soft.

"And why did you keep trying to move around her?" Doc asked.

"Because I didn't . . . I didn't trust her," I admitted, the relief slamming into me. "I didn't trust her. I didn't trust her at all, but I didn't know why." Wetness had gathered at the corner of my own damn eyes. Seeing Luke in the situation instead of myself had allowed me to slow down the memories and home in on the details.

"I didn't trust her, and I tried to move around her," I said to the screen with Doc waiting patiently for me.

"And if it were Luke, what would you tell him?" She was relentless.

"I'd tell him that it was obvious that he'd tried to move on and that, clearly, whoever had set us up had done so expertly. Quickly, well-planned. Designed to the second, executed perfectly."

"And would you hate Luke for how fast or slow he had moved around the woman?" she asked.

"No, I'd know that he had done his best to move around her."

"Ah, there you go, Theo. There you go. Now, tell me again,

why did you try to move around her so quickly?" she hounded me on this point, but I knew why.

"Because I didn't trust her. I knew something was off," I said, stronger this time.

"Okay, and did you trust Hensley when you fished her out of the Channel? When she told you everything? In the quiet moments when it was only the two of you in that safe house in Normandy?" Her voice was lower again, and again, the steel underlying her words smacked me in the face.

"Yes, of course. Completely." The answer was automatic on my lips and, most importantly, within me. I had trusted her. And I was someone who could discern a liar. I had known that day in Mosul that something was afoot. I hadn't trusted the woman, even though she'd tried to lure me in. I knew Hensley was genuine. I knew her at her core, who she was under the layers of corporate polish, under the money, to her very being. She was good. She was strong. She was being hunted and framed, and I had almost let some asshole deter me from what I had known. What I knew, what I personally had experienced.

The doc's face was smirking on the screen when I looked back up at her. I opened my mouth to tell her I finally got it, yet I couldn't even bring the words up and out from where they were festering low in my belly. I was a dumbass.

My admission, my breakthrough on what had happened in Mosul, had struck me speechless, apparently. All I could do was nod at the doc. Nausea cramped my belly at how I'd pushed Hensley away when she needed me most.

"Theo. I love you as a brother, you know that. I'm proud of you, you should know that, but I'm going to say it out loud again now because you boys have to hear words clearly spoken multiple times to get some things. I trust you with my life. I trust you with their lives. Do you see what we see now?" Kindness and laughter had started to poke through her tone the more she talked.

"I think so, but I'll probably need you to remind me, at least once," I replied. The band around my chest for the last two years, the invisible shackles, had eased in the last hour. I was lighter, sure, but more than that, there was a peace that had settled into the cracks around my heart. A hope was stirring even deeper, a tiny prickle of light I could anchor to.

"I'll tell you as often as I need to, Theo. That's part of my job. But you, you have to continue to do this work. You called me. You were ready to see this finally. You knew not to trust that woman in Mosul, just as surely as you know you can trust Hensley. As surely as you know you can trust yourself."

I dropped my head into my hands, tears of fucking relief dampening my cheeks, the absolution with which she spoke grounding me to my chair. Self-forgiveness racked my shoulders as I cried into my hands. I pressed my fingers tightly to my own face to trap the moisture, attempting to get myself under control, but still the tears came. Doc was quiet, but I knew she was still there. With me, from a thousand miles away, just like my team had me from wherever they were. Snot was threatening to drip from my damn nose when I looked back up at the screen.

"Thank you." The words were simple, yet the gratitude infinite.

"You did this, Theo. I just helped reframe the puzzle pieces for you," she said.

"I finally got my head out of my own ass, I guess," I laughed.

"Exactly. You got some altitude. Saw it more clearly from a different vantage point. Nicely done. Now, go figure this out. I want to meet Hensley some day and I have a feeling you have more to work through with her now that is unrelated to finding her brother or saving her company."

"Yes, I definitely do. Thanks, Doc. I love ya."

"Same, you big lug. Stay safe, and I'll see you stateside soon." She pressed her own fingers to her lips and mimicked blowing me a kiss as she disconnected.

It could have been minutes or seconds before I heard Hensley's steps coming into the open kitchen. I'd never know how long it had been. Inside my own head, it felt like a lifetime. *Before* I had 'gotten some altitude,' and *after*. I found myself shy now, not sure where to even begin. What did you say to someone who trusted you to rescue them, then felt like part of your lost soul, then you pushed them away in distrust? Was there a Hallmark card for this? I sure as hell didn't know what to say, so I stayed silent until I could figure it out. The least I could do was keep my dumb mouth shut until I thought of something decent to say.

I watched her as she grabbed an espresso and sat down across from me. She had an energy coming off her in waves, some badassery. She was in a mood, and I liked it. She staked her claim to her company, her future and her role in this insanity, and after she'd finished her declaration, I acted without thinking.

TWENTY-FIVE

HENSLEY

After declaring what was mine, I set the warm cup back down, resting my hands alongside the saucer. Theo had been watching me intently, those hazel eyes never leaving my own.

He reached across the table and grabbed both of my hands in his. The warmth from his hands seeping into my own colder hands, the calluses against my smooth skin, his thumb rubbing along my pulse points.

"Hensley, you are incredible. I'm sorry I've been distant over the last day. I needed to process through some of what we are learning." His words were clear, and the comfort they brought me so quickly was almost annoying.

"Like what, Theo? Something I did?" I asked him. I was curious, determined to speak plainly with each other from this moment on.

"No, you did nothing wrong. I needed to work through a few things, and I did that clumsily. I'm sorry about that. I think you are brave, brilliant and you do own those things that are yours. If you'll let me, I'll help you reclaim what is yours. I'm with you, I promise. Whatever it takes, we'll see this through."

I tightened my own fingers, gripping his. "Thank you, Theo. Thank you." There he was—my rock in the storm. The lighthouse that I'd crashed upon in the dark waves.

"Oh good, you're both up. All good?" Seb's voice cut through the moment, and I tried to pull my hands back into my own lap. Theo held tight though and raised one to his mouth, kissing my knuckles before releasing me. His lips were tender on my skin, and goosebumps lit across my arms before I faced Seb.

"All good here. Time for you to get your ass out of bed and help us solve this shitshow." Theo said to Seb.

That made me laugh, which I think was the intention. Seb laughed too and set about pulling out items to make sandwiches for all three of us.

"I'll make dinner. You lay out what we know now," he commanded Theo.

"Copy. We know that Hensley was the target of an attempted murder, in a location and on a boat only her brother should know about. We know her brother has been in over his head in some unknown capacity at work, dealing with unsavory people. We know he has been missing since Hensley overheard a vague threat and that there might be a 'Project Liberty,' which has the same name as a company Richard Companies bought in the last three years, one that is here in Lyon. We know Adrien has been around some seriously sketchy people in the last year and that some guy named Ken is acting as VP of Hensley's company, yet she's never heard of him," Theo rattled off.

"Okay, damn, slow down. Sebby needs food to process all of that information," Seb spoke about himself, making me laugh out loud. He was a lovable guy too. I could see why these men were like brothers.

We talked over the details Theo recounted and ate the delicious spread Seb had gotten out. Luke really knew how to provision a home. We had a planned call with the team in their respective locations soon and after that, it sounded like we'd, or they'd, I wasn't clear on that detail yet, would go to my house and see what they could find in notes. I had notebooks, literal old-school notebooks, yet I didn't know if they were still there, if someone had taken them, tossed them, or what. I was nervous about what had happened to my home, yet I could fix all of that if we survived this.

I was thinking in terms of *we* again, which was kind of dumb of me, I know.

When I envisioned surviving this mess, I saw Theo sitting at the breakfast nook table across from me again, this time as a partner. His glorious bedhead tousled about, maybe a bit of scruff on his unshaven face, a throaty laugh as he picked me up and sat me on his lap to watch the world awaken below us. Safe and sound, Richard Companies secured, Adrien safe and/or locked up (I wasn't sure which yet), and Theo and me together drinking our espresso. Me, in his shirt and nothing else, and him in those low-slung gray sweats and nothing else but his miles of muscles and that adorable dimple.

Like I said, dumb. Even I knew that was farfetched, and I laughed to myself at the daydream. I was in the mood to figure this out, and I was grateful Theo had apologized for being weird lately, yet I had to focus. I was committed. Like I told Theo earlier, this was mine to get through, and I would get through this.

It was time for us to connect with the team and get an update on Adrien's apartment and Adrien himself. I wondered also if they'd found anything in the acquisitions that we'd talked about.

"Hey, guys. Hey, Hen!" Mila's sunny voice greeted us all. "How is the place there?"

"As expected. Safe, super nice, great food supplies," Seb replied.

Mila laughed as Wills popped into the frame next to her. "We are well aware of how great Luke is at provisioning food, or finding someone who is good at it anywhere in the world, even in a tiny snowbound cabin along the water of Maryland. And we are grateful for it," he added.

They laughed together as I glanced questioningly over at Seb and Theo. Theo whispered, "I'll tell you more about that later." I got the feeling that these people had many 'inside stories' and, for the briefest of moments, all I felt was jealousy at this group who were so close to each other. I'd ended up a loner, who wanted to be a joiner, part of a huge family. I envied them their closeness.

Tad's voice broke through more of my wishful thinking, updating everyone that although they hadn't found Adrien himself, Tad had dug through the ashes in his home office fireplace and they believed they had some interesting fragments.

"What do you mean? Interesting fragments? Wouldn't any important information be on his computer?" Theo asked.

Before Tad could respond, I weighed in, knowing Adrien. "Not necessarily. Most of it, sure, yet Adrien is prone to headaches when he reads or studies screens for too long. Ever since he was a teenager, he'd print key things to read after he shut his screens down for the day. He was old-school for his age in that regard."

"That explains it then," Tad said. "We have what look like schematics of devices. I guess, your devices, Hensley."

"What type of schematics?" Theo asked.

"From what we can tell from what wasn't torched is that these are the inner mechanics of the devices that Liberty manufactures in Lyon. It looks like ideas on how to connect them all to one system, like all activated or deactivated at once. For what it's worth, I also think that Adrien himself burned these. The fire was long cold, and these were at the bottom, not cleaned out yet. His home was otherwise immaculate," Tad said.

"It would track for Adrien to do it too," I added. "He's always been embarrassed about the headaches with screen time, so no one else knows that about him. Anyone he does business with would never guess that he still prints documents and then tosses them in the fireplace when he is done."

"Hensley, what is your largest contract right now?" Violet's voice piped up from the screen. She was in the DC headquarters, and I noted she was wearing a baby carrier with a sleeping infant and had a black lab at her side. She didn't talk as much as the others, she was typically with her son when we had these calls, so I didn't know her as well. I paused to consider her words while the others waited patiently.

"That's an easy answer. Right now, our largest contract is with the French government and Paris city officials for security measures surrounding the Olympics in Paris. We've got various devices all over France, facial tech across the EU scanning faces, you name it," I answered the gorgeous woman who had leaned down to kiss her infant on his little downy head.

"There you go, boys, that's your angle. Adrien, or Ken, or both, have something nefarious planned for the Olympics, and the only person who may know that is Hensley, ergo, they need her dead. They own the security measures, so they can be the bad guy the easiest," Vi said. She'd been standing but after dropping that little bomb, made her way over to Max and sat on his lap, the man's arms coming around her automatically.

"Holy shit, Vi. Thanks for joining the party here," Luke said.

"She's a journalist, smartest one here. Sorry not sorry, Hazel," Max said, smug in his confidence. It was to his credit he added the false apology to his sister-in-law Hazel, and from what I could see, Hazel agreed with him because she laughed and nodded.

"But I don't know." I broke through the excitement that had gathered with Vi's words. "I don't know what they are doing, or how they are going to do it." Despair made me a little light-headed at the admission, yet I couldn't give these people false hope when I had zero clue about what Adrien had planned.

"You always know more than you think you do." Theo's

quiet conviction shocked me. He was dead serious, and I couldn't look away from the intensity in his eyes as they bored into mine.

"He's right too," Tad said. "You guys work on any notes in Hensley's apartment, we'll keep going on Adrien and Ken, and the team back in DC will keep working on all of it." Heads were nodding around me, and although they all acted assured I knew more than I realized, I was doubtful. I'd been taking notes on our Olympic coverage for months, but I wasn't sure how they could help, or if I could even find them again.

We decided that it was safest for all three of us to go to my home around 3:00 the next morning, when it was darkest. If we split up, we were weaker, so we were all going together.

Brian was here somewhere, yet he was on "overwatch," whatever that meant. I assumed we'd see him if we needed him and otherwise, he wasn't to tip off anyone who found us that we had backup so close. Theo had explained that part to me earlier over dinner, and it made sense to me. Having heroes hidden about the city sounded reassuring, and I was eager to get back into my home. My beautiful space that I had spent so much of my time creating and curating. My haven. I'd seen what these assholes did to my boat, so I knew what they were capable of.

The cameras that Seb had set up before joining us in Normandy hadn't picked up any activity, yet that didn't mean that whoever was after me hadn't been in my space before he'd arrived. The guys were relatively sure it was safe right now, yet tension was woven tightly within me at not knowing how my home had fared thus far.

When the clock struck 0300, we left the townhome through a door a few facades down from the main townhome we'd been staying in. Seb was leading the way, and Theo was at my back. It was quiet, quick and tense. I was so busy focusing on what was happening around me that I missed a stone sticking up higher than others, common among the streets of Vieux Lyon. I stumbled and almost went down, brought up right before slamming into the hard stones by strong arms banded around my hips. Theo pulled me up, and held me against himself, whispering into my ear as goosebumps skated along my neck. I could see that Seb had stopped and was watching ahead of him to ensure we were safe, yet in that moment all I could feel or smell was Theo.

"Are you okay?" His words were practically breathed into the shell of my ear, carried in the stillness of the night versus spoken out loud. His hand had splayed open on my belly, anchoring me to him. His touch promised safety, and his words carried care for me, something he'd shown countless times since apologizing hours earlier. Wishing I could stay in that promise forever, I nodded that I was fine. I thought the words instead of saying them, and he seemed to hear them. His hand tightened against my stomach, his biceps bulging where I'd laid my hands, and I could have sworn his lips grazed my neck before he released me and stepped back.

We continued on, around another tight corner and up the hill toward my home. When we got close, Seb ducked into a little notch in the storefronts, and we followed him into the darkness. Still as statues, the three of us waited and watched the area around my home. My lungs were burning from trying to breathe as quietly as possible, and my body was sore from holding myself steady by the time Seb nodded and our trio stepped away from the darkness and toward my door. Seb pressed himself against the wall outside my door and turned, covering our backs while Theo produced a device that unlocked my door. He had my entire security system dismantled before I even realized we were standing inside my foyer.

"I could have helped with that. I do own this place," I said quietly.

"No need, we've got you." Theo smirked at me and instead of being annoyed, I was struck by his surety that he knew what he was doing. A man who knew what to do and when to do it was a heady thing.

Seb ushered us up the stairs to my office. We didn't turn on any lights, yet I could see that my home, another one of my havens, had been destroyed by someone. Some faceless asshole who was always a step ahead. They had been in my home, had violated my most private space. My bedroom was torn apart, the down comforter slashed, feathers everywhere. My clothes had been ripped from the closet rods and out of the drawers. My bras and underwear pawed through by an unknown hand.

Flames of anger were building within me. When I finally got my hands on this person, I was going to do some damage of my own.

Photographs were pulled from side tables and my mantle, artwork yanked from the walls and broken. Theo murmured at me to watch my step, lest I step on shards of glass littering the floors.

My own home had picture windows, similar to the safe house. Yet now, in this cold and dark, broken space, the blinds were all drawn and shut tightly. I had left them open, I know I had. No one could see in here as I'd had special glass installed, and it was on the side of the hill overlooking the river and the city. The view is what had drawn me to this place when I moved here. Now, it was a wall of blinds, trapping the darkness in this space of mine with us.

We made our way to my office, the door ajar. It was exactly as ransacked as I could have guessed it would be. My computer was long gone, the cup I had been drinking tea from when I decided to head to London smashed against the surface of my desk. Papers were everywhere, drawers were pulled out, the gorgeous velvet chairs flanking my fireplace slashed, the green fabric gaping open.

"I'm sorry Hensley, whoever did this was thorough," Seb whispered.

I couldn't find the words so I nodded at him. He was right, the asshole who did this was thorough. Theo's strong hand was at the small of my back, anchoring me to the present, to him. His strength fueled my own.

"I'll buy more when we find this asshole and put them in jail." My jaw hurt from clenching my teeth together too tightly going through my apartment. My head was pounding and if it weren't for Theo's sentry at my back, I might have crumbled then and there. For all of my bravado in the shower this morning, I was bereft of it now, facing the violence with which my home had seen. I'd been focused on my own survival when I was on my boat, and then it exploded and I'd been out of it. I hadn't had to face the sheer hate someone clearly had for me like I was now.

"Thatta girl, Hen. You got this, we've got you. Where would you have kept your notes?" Theo's calm question gave me something to latch onto, which I did gratefully.

"Right. Okay, I take notes in little paper notebooks that I can easily carry in my purse so that whenever I get an idea or remember something I need to follow up on, I can make a note. I started doing that when Adrien and I first started working together so I could leave him a handwritten note if he was having a migraine. The morning I left for London to confront Adrien, I made the decision and then acted on it almost immediately. I needed to hurry to make the TGV up to Paris and then the afternoon Eurostar over to London. I was distracted, or I would have grabbed my notebook. It was stupid of me to leave it, when I was heading there to talk to him, in hindsight." Damn, I had been naive.

"I forgot about the TGV, the train of great speeds. It isn't something we think about in America, yet you moved from the South of France, up to Paris and over to London in one day," Seb murmured, looking around the wreckage of my office.

"I did. I made up my mind, set my tea down and then booked my ticket online. I only booked one way, grabbed my purse and headed out to catch the TGV out of Lyon. That's how I know I didn't close my blinds before I left. One, because I never do and two, because I left in a hurry. I didn't even grab a jacket and I never leave here without my jacket. Wait!" Hope almost brought me to my knees. I ran from the room, not caring about the glass crunching under my shoes. The guys were both right behind me and I prayed that I was right, that I was finally catching a break.

"Here, it could be in here," I said as I opened the closet door. There it was, right where I left it. My market bag. I pulled it from the hook I always hung it on and sent up a prayer of thanks. When I bought this place and renovated it, I kept many of the tiny, quirky details that made it quintessential Lyon, quintessential old home. The hook for my market bag was *behind* my jackets. And yep, there it was, my notebook. I pulled it out and whirled around to show them.

"I'd been at the market that morning, with this bag and some cash instead of my purse. Remember when I told you I thought someone had been following me?" I asked them.

Both men nodded, patiently waiting for me to explain.

"I'd seen a man in the market that looked like someone Adrien had around him all the time before that day. I had taken my notebook from my purse to notate that, what he was wearing, you know the drill. At the time I took the notes, I felt paranoid and yet I wrote it all down. I put the same notebook in my market bag that morning because I didn't take my normal purse, just some cash for a coffee and a pastry. My intention was to walk and think, but after seeing the guy, I came back here, then decided to head up to Paris and over to London to talk with Adrien."

"Hensley! Nice work! Now, I don't know about you guys, but every suspense movie I've ever seen has a scene where the good guys think they're in the clear and then bad guys surprise them. I'd prefer to not fall into that trope so let's get out of here before a villain twists his mustache, asks for the notebook and shoots us all." Seb whispered.

"Copy," I said, and giggled. Actually freaking giggled. I was so ready to grasp onto a break in this insanity and solve this giant puzzle that had become my life.

We made our way back out of my home, my heart both heavy and thirsty for good news. Inching our way through the dark streets was quicker on the way back to the safe house and even though I knew Brian was watching out for us, I was scared of that mythical villain jumping out at us too.

"Let's crank that espresso up and check in with the team." Seb said. He'd climbed the stairs once we were safely inside. Theo told him we'd be up in a moment and then turned to me.

"Hensley, I am so proud of you right now. You picked yourself up back there and remembered what could be a critical detail. Well done you," he whispered, stepping against me.

"I'm glad I remembered it, but it might not tell us anything Theo. What if it doesn't?" The hope was just there in my grasp, but it was as if I was trying to hold on to fine grains of sand slipping through my fingers. And after that? Darkness, fear, death, destruction. A real punch in the gut of hope.

"Then we keep looking. Together. I've got your back," he replied, his arms coming around my waist and pulling me flush to his body. His nose grazed my own and his hazel eyes caught me in their trance.

"Titan Group has us covered, and I have you covered. I promise." His lips found mine. Theo was a confident kisser and coaxed my mouth open, his tongue curling along mine. Mon Dieu, the man could kiss.

I brought my hands up along his sides, running my fingertips up his muscles and then to his face to frame it. His hair was soft under my fingertips and he was consuming me. I held on, my body held tightly to his hardness and his lips devouring.

"Guys, Tad is on the line, you need to hear this. Get up here." Seb's voice yelled down the stairs. It was a bucket of ice on an inferno, it sputtered the flames and yet still they raged, hotter and higher.

The buzzing in Theo's pocket is what finally broke us apart.

With chagrin on his handsome face and that dimple popping, he apologized for losing his head and kissed me one more time before pulling away slightly.

Wordlessly, he took my hand in his, squeezing reassuringly, and turned me toward the stairs, following me up, putting himself between the outside world and me.

TWENTY-SIX

THEO

Seb shot me a look when Hensley and I made our way into the kitchen upstairs. I couldn't help myself, I grinned back at him. It was enough that he relaxed and switched gears to patiently waiting. Seb could read anyone, even the unspoken pieces that didn't make sense to anyone else. If anyone could tell that I'd had an incredible breakthrough with the doc earlier, it would be him.

The rest of the team was already on the call and I almost felt guilty for making them all wait, but then Hensley's hand squeezed mine again and I gave up that guilt. It wouldn't serve us now and frankly, I'd do it again in a heartbeat, hoped to have the chance to do it again later. I hoped to get a chance to do much more with my mouth and her body later.

It took Luke twenty-three seconds to pop my bubble of happiness.

"Hazel talked to Anton earlier, and he confirmed what we had already learned about Ken. Ruthless oil and gas guy, left that life to raise a family after falling in love. But, sadly, Anton heard that Ken's wife died about a year and a half ago," Luke shared. Quiet murmurs sounded throughout the group, uneasiness rising.

"That sucks. What happened?" Seb asked.

"It sounds fairly awful. She was killed in a freak boating accident while with Ken and their kids. Sounds like Ken lost his mind after, hasn't been the same. Anton says he heard it was like the Ken before he met her, but a million times worse."

"Good Lord, that's awful," I replied.

Quiet murmurs of agreement sounded from every corner of our group. "Apparently Ken blamed everyone," Hazel said.

"What do you mean everyone? It was a freak accident, who is there to blame?" Hensley's question echoed my own curiosity, but I had a niggling thought, and glancing at the surrounding faces, I knew I wasn't alone.

"I'm not saying it's right, but I will say that if something happened to Vi, I'd lose my mind too." Max's quiet admission caused almost every guy on our team to nod at him.

"I wouldn't turn into a psychopath, but I don't know what I would do. That level of grief is deadly itself, coupled with an already ruthless temperament? It could be the perfect cocktail for destruction," he added.

"That level of grief would make a man illogical, which all of this seems to be. It is illogical for a very rich oil and gas guy to pop as the VP of Richard Companies, and yet the illogical behavior fits perfectly," Luke added.

"I'd agree with the illogical part, because he doesn't work for us. He never has. I feel for this man and his loss, I grieve with him, yet I don't know him," Hensley said from beside me.

"Wait, so now, here he is popping up as a VP for a tech systems and safety device company who has the largest contract for the Olympics and he is completely off the rails? The company practically responsible for the safety of millions of global citizens?" I asked incredulously. That altitude that Doc always talked about was paying off here. In my mind's eye, there were these giant puzzle pieces coming together. The corners were in place, the edges laid, more of the image was coming into focus.

It hit me then, we were on to something. I just didn't know how it all fit together. "How does Hensley's brother factor in?" I asked the room at large.

"Adrien is our VP, not this Ken guy. The guy saying he is the VP and spokesperson is using Adren too." Hensley's words were softly spoken, almost like she was still in shock.

"I think there is something in the acquisitions from about a year ago," Tad said.

"Wills, you mentioned to me earlier that the very first acquisition Adrien worked on was something out of the ordinary scope of Richard Companies, what was that?" he asked.

"Ya, that's right. When Hensley told us to dig into acquisitions, we found that Adrien had only been working on one large one initially. It turned out to be a red herring though because every lead we chased turned up empty," Wills replied.

"What was the name of the company?" Hensley asked.

"Well, that's where it really doesn't make any sense. It was Liberty Tech. Odd to have another company with the name 'liberty' in it, yet every path led to nowhere when we tried to trace it back."

"Nowhere? As in that company could have just been a shell for something else?" Hensley asked.

"Yes, it could have been. Maybe that's where Ken comes into play with Adrien?" Wills asked.

There was a beat of silence as we all considered that. Hensley was the first to break the quiet engulfing us. "I've never heard of that Liberty Tech. If Adrien had been working to acquire them, he was doing it alone."

"What was he doing?" She had turned to me then, pain naked in her eyes and in the way her voice broke.

"I don't know yet Hen, but we will. I promise you, we will get to the bottom of this," I vowed.

"Listen, I need to call my dad about this and have him give

Interpol a heads up. There's too much risk," Tad said to the room at large from the phone.

"Agreed. We'll keep tracking Ken, and this potential shell company, with everything we have here. You guys stay safe there. If what we are talking about has even a kernel of potential to be right, and Hensley is the only loose thread, Ken will cut it without thought," Luke said.

Hensley. The loose thread in a potential international safety issue. One that we knew just enough about to sound crazy if we broadcast it. It would cause panic in the streets, mass chaos and Ken, and his people would go to ground. We had to know more. Not only did Hensley's company depend on me to do so, millions of lives could also be riding on me to figure this out. On us. Lost in thought, I murmured my own assurances that we'd of course be careful and signed off the call with my team.

"Well fuck," Seb said, cutting straight to the heart of the matter.

"Yep, fuckery. You were right, Sebby," I said.

"I know, Baby Theo, sadly, I know. It's late, almost morning again. Why don't you guys get some rest and I'll take watch." He stood and stretched before moving over to the espresso machine.

"You sure?" I asked. Hensley had gone quiet at the realization that she could be the only loose thread for a very smart and very rich man. Hell, she was smart to be scared. This guy taking over her company and announcing to the world at large that she was a murderer, then offering a reward, was brilliant. Devious, yet brilliant. It's too bad that so many of the smartest minds in history were diabolical, or dictators, or both as it often happened.

"I'm good, you guys rest and I'll hold down the fort here. I'll go back through the footage we have of Hensley's apartment that I left cameras on shortly after her call. If we're lucky, whoever trashed her place did so after I had cameras recording and we can recover something," he said.

"Wouldn't you have gotten an alert if that were the case?" I checked him. I knew the answer, but had I missed something while I worked through my trust issues?

"Ya, we would have. I'm assuming whoever trashed it was there the day she was in London, which is why we haven't seen anything. The only hope I have in that footage is that someone comes back. They have to be getting desperate to find her. Maybe they'll go back and see if they missed something too."

"They can have it all. I don't know if I can go back there, ever again," Hensley added. "Thanks, Seb. Thank you, Theo. I'm going to head up." She was quiet. Contemplative. I wanted to go to her, assure her, promise her I would protect her.

I waited until I knew she was out of earshot and then as low as possible, I told Seb to sound the alarms as loudly as possible if he needed us, but he'd have to be loud. I was going to Hensley. If shit hit the fan in the coming hours, he'd have to pry me away from her and he needed to know I was tapping out to be with her.

"I know, Baby Theo, I know. Damn, man, am I glad to have you back. Go. I've got us covered here, Brian is back on and the team has us covered."

His words were all I needed. I stood, clapped him on the shoulder and made my way upstairs to Hensley.

She was stepping out of a hot shower when I knocked. I heard the water turn off and her soft invitation to come in.

"It's me. Are you okay?" I asked as I walked in. She was covered, mostly. The towel was tied around her and she'd pulled her hair up into one of those piled high buns girls did. Little wisps of hair had fallen out and were sticking to her damp skin. Her skin was pink from the heat of the water and she was regarding me silently from the doorway leading into the bedroom I'd come into.

"Not really if I'm being honest. I was hopeful before, yet now, knowing that this guy has completely taken over my brother, my company, turned the world against me and millions of lives are on the line, I could be better. So no, not really okay." She stepped toward me, toward the bed. She was graceful in her movements, even with her honesty.

I met her by the bed and gathered her in my arms, hers immediately coming around me to squeeze me tightly to herself. She kissed me first this time, her emotions pouring into her actions. When she pulled back to look up at me with those melty chocolate eyes, I was sunk.

I sat down on the side of the bed, adjusting her as I gently tugged her to stand between my knees, giving her the advantage of height now. She was still standing, and I looked up at her for permission. Unspoken, she granted it. Her hands came to the towel knotted just below that luscious collarbone and her fingers untied the knot slowly, the towel dropping to reveal her gorgeous breasts.

She dragged the towel along her own skin, further down and I watched as it revealed each glorious inch of her. It was practically impossible for me not to take her into my own hands then, to feast upon her, but I wanted her to know she had the power here. I was game for anything with her, everything. I wanted her, I wanted to feel her, and I wanted her to feel amazing.

That tortuous towel fell away from her hips, and she reached out toward me, resting her hands on my shoulders. I took my time, memorizing every dip, valley and curve. I traced my fingertip from her knee, up along her inner thigh, then swept out to lightly tickle her hip before sweeping back in to lightly dance up the very center of her stomach, up between her breasts, those pink nipples puckered with need. I dragged the pad of my index finger outward to her side, along her obliques. With her hands resting on my shoulders, her arms were raised enough for me to make out tiny words inked along her side. *Tu me manques.*

Locked on to my actions, she waited for me to meet her eyes and then she whispered. "In French, we don't say, I miss you. We say, you are missing from me. It's more than an I miss you, it's that without you, I am never the same again. You are forever missing from me."

Solemnly, I broke eye contact and kissed along the edge of the words, my attempt at soothing her heartbreak. My silent promise that I would never leave her. I couldn't say the words yet, the moment was raw, and heavy, and yet we were deeply connected in our want for each other. I needed to apologize to her for my doubt yesterday, for stretching the tie that bound us, yet not right now. Right now was for promises.

I kept my touch light as I continued up, along her collarbone and then up to her ear. A shudder racked her body, and she swayed more closely to me. I used my other hand to come up on her opposite hip and anchor her. With my fingertips still tracing her ear, I opened up my hand and brought it around her neck, resting my thumb at the hammering pulse fluttering there.

"I don't deserve you, Hensley," I admitted. "But I need you. I want you. Please."

I needed her to know that before we did this, before I claimed her fully. I didn't deserve her at all, yet I wanted her desperately. I fucking needed her.

Her eyes hadn't left my own at my admission, yet her hand came up from my shoulder and her fingers scratched lightly through the hair at the nape of my neck.

"Theo." My Goddamn name again, a command. A plea. Permission. Lust rocked through me, hot and intense. I used the hand anchoring her hip to bring her fully to my lips. I dropped my other hand to her other hip, notching my thumbs along her hip bones.

I kissed her gently at first, swirling my tongue along those hip bones, nuzzling my face into her, nipping at her as I worked my way to her core. Her hands had gone to my head fully, her hands wrapped up in my hair as she guided me to where she wanted me. I was many things in that moment. Undeserving, unworthy, drowned in need for her, hungry for her and only her.

I was all of those things, but I wasn't stupid. This woman was giving me a chance, and I'd go to my fucking grave before I wasted that chance.

Lowering my lips, I devoured.

TWENTY-SEVEN

HENSLEY

THEO'S TONGUE WAS MEANT FOR ME. OF THAT, I HAD NO DOUBT. IN my life of prim and proper, of control and serenity, I had never experienced what I did in those moments. I couldn't get close enough to him, my legs were shaking, I needed him. Every moment I thought I needed something more from him, no sooner had the thought formed than he did that very thing. I was going to combust.

Tightening my grip on his soft hair, the strands curled around my fingers, I pressed myself into him, wanton and wild. I craved that mouth, that tongue. He was relentless. The onslaught of nerves riding an edge that I hadn't known was within me. "Theo," I gasped as I watched his head devour me.

His name fueled him on and the pressure built within me until I exploded. La Petit Mort, the French called it. The little death. Yes, I had died in a black and white world and this man's tongue had brought me back to life in a kaleidoscope of colors. I giggled and looked down at him, this man who had saved my life.

Hazel eyes met mine and then returned to kissing a path

upward to my breasts. He stood then and turned, pushing me down as gently as possible and laying me out on the bed. I became a feast laid upon a holiday table so hungry were his eyes on my skin.

The scrape of his jeans against my bare legs disappeared briefly as he stepped back to undo them and drag them down his own legs. I watched him reach down and yank his henley up and over his head, his eyes barely leaving my body. He'd pulled a condom from his wallet before stepping out of his pants and he quickly sheathed himself.

He stepped back into me, the hair on his legs prickling against my smoother skin, the size of him pressing against my core. He was hot against my already swollen center and I expected him to push deeply inside of me, yet he held still at my entrance.

He was watchful, practically reverent in his gaze. I bent my knee, bringing one of my feet up to rest on the bed and then propped myself up on my elbows. The movement brought him closer to me, to where I was desperate for him.

"Theo?" I asked him.

"Hensley. I don't deserve you, but I swear I will spend however long you let me worshipping you." His tone was serious and his eyes found mine, a promise there.

"Then get to it," I commanded. He enabled me to wield my power. I know that may sound crazy, yet I was not typically a dominant person in the bedroom, only in the boardroom. I knew I had control of this situation, yet I also knew that I did so because I had earned it from him. He was a warrior, an elite operator and I had him at my mercy. That empowerment surged through me and I sat up straighter and scooted back on the bed. I came up on my own knees and kissed him deeply, my arms twining around his neck. My tongue found his, and I was lit from within. I couldn't get enough of him.

I started to lay back, to pull him with me. He complied, trying not to crush me. I was caged in those glorious arms of his.

Muscles ensnaring me, his hips pinning me to the bed. I opened my legs again, bringing them up around his lean hips.

I met his eyes. "Worship me."

And he did.

Theo nudged himself inside of me firmly, his length stretching me and filling me. Once he was fully engulfed in me, he ground his hips more deeply against mine, shifting his length inside of me to hit right where I needed him.

I murmured words of praise, of thanks, of so many things. I didn't even know what I was saying as he drove into me, grinding against my clit, his lips having found my breasts. He growled against them as he licked and laved, his arms rippling with the force of his body coming into mine. I lost all sense of time, pleasure my only marker. He pulled one of my legs up higher from the knee, changing the angle he was driving into me. His mouth was everywhere. He nipped at me, suckled lightly on my neck, drove me wild.

For the second time that night, I died a death of color and light. Of pleasure and joy. And Theo was right there with me. The second I came again, he came too, my name on his lips as his hips slowed their feverish movement.

He dropped to the side and rolled over to his back, bringing me on top of him. His mouth found mine, one of his hands tangled in my hair, the other on my hip. He was still inside of me and I felt him hardening again against the overly sensitive inner walls of my core.

A yawn slipped out before I could stop it and Theo chuckled. "You need rest, and here I am being a brute."

"No, this is the worshipping I was hearing so much about and I love it." I giggled and then that was interrupted by another damn yawn.

"Stay here." He disentangled from me and went into the adjoining bathroom. He returned a moment later with a hot washcloth and slowly dragged it against my well-loved skin. It was incredible and the care behind it almost brought tears back to my eyes. Being worshipped by this man was indeed an experience. One that made my eyes heavy, my satiated limbs practically weights, and an inner comfort overtake me.

He slid back into bed behind me before I finally gave up on staying awake. I was tucked against his heat and strength, and it felt like home.

I awoke a few hours later. I could tell it was still early in the morning based on the light coming in from behind the blinds on the window. Reinvigorated by what had happened with Theo, I threw on some clothes and went downstairs to find him, and read through all of my notes.

I must have been quieter than normal because I heard Theo and Seb talking in hushed voices before I rounded the corner. Something in their tone made me stop, made me listen closely without letting them know I was near.

"I'm glad you pulled your head out of your ass before you messed something that could be perfect up. Hensley is amazing. Out of your league, but I'm happy for you, nonetheless." Seb's voice floated to my inadvertent hiding place.

"She is incredible and so far out of my league. I can't believe that I thought she was lying, that she was caught up in this madness somehow and playing us all. I didn't trust her there momentarily, but Doc finally made me see the light." Theo's voice carried, the smile it had brought to my face when I heard his first words dying a quick and painful death as he finished his sentence.

Seb replied, but I was caught in my own head, my thoughts and memories swirling together. That was what had happened! Mon Dieu, the man had thought I was capable of this? A liar? Worse, a murderess? My throat was closing, gray spots were crowding the edges of my vision. I forced myself to retreat to the room I was in earlier, to put on my tennis shoes and to retrace my steps.

The guys were still talking. Because I had watched them

earlier when we went to my house, I knew how to leave quietly, so I did.

If I had was a mess after being blown up on my boat, this was a death knell. I had envisioned Theo as my hero, as part of my heart, as my home, and he'd doubted me the first time he could. He'd believed some insane monster over me, the person he'd spent hours with by then.

And last night! Or earlier this morning rather, I'd thought he was promising me glimpses of forever. Glimpses of a dream I'd barely dared to think could be mine. But, he didn't even trust me. Maybe he did now? When would he lose that trust again? Was he this mercurial all the time? I had unknowingly risked my heart last night, I wasn't about to sit around and risk my life too.

Pulling my hood up over my hair, I turned toward the train station. I'd make my own way to Paris and find Adrien. I'd call Tad and thank him, write him a check for everything Titan Group had done and get them out of my life, get him out of my life. I'd forget Theo.

It was the last vow I made before someone at my back dropped a scratchy black bag down around my head. I thrashed against my assailant, not knowing where to kick or punch, but swinging as hard as I could.

I heard a man yelling about capturing the money, the murderer, but I was losing air inside of that damn bag. I kicked out sharply, desperate to stay awake and fight. Connecting with a shin, I heard an American man's voice pleating about how the bitch kicked him and better be worth the reward.

Oh shit. The bounty. Some asshole had hunted me for money, and that asshole was winning. I threw my head back and bingo! Connected with the asshole's nose. He was screaming, and it was all I needed to get away.

I ran. I ran as hard as I could along the narrow stone street until I saw one of Lyon's famous traboules. I ducked inside as fast as I could. I could hear footsteps chasing me and I pulled my hood back up as fast as I could to avoid even more people trying to cash in on that crazy bounty.

For a brief, shining moment, I thought I had made it. I could see sunlight at the end of the tunnel ahead of me. The traboule was almost to the connecting street. I could hide in these all over the city, making my way across town to the train station from traboule to traboule.

Popping out of the "hidden" passageway, I careened around the corner. Right into the waiting arms of a madman. Ken Seimers. I recognized him from the news, that bastard!

I pulled up short, but it was too late. Two men had come from the walls of the passage way and had my arms pinned back. Zip ties had already been ratcheted down, cutting through my skin. Great, another familiar asshole, the guy who had been following me in Lyon before I went to London. This day was getting worse and worse.

"You're a tough woman to take down Hensley Richard, and I hated to do it," Ken said.

"I don't even know you, what have I ever done to make you want to take me down?" I asked. I was over men at this point in my life. Always jumping to the wrong conclusions, always blaming others, always doubting. Fuck that. I spit at his feet. "Fuck you!"

His hand connected with my face faster than I expected, had I expected it. Stars danced in my vision, those damn gray spots back.

"You exist while she doesn't. Isn't that enough?" he roared. Oh. Oh shit. This man was completely unhinged.

"You exist and have been nothing but a thorn in my side. It's time to execute on our plan and to do that, I need you taken care of. Your fucking brother couldn't keep you controlled, but I can," he ranted in my face, the purple veins around his nose bulging, his eyes unfocused, pupils blown.

Oh my God, Adrien. Was he alive? He didn't try to kill me

after all? A tiny flame of hope lit throughout me before someone grabbed my elbow roughly.

"Get her in the car," he commanded to the men standing behind me, one of which had zip-tied my wrists together. He pushed me toward the car, and I knew, without a shadow of doubt, that they would kill me. I tried to think through the fuzziness that was my head as they tossed me in.

Like an old raggedy stuffed animal tossed in a closet, I hit the other door of that car hard. My ears were ringing, yet for the second, maybe third, was it fourth? Damn. For the millionth time that day, I struggled to stay awake. I needed to make myself valuable.

"Safeguard," I tried to force out through stiff lips. "I have a safeguard." It was all I could get out before darkness stealing into my limbs claimed me. What had I done? With danger, came clarity. Why had I left the damn apartment without simply having it out with Theo about his trust? He'd had a terrible experience, and I hadn't offered a shred of grace based on that experience. I'd done the same to him that I was pissed about, not freaking communicating, nor trusting. I'd simply left to handle things on my own rather than stay and fight. Now look, the fight had found me.

TWENTY-EIGHT

THEO

SEB AND I WERE TALKING QUIETLY ABOUT WHAT A DUMBASS I HAD been and how lucky I was not to have fucked it up when all hell broke loose. Brian was calling, Luke was calling, Tad was sending alarms through the house.

Damn, was that Luke's voice too? He had speakers in the main rooms of the house. I had my gun in hand before I understood the words, and once I understood them, it was as if the world stopped spinning. One moment it was in motion; the next, it wasn't. My vision blurred at the edges, the cacophony of voices around me growing, suffocating, smothering.

"She's gone. We lost her trail in one of the traboules, but the guy who initially took her is down. Brian has handed him over to the police, but he was only a bounty hunter trying to make a payday," Tad was saying to Seb. Only a bounty hunter? That was a good thing now?

Lights were bright, then dim. Sounds were loud, and then quiet. The pain was lancing through me. She was gone. But how?

"How did they get to her? She was upstairs in bed," I asked. I met Seb's eyes. "Right? She was upstairs," I pleaded with him to say that yes, she was upstairs and that no, all the others were wrong. I'd left her naked in bed, the smell of her still imprinted on my skin and in my heart. Her love making me whole. Not missing from me.

"She was, yes. But she left." Seb tried again, but again, I cut him off.

"Left? When? Why? What do you mean she left? She isn't stupid. She wouldn't have done that," I reasoned.

"She did Theo. Something sent her out of here, and although she got away from the first guy and was in the traboule, we lost her after that. Every camera in the area went down at once. They're back up now, yet she's nowhere. The alleyway from the traboule she was in is empty now," Luke said calmly. "We're checking camera feeds all over France, man. She can't be far."

"What the fuck do you even mean, she's missing? HOW?" I screamed. It was as if Seb had reached down my throat and pulled my heart out, still beating, scraping my vocal cords as he dragged it back out to stomp on it.

"She left. We don't know why. Did you guys fight? Did something happen? Did she get a message of some sort?" Luke was still calm, and that was pissing me off. Theories were still flying around the room, some talking about camera angles, others questioning how she could've simply walked out.

Mentally, I was at the bottom of a stampede, millions of boot heels grounding into my empty chest where that heart had once beat, crushing my windpipe, digging into my side, shattering my bones, leaving me broken, unable to yell out. I had done this to her. I had caused this, and now, now she was gone. Now, she was in danger.

"She did this because of me." The words were gravely and low; they scratched against the sides of my throat as they came out. I said it again, the pain of it no less than what I deserved. "She did this because of me."

Seb's quiet stare pinned me like a fucking butterfly to a board. His eyes were stark, empathetic. Luke's sigh could be heard in the quiet that followed. It was like that in an emergency. So much noise and then nothing. Quiet. Suffocating quiet. Deathly stillness where moments before had been laughter, the love at the heart of a human for another human.

Tad tried again after a few moments of stillness. "Brother, we were ready to burn the world down for Hazel, and we'll do the same thing to find Hensley, I promise you. But, man, you have to hear me now. You have to quiet the rage in your brain, the fear and anger clawing at your heart. You have to tell us what happened, and then you have to fight like hell to go get her. What do you mean you did this?"

"I'm an idiot. I left her sleeping in bed after hours spent together, after making promises. I came back into the kitchen and was here with Seb. We were talking about how glad I am that I got my head out of my ass and decided to trust her. To trust myself and my own judgment. I was openly talking about how I hadn't trusted her there for a while, out loud."

"I was coming clean about it to Seb. She had to have heard me. She heard my colossal stupidity relayed to Seb before I talked to her about it. After we'd been together. Fuck!" Seb had crossed over to me. He put his hands on my shoulders, practically mimicking what Hensley had done earlier. He waited for me to meet his eyes.

"We'll fix this, Baby Theo. We've got your girl and we've got you," he said.

"But we don't have her. Someone else does," I said, the words making it even more real.

"Could she have been in on it at all? Has she simply rejoined her original crew?" It was Brian's softly asked question as he joined us from downstairs that did me in. I had never been a bigger hypocrite in my life than in that moment when I turned and lunged for him. His question sparked at the root of what had driven her from my arms, my own stupidity.

Thankfully, Brian was solid. He waited until the last minute of my crazed advance and ducked, turning in a flash and pinning my own arm against my back. "Easy killer. I've got you." He meant the words in a reassuring way, like it was all a walk in the park for him. As if I were his child, desolate and crying out, and he were calming me. And, fuck me, it worked.

I stood down. "Sorry, man. No, she's innocent. She'd never hurt anyone. Someone took her."

"I figured, but had to ask. You should see the guy currently on his way to the police station. His arms are scratched to shit, his nose is broken, and he lost a few teeth in the scuffle." His words didn't make anything better. Her head had to hurt from hitting that asshole so hard; maybe she was concussed.

She was hurt and alone, and it was all my fault. I had promised to worship her, and that meant more than her body. Most importantly, it meant her heart. I had failed her. I'd failed myself.

Tad was right, I would burn the world down to find her. I was going to murder Ken. I didn't know how yet, or when, but that guy had signed his own death certificate sending everyone and their dog after Hensley. I would make damn sure he paid for that. And if it was him who had her, I would relish the killing.

"Paris. Whatever clusterfuck is going down, it's going down in Paris. That's where he'd take her. We need to head there. I know it."

TWENTY-NINE

MIRACLE OF MIRACLES, I WOKE UP. I WASN'T SURE IF I EVER WOULD.

"Ah, I see you're awake, good. Let's talk about this safeguard you have." Ken's voice was right next to me, and we had to be on a train based on the way our little compartment was shifting. It felt like the TGV, which could only mean we were on our way to Paris. Good. The longer I was alive, the better my chances were. I motioned to my throat, indicating that I needed a drink. I didn't, but my mind was racing with a plausible story.

"Get her some water," Ken murmured to someone out of sight as I struggled to right myself. My hands were still tied, and the cramps in my elbows were excruciating. My mouth really did feel as if I had swallowed a wad of cotton. My arms were heavy. My legs were slow to respond to my brain. They had to have drugged me. That was good too, I hoped. It meant that I was in a public place. If we were on the TGV, as I was certain we were, that meant we were in a private train compartment on our way to Paris. There had to be tons of other people doing the same thing.

"I've been on to you," I said the first thing that popped into my head. I hadn't been on to him. I still wasn't sure what was going on completely, yet his comment about a "her" resonated within me. He'd had a wife—that was what Titan Group had learned after he'd been on the news.

"I'm sorry about your wife," I tried.

"Sorry? You're sorry?" He laughed, but there was no joy in that laughter. "You will be sorry, make no mistake about that."

I tried again. I had found that with some men, repeating them made them want to explain more. They couldn't help themselves.

"I am sorry, so very sorry." I tried to sound contrite. If I acted meek now, and controlled, it would be easier to get away later, once we hit Paris. Now, I was trapped on a high-speed train, hands zip-tied, nowhere to go and frankly, no way out but through. I had to save myself here, but I had to figure this out to do it. Pain lanced through me briefly as Theo's words from earlier resounded in my memory, and yet the feel of him against me earlier in the night had been real, I knew it. I had to save myself, and yet, I knew he'd be coming for me too. I just needed to keep myself alive long enough to figure some of this out.

If I knew what the hell was happening, I could use it once I could get free. Maybe even save my brother. If he were still alive.

"I'm sorry we couldn't make it right, neither Adrien nor I." I had to start somewhere, might as well start with the hardest part.

"Adrien couldn't make it right if he tried, too ethical. He thought he could lead me away from my ultimate plan once he figured out he'd been trapped, but he was wrong. No one will get in my way. Not him, not you," he said. He sounded almost bored, but there was a current running beneath his voice, a riptide waiting to pull me under. I'd seen his rage in Lyon. I knew it was a quick trigger. Now, I also knew that Adrien had indeed been trapped into something. That kernel of hope flared again, the little wisp of light growing stronger within me.

I went for the old repeating trick again. "He tried to lead you away. I'm sorry for that."

"He thought he was a clever boy, and he cost me months! Chasing patents, getting contracts in line!" He chuckled then, as if he was almost entertained by Adrien's actions. "Alas, time is almost up. I will not be deterred. Everything is in place now, and neither you nor your brother will stop me. We have the devices altered. They are in place, and soon, the world will know just how important safety measures are. They will know that they could prevent senseless deaths if they really wanted to spend the money to do so, and guess who they'll spend that money with? Now, you and I are going to chat about your safeguard, and then you can die with your brother. I'm not a monster after all, simply proving a point." He steepled his fingers under his chin, his gaze fixed outside as the countryside raced by.

I didn't know how long we'd been on the train, yet from what I could tell, we were getting into Paris and couldn't be far from Gare Nord, where the TGV docked. I had about ten minutes to get as much information as possible out of this man and come up with a plan to get away from him. This is what I could control, what I could do. The rest I didn't know about yet. For now, I had to get as much of this story as possible.

"You are not a monster," I took a guess, one I was pretty confident in at this point. "Your wife's death was senseless. It didn't need to happen."

"Don't say one more fucking word about my wife. You don't have the right." His words were quiet, almost reverent.

This man was a broken man, and his pain had destroyed him. I saw it in his eyes. I heard it in his words. He was a cornered, wounded animal—the most dangerous animal. Grand-père had been a hunter; it was from him that I knew that an animal cornered, believing itself out of options, could not be taken easily. They were stronger, they were cunning, the fight for life and death in full color in front of them. Ken Siemers was a cornered animal, willing to take everything out with him in his pain.

"I'm so sorry about your wife, but there is more to live for. You have children, right? A family?"

I really was sorry for him, for her, for their family. I simply wasn't willing to be collateral damage in his revenge-fueled plot. For so long, I'd done my best to live up to the legacy of my own family, in the face of my own pain. Losing my own family had taught me a great deal, and yet I was still standing.

Metaphorically, of course. I was currently tied and at his mercy, like prey physically, but I had strength too.

I almost even understood this man before me, responsible for so much. He'd let his pain awaken a monster inside of himself, no matter what he said. I thought of Theo, a wave of understanding washing over me. Theo had felt like a cornered animal too, scared of trusting himself, incapable of trusting me to a degree. And yet, he hadn't let the monster win. He was fighting to overcome the pain every day, just like me. We were bumbling through this path, scraping along each other's most tender parts. I sincerely hoped I survived this, then he and I could talk openly. No more wounded darkness. Maybe we'd have the time I was desperate for.

"I almost believe you, and for that, I'll say thank you. It's a shame you and I didn't meet before now. Perhaps you are more reasonable than your brother. He assured me you couldn't be part of this, said you'd go to the authorities. He was perhaps lying, not that I can blame him, I guess. I gave him no choice, you see. I can be persuasive in taking what I want," he replied.

"Was it your idea to kill me in Normandy?" I asked, genuinely curious.

"Of course. Your noble brother had tried to keep you out of it, but you were a bloodhound. You can apologize to him in Paris before it's all over." He said it almost magnanimously. The relief that surged within me at Adrien still being alive was short-lived as a new thought struck me.

"With the world watching Paris for the Olympics, everyone will scramble for more safety measures." I was fishing here, but it felt right.

"They absolutely will. Then, your devices will have failed to save people, I'll buy everything for pennies on the dollar and build it back up, using your technology. It'll be too late for quite a few people in Paris, but apparently it takes a major event to inspire real action these days. Real action is what they want to see; real action is what they will get, and long term, I'll get your company for practically nothing, and make it my own."

Oh my Lord, he was going to kill people on the world stage of the Paris Olympics. But why us? Was this about money? I was so lost, and I was running out of time. He was using our devices that should detect bombs, but wouldn't? I had to keep trying with him.

"Did Adrien know what you were planning all along, with the bombs?" I asked.

"God no, not at first. He was lulled in by the money and power another acquisition would bring him, like everyone else. Once he figured it out, it was too late. I had already taken what I needed from your company. He tried to slow me down, and in some ways, it worked. He could have gone to the authorities, but I made it clear what would happen to your employees and you if he did."

"Honestly, I can't believe how easy it was to find you and follow you. Blowing up your boat was meant to be a lesson for him and poetic justice for me, but then you survived, and I'll admit, I did have a moment of panic, but not for long. Putting a bounty on you paid off, as did taking over so much of your tech while Adrien tried to send us on a goose chase. Your own facial recognition software picked you up on screen in Dieppe. You're smart. I'll give you that. I thought we'd lost you, but there you were on some tourist's Instagram story in the background. People just have no idea how often they are filmed, you included."

Damn, he was right. I had done everything I could, and I'd still been caught. How did anyone go off-grid these days?

"But why?" My ultimate question, I spit it out with zero finesse. I simply didn't understand. "What poetic justice?" I asked.

"You're a smart girl, Hensley. Think about it. Port security ring a bell? Richard Companies covers all the ports on the coasts throughout the European Union. And yet, you failed when it mattered most." He'd lost interest in talking to me, it was obvious, but I was starting to understand. Ajaccio.

"Your wife was killed in Ajaccio," I guessed.

I'd pushed him. He went from still and bored to rage instantly. I didn't have time to react before the back of his hand slammed across my face.

THIRTY

THEO

THERE WAS STILL NO SIGN OF HENSLEY ON ANY VIDEO FEEDS, EVEN though it had been almost an hour since she'd gotten away from the dipshit who had tried to grab her for the bounty. I knew she could take care of herself, and yet she shouldn't have to. I had made her promises, and I intended to keep them. I should have told her the whole truth before we were intimate. I knew that rationally. I just hadn't been thinking rationally earlier. Trusting myself was new; forgiving myself might never happen if I kept repeating the same stupid patterns.

My head was a mess. The team was frenzied around me, and I had practically paced a hole in the floor while we prepared to head to Paris. We weren't sure what was awaiting us there; we were only going on instinct. No one knew where Ken was, where Adrien was, or where Hensley was. If only I had trusted her, or even talked to her about it, maybe we wouldn't be here. I felt it in my bones too; something was very wrong. I ached.

"How much longer before we leave?" I asked Seb.

"Ten minutes, waiting on tickets. Trying to figure out the

fastest way to Paris, and that's the train. The high-speed, TGV, leaves here every hour today, and that is our fastest way to the heart of Paris. Mila has an address for us in Montmartre, an apartment of Adrien's. We'll head there first."

I nodded at him. It was a solid plan, and I knew that Tad and Nate were meeting us in Paris. I couldn't shake the ominous sense that had taken root within me. And why were they all being nice to me? Hadn't they seen that this was my fault? If nothing else, I was shit at personal protection too. I had failed at my job. Again.

"Grab Hen's stuff and let's get down to the car. Brian is ready for us."

I nodded at Seb and went to gather her things. She didn't have much, just the items Luke had provisioned in the Normandy house for her. They were still hers though, and her scent enveloped me, her warmth warring with the shame I was drowning in. I sent up a prayer that she was safe, that I would have the time to apologize, the time to prove to her that I was done letting people down. Done letting her down.

Walking back out to the kitchen, I snagged her market bag and notebook off the table before I joined the guys in the car. It would take us two hours to get to Paris, and I'd spend every moment working through contingency plans for finding her.

We made our way to the train station, circumnavigating security checkpoints in part due to knowing how to and in part via a contact of Tad's letting us through. Thirty minutes later we were hurtling through the valleys and hills of southern France, making our way to Paris. We'd taken a small compartment and had immediately secured it, then dialed in the rest of the team. Tad and Nate were in motion, so it was just the crew in DC and us.

"I have bad news. Ken has Hensley, yet she is alive." Luke didn't waste any fucking time in telling us what he knew. "The good news is that they are also on their way to Paris and they are on the train in front of you. Because of the Olympics, they're running every hour, so you aren't too far behind."

I had sent her running straight into the arms of a killer.

Dropping my head into my hands, I squeezed my eyes shut against the wetness trying to leak out. Fuck. I had failed everyone around me.

"We'll find her brother. That's what we do. We can do this." Brian's quiet voice next to me made me feel worse. I didn't deserve this brotherhood. The dam within me broke, and I raised my head. I took stock of every single face around me and on the screen. I saw the trust in their eyes as it washed over me, seeping into the nooks and crannies within my broken-ness. They trusted me. These men, they'd been through hell with me, carried me, believed in me. Their strength propped me up, reminding me that I was worthy. I was an elite operator. I was not un-redeemable.

"Double the bounty," I said to these faces that I loved so much and owed so much to.

"Double the bounty?" Luke asked. "Okay, but can you give me a little more, Baby Theo?"

"He's right. Doubling the bounty gets even more people in the world looking for Hensley," Brian said. "Genius."

"Use their weapon against them. I love it," Seb added.

"Double it, triple it, fucking quadruple it, I don't care. There is no amount too large to find her," I said.

Luke was already nodding, talking to Wills offscreen.

"Good Theo, good. We're on it now, in real time," he said.

"It's all we've got right now. Any sign of Adrien?" I asked.

"None. However he got where he is now, he did it without anyone seeing him. That's not an easy thing these days," Luke said.

"In fact, it's more than not easy. It's practically impossible. Unless, of course, you own a tech company and know how to avoid cameras," Wills said.

"We're missing something, something big," I stated the obvious, turning to look out the window. I wondered where Hensley was, whether she was safe, if she was scared. She was strong, I had to keep believing that she was okay or I'd go crazy.

"Hensley! That's it!" I dug around for her market bag, pulling it up onto my lap. I grabbed onto the notebook and pulled it out.

"Hensley took notes of everything. She had to have known something that she didn't even realize." I was speed-reading her notes, studying her drawings.

"Guys, she has a hand-drawn map of Paris in here, and she's put a star everywhere they put . . ." I tried to read faster, mumbling out loud as I did.

A-fucking-ha, found it! The stars followed the river Seine, the river flowing through the heart of the city.

"She put a star everywhere in Paris that they put one of the Liberty Devices, everywhere they'd want to scan underwater for bombs. That's it! They are the only people in the world who have both underwater capabilities from the founding of their company and bomb-scanning devices."

"And the epicenter of the Olympics is the Seine. Everyone will be gathered there for the opening ceremonies. Paris started as an island in the middle of the river, so they have everything planned along it," Luke said.

"So if the devices in place to detect underwater bombs are in the hands of a madman, and the world is watching, and these devices aren't working properly, what happens?"

The train car was silent as we considered the question, looked to one another.

"Lots of people die. Richard Companies folds, but the tech itself wasn't really to blame," Seb said. "So the tech is dirt cheap, Ken effectively rides off into the sunset with a billion-dollar empire for nothing."

"And he doesn't care that people died for it because in his warped mind, people die all the time." Brian added.

"Why Richard Companies, though? That doesn't make sense to me at all," Seb asked. "What's the connection?"

"You said Ken's wife died in a boating accident, right? Where? What are the details? It can't be a coincidence that Richard Companies covers port security, and she died on the water," I guessed.

"She died in Ajaccio," Luke started before he trailed off. "Oh shit, you hit the nail on the head, Theo. She was killed when their boat was docked in Ajaccio. A small bomb went off that day in the port, part of a mob hit gone wrong, apparently. The bomb was on the wrong boat, and she had stayed behind while Ken took the kids into town." I could hear Luke reading aloud what happened, and everything was clicking into place while he did so.

"So he blames Richard Companies for not finding the bomb?" I assumed.

"He must. Their tech was down for a stretch of days, not working at all," he added.

"You said mob though, right? Was it even Richard Companies who failed Ken?" Seb questioned.

"No, it wasn't. There's been a trial, and all of this is fact, not supposition. The guy who planted the bomb made a plea deal and confessed everything, including taking their tech offline to do so," Luke said. "Aaaand that guy was killed in a random mugging three months later, while out on parole. Random mugging my ass."

"But it didn't matter to Ken. His wife was already dead, and he'd learned how easy it was to turn off the devices, to override the device." I was guessing again, but it felt right.

"He used his grief for revenge, because it was too easy to override the system, or to get rich once it fails in Paris? I don't get it," Brian said.

"He's a diabolical fucker. Yes, to both guys. He has the resources for both. Luke, you said earlier that illogical patterns are expected when it comes to the mind, and this fits right? It doesn't make logical sense, but it wouldn't to us. Getting twisted revenge against a company he can hold accountable, killing off the guy who confessed, and taking the tech for himself for pennies on the dollar. It fits," Seb said.

"And he can fix what killed her. It does fit. I mean, the device didn't kill her, but it made it easier for the shitshow to play out," I said. This was the guy who had Hensley. This was the man who held my world in his hands.

"We're getting hits!" Wills shouted throughout the train car from the DC office. "She's in Paris. They were on the TGV and have left Gare du Nord, but a spotter lost them in a private car from there. The increase in bounty is working. There is now a group of people working together to try and find her."

Fuck, my gut clenched again. I hoped that I hadn't unleashed anything more on her. We needed the spotters, but we had to beat them to her to keep her safe.

"The bounty is only good if she's alive and unharmed," Luke said, reading my mind. "Mila has also fed that soundbite to every news channel in the world, so it is well known."

I nodded at him, even though worry was my constant companion. It would be until I held her in my arms again.

"Wills, where is Adrien's place in Paris?" I asked.

"Montmartre." His singular response indicated he knew where I was going with this.

"We'll head there. Shoot me the address." Luke nodded, and I saw the address pop up on my phone as he did so. We'd be in Paris in approximately twenty minutes ourselves, and I'd turn the city upside down to find her. The guys were murmuring around me as I pulled up Adrien's address and began studying the map of the surrounding area.

Silently, I pleaded with God to keep Hensley safe. I told him I'd double down on my vow if that is what it took. I'd give anything to see her safe. Whatever it took. I apologized in advance for likely killing another human. I wouldn't seek to do so, yet if I had to in order to protect or save Hensley, I'd do it without remorse. Sorry God. Hensley was missing from me and I would never again be whole without her.

Heaven help them if Ken or Adrien hurt one single hair on her head.

THIRTY-ONE

HENSLEY

THE LONGER I WAS HELD BY KEN AND HIS MEN, THE MORE I realized that the man was ravaged by insanity. He'd grown bored with talking to me, but not before a cryptic comment about the opening ceremony, scheduled to take place later tonight. I'd clearly missed something in my notes, and I was racking my brain to figure it out before it was too late.

I'd been bundled into a dark car immediately outside of Gare Nord. We were headed toward the river Seine, which I didn't quite understand. Adrien's old apartment was in Montmartre, a solid twenty-minute drive away from the river. His apartment was between Moulin Rouge and Sacré-Cœur, a beautiful part of Paris that had originally been far away from the city center. He'd inherited that from the same Tante Louise that I had inherited the boat from.

Paris was laid out in a turret seashell pattern, spiraling out from the center, an island in the middle of the Seine where the city had begun. It was called Ile de la Cite, most famous for Notre Dame, the heart of France. Each neighborhood in Paris had its own distinct culture and personality, and I loved them all. Similar to Lyon, I could wander forever here. I just couldn't figure out why we were cutting through the seashell shape down to the Seine instead of up to Montmartre. Ken had said that I would be seeing Adrien soon, so I had assumed he was taking me to him in his apartment, but apparently, I had assumed that incorrectly.

I thought back to my little notepad, one I hadn't read through in the rush of being with Theo finally, and then hearing his words lance through my heart before I ran. I tried again to get more information out of Ken.

"*Liberte*. I think it's interesting when a word is reclaimed. There is power in that, no? You aren't liberating anything, or protecting freedoms, and yet you tried to take the word and weaponize it. You almost succeeded too." I was fishing, but I needed to know more.

"Almost succeeded, Hensley? Look around you. I've won. Before too long, neither you nor Adrien will be my problem, and the rest of the world will be falling all over themselves to buy one of my devices, but after this, they will actually work. You see, Hensley, it's a solid plan. Kill some people, save the rest, fix what doesn't work on your devices and then scale them. Those that died? It happens," he said. His voice was even, not one iota of inflection. He simply didn't care that he was going to kill other people. Human life held no value to him any longer.

"That won't bring her back, you know." I had to try one more time. Perhaps break through to his humanity, if that was possible.

The back of his hand hit my face hard enough that I fought to stay awake. How had I not seen that coming again, and *merde*! It hurt. My eyes were watering, and my jaw felt like he'd broken it, although I knew he hadn't. I shrank against the door even tighter than before.

"Shut the fuck up, Hensley." His voice was as even as before, no change in the tone. I had learned my lesson the hard way, as I typically did. For the millionth time, I wondered where we were going.

I guess I was about to find out as the car slowed along the river's edge. We'd exited the busy street and taken one of the smaller boat ramps down toward the water, something we would only do if we were boarding a boat. Sure enough, the car came to a lurching stop alongside a boat anchored at the water's edge. Many people lived in boats along the Seine in Paris, much like Amsterdam, the regulations had made living there infinitely cheaper than apartments in the same area. People could live in one of the most desired real estate areas in the world for a fraction of what their neighbors on land were paying. The river's edges were already starting to get crowded as the afternoon waned.

Abruptly, light flooded the dim car, and Ken reached over to drag me out.

"Scream for help and more people will die. I will kill anyone who tries to help you right now, right here, right in front of you." Ken's threat, whether real or not, was enough to make me stay quiet as I was unceremoniously dragged toward the boat, looking to anyone who may have seen us as two lovers walking quickly together, tethered almost. Once on board, we descended into a galley, stopping at a cabin door, portside. Making sure to orient myself, I tried to remember where I was in relationship to the bank, and to the water. I've been taken to a cabin facing the water, and as Ken unceremoniously unlocked the door and shoved me in, slamming the door behind me, it took me a minute for my eyes to adjust.

"Hensley!" His voice brought me to my knees in relief. I hadn't wanted to get my hopes up and yet I had. I couldn't help it. My brother was part of me, the only family I had left and thankfully, I still had him.

"Oh my God, Adrien! You're alive!"

"I could say the same for you! I'm so sorry. I am so, so sorry. I tried to keep you safe, but I should have told you the truth as soon as I figured it out." Adrien had rushed over to me and was pulling me up and against him, hugging me in what appeared to be genuine relief. I wanted to sink into him, believe in the best possible scenario of my brother's involvement, and yet I couldn't just yet. I pulled back slightly and regarded him warily.

"I take it that you did not try to have me killed?" I asked bluntly. My heart could take it. I had to know.

"Have you killed?! I've been trying to protect you for ten months. I've been laying off employees and giving them severances so that they would not be in the path of Ken's ire, and I've tried to distance myself from you as much as I could, but I should have known you would keep asking questions. I'm sorry, Hensley. I should've trusted you with the truth. I am just so sorry." He came across as genuinely contrite, the truth hovering between us. Another wave of relief rolled over me.

"What truth Adrien? What truth should you have told me?" I asked, trusting him now, yet still desperate for the truth.

"I brought a madman into our company Hensley. I was like a fucking lamb to slaughter following a potential acquisition that I thought would make you proud of me. It was meant as a boon, a way for us to work together more, get to know each other as adults. I made a bid for a company that I thought was way too big, thinking I would at least get some experience and be able to talk the language you traverse with ease. Before I knew it, the owner had personally pulled me in." He trailed off and my heart flopped over at his words of wanting to be closer, get to know me as an adult.

"Ken." I didn't even need to ask. It was that simple.

"Yes, Ken. From what just happened, I'll assume that distancing myself was for naught. He didn't hurt you did he?" Adrien's countenance had darkened, and I was reminded again of Theo. My Theo, he was probably tearing Lyon apart for me. I hoped he was anyway. There had to be a way to signal him, or Mila. I knew she was watching feeds with Wills. One of them would see us if we could get into a crowd.

"How long have you been here Adrien?" I asked.

"Since the night you ran from our London offices. I called Ken to threaten him that if anything happened to you at the hands of his goons, that I would expose him. I have back up print outs stashed in my place here in Montmartre, the one *Tante Louise* left me in her trust. I just need those to prove how he deactivated the devices. Hopefully, before they are deactivated." His shoulders dropped before his next admission.

"I was so fucking naïve! He was sitting in a car outside of our building when I left that night, eager to get to you. I was gagged and bound, then left here. Today, when he brought you in, is the first time I've seen him since then."

"Ya, he was in Normandy, blowing up my boat, shooting at me, then finding me in Lyon and kidnapping me. Busy guy," I deadpanned.

"He blew up your boat?!" Adrien bellowed, then caught himself. "He shot at you?!"

"Indeed. I've been a busy woman trying to stay alive, yet I've had help." I gave him some high points of Titan Group and the connection via Tad, whom he knew of. Tad was from an extremely wealthy and famous American family. At our level, it was a small world.

"Well, thank goodness you've had Titan Group," he said.

"Yes, thank goodness for Titan Group, for Theo." My mind snagged on Theo again, my heart clenching. I had to figure out how to signal him, signal the team. Right now, I had more questions than I had answers, and it was pissing me off.

Maybe it was time Adrien, and I finally worked together.

"Adrien, does Ken know about your trust? About the apartment?" I asked him. "He had found me via facial recognition software, our own as a matter of fact, in Dieppe. He didn't say anything about knowing about the boat beforehand."

"He doesn't, or he wouldn't have kept me alive. Ken is ruthless. He would have killed me and then gone for you. He needs us alive right now," Adrien answered. "Oh Hensley, I am fucking sorry." His deep sigh rattled throughout me. His anguish my own.

"By the time I figured his plan out, Ken had used me to learn how to deactivate the scanners along the river for the opening ceremony. It was too late to warn anyone. I tried to send you away, but I did a shit job of it and should've been honest with you. And now here we are, locked here together, going to die together. He's put bombs under boats throughout the Seine. They're set to go off tonight at the height of the opening ceremony, right next to us at the base of the Eiffel Tower and with no devices active to scan for them, no one will know what hit them until it is too late. French authorities won't even think to check something they think is already covered."

Ken's words from earlier sliced through me. "I think if all goes according to plan, we will actually be part of the bomb Adrien."

"We will definitely be part of the fireworks. One of the largest bombs in the city is on the bottom of this boat," he replied, finality sinking into his words.

Despair threatened to overtake me. The last days of my life had been insane, and yet along with the insanity had come a gift that I had never expected. One I had dreamed of, yearned for, yet had never gotten close to having. Theo.

God knows we both had some trauma to work through, and some trust issues, but I knew he was my person. Our edges just fit, brought together by madness and one man's revenge, yet locked into place naturally and effortlessly. I kicked myself for not confronting him this morning, which now felt like a lifetime ago.

Today could've gone much differently had I simply asked him what he was talking about, or he had simply talked to me about his trust issues. So much miscommunication, but with goodness at its core, as it happens sometimes. That was life, right? Sometimes, we hurt people that we may even love. The ones we loved the most were typically the ones we hurt the most.

Love? Already? Did I love Theo? His strength called to me, his steadfastness of protecting me, even when he wasn't sure he could trust me, amazed me, and he lit a fire inside of me that I didn't believe possible. Did I love him?

I did, even if it was inexplicable. I've known him less than a week, and yet I knew deep within myself that he was my person. All of those platitudes you could give about loving someone flooded my mind, yet one stood out among all the rest. He was the safety in the storm, always. We only needed more time.

"For now, we are sitting ducks." Adrien's morose words broke though my revelations about loving Theo.

"Not if I can help it Adrien. We aren't in this alone anymore. We have friends now, friends who are looking for us, friends who will not let us down, no matter what. We need to help ourselves first, to give them some time to find us." The words coming from my own lips conveyed my conviction. We were fighters, and I for one, was not going down without a fight.

"Adrien, Ken won't be here the closer we get to the Olympics' opening, on the boat. He'll need to be on a public stage so that he can take our company after neither one of us returns. He's got to be at the VIP space with the officials we contracted with, he won't miss that. Sure, he gets his revenge, but to the tune of a multibillion-dollar company for practically nothing when we die and it comes out about a supposed failure of our tech. One only a newly-named VP can fix, as he'll tell the world. No one will know we are here or that we were part of the damage." A plan was coming together in my mind, the words tumbling out as they came to me. I didn't have time to second guess myself as most of the day had flown by while I'd been held hostage in the train, the car, and now the boat.

"Right, if we can overpower the guard, there's hope that we can at least get to the shore and cause a ruckus. We just need one camera to see us. I know Titan Group will see it."

"How will Titan Group see one camera in the world in Paris?" Adrien asked. "Do they have our tech?"

"Trust me. If I've learned anything in this, it's that we are always on film. I know Titan Group is monitoring it and I know they are searching everywhere for me. Theo won't let me go without a fight." The absolute clarity I had on that as I said the words would have brought tears to my eyes if I had taken the time to stop and let it sink in. I didn't have that luxury of time just yet though, so I squared my shoulders.

"Even when Theo didn't trust me, he made sure to take care of me. We are going to get to the bottom of that trust, because I'm not going to walk away again. It's my own damn fault that I'm in this mess right now, and I won't walk away again without asking hard questions. What we have is worth staying around for and talking through. He'll find me, he will come for me, he only needs to know where to look."

"Okay. Let's do it, how can we cause a ruckus and send that signal?" Adrien's immediate acceptance of my reasoning warmed me, it gave me courage.

"Causing a ruckus is the easy part." I grinned at my brother. That little flicker of hope continuing to grow deep within me.

"I'm going to start yelling for all I'm worth Adrien, and when that guard opens the door to ask why, you're gonna hit him over the head as hard as you can. Wait till he gets in the room a step, so you can really hit him hard. I will be right behind you, and as soon as we get off this boat, we both need to start yelling for help. With all the tourists in town for the Olympics, and all the cameras along the Seine, they'll find us." I was sure of it.

"We can do that. Hensley, just promise me you'll be okay." Adrien's quiet acceptance and concern settled in my heart.

"You promise me! I have to think that we aren't finally having this conversation with each other only lose each other again Adrien."

"Agreed. And Hensley, as soon as we make for the bank, start yelling and run toward the bridge. We can't sit here and yell, we have to keep moving."

"*D'accord*, let's do this," I agreed.

He hugged me tightly to him and kissed my temple. "I love you, Henny."

"I love you too, Adrien."

With one more squeeze to him, I stepped back and screamed for all I was worth. It took less than thirty seconds and a guard came running. Adrien had him knocked out and was above deck in moments, with me hot on his heels.

Neither of us saw the other guard until it was too late, until he had me in a choke hold before I could get clear of the walls of the boat to see the bank. I only had a fleeting glance of Adrien's pale face as he frantically looked back for me.

"Go!" I mouthed. I knew our best chance now wasn't him coming for me, he had nothing to defend himself or me with. Not against the guard. No, our best hope now was the ruckus.

THIRTY-TWO

THEO

WE'D GONE INTO ADRIEN'S MONTMARTRE APARTMENT QUIET AS church mice, expecting to find Hensley and whoever had her. What we didn't expect to find was a peaceful stillness, and an apartment that hadn't been touched.

It was tidy, yet with a fine layer of dust. Adrien hadn't been here in recent weeks, no one had. I huffed out a quiet, "Fuck," in my own rage and called Luke to let him know she wasn't there. Seb was checking the apartment, and Brian had gone back to the door to cover us.

"Any word from the bounty?" I asked without preamble.

"Not yet, but it will work. I know it will. Also, Tad and Nate are on their way. Tad has the notes from Adrien's London flat with him. They've been trying to piece together the burned fragments."

I was listening to Luke, but my mind was already three steps ahead.

Hen, baby, send me something. I know I let you down, but I won't do it again. The mantra was on a quiet loop in my head, my heart refusing to accept any other outcome.

I ran my hand along the man's desk. Who was Adrien Richard? Monster? Greedy asshole? Interestingly, he had a photo of himself with his grandparents and a very tiny Hensley on his desk. I picked it up, running my finger over Hensley's little face. 'I promise I'll find you. I will not leave a single inch of Paris unturned.' I vowed to her again. *Tu me manques.*

Setting the frame back on the desk, I heard the clinking sound of something falling. Glancing at the floor, my eyes snagged on the jump drive that had fallen off the back of the frame. Interesting. Why would somebody hide that in such a location?

"Luke, I might have something here. Hang tight. Seb!" I yelled for Seb to join me and Adrien's office.

"I need the computer," I rushed out.

Seb plopped it on the desk and I immediately put the thumb drive into it.

"Luke, we're hooked up, tell me you can crack it."

"Boys, I'm no nerd. Wills, man, we need you here," Luke yelled at Wills, whom I knew to be sitting next to him in DC.

"Good grief, Luke, even in a time like this you're calling us nerds. I love you, you dumbass, and this nerd is happy to save the day." Wills was calm, which gave me hope. The man could crack anything, and if he needed help, Mila was the techiest person I'd ever met.

"Theo, Seb, give me a couple of minutes, I know I can hack this," Wills said.

I could hear his fingers clacking at rapid speed as he did so, murmurs to Mila in the background and her responses.

"Got it!" I heard his words at the same time photos flashed across the screen of different locations along the river. Holy shit, Adrien had laid out where he believed Ken would put the bombs, inside of the very devices that should have been scanning for them. Diabolical fucker was a genius too. They all were, sadly.

"Well, the good news is that we were right: Adrien was trying to prevent something. Ken is avenging his wife," Seb said.

"Yeah, and the bad news is that we were right. Adrien was trying to avert something and doesn't seem to have done it," I added.

"Holy shit, I've got to get Tad's dad and Interpol in on this. Hang tight," Luke added.

Tad's dad was one of our "handlers" with the Pentagon, and Luke was right to get him, as well as Interpol, updated in real time. We had an international shitshow on our hands, one of epic proportions.

What came up in front of us were schematics on how to bomb the opening games, laid out completely. It appeared as if every scanning device had been not only deactivated but also armed. The very machines meant to keep people safe would be the ones that killed them. Holy shit, indeed. I glanced at my watch, the time confirming what I already knew—we were almost out of time. The bombs would start with the setting sun, coinciding with the fireworks meant to open the Olympics.

It still didn't tell me where Hensley was, though. I was ice-skating along the razors edge, to one side an infinite abyss of ice and sharpness, to the other, safety, Hensley. I just couldn't get off the edge of the razor. Sunset was closing in.

"Theo! Guys! There's a man yelling for help and running alongside the Seine, he's making his way haphazardly in the direction of Montmartre. I'm pulling facial recognition now, but this is the biggest commotion we've seen all day." Mila's excited voice was clear across the comms and I knew in my gut that this was my girl.

"It's Hensley—it has to be. She's trying to send us a signal." I was confident about that. She'd find a way.

"If she's sending us a signal, she's sending us her brother. Facial recognition is lighting up with Adrien Richard's face," Mila said.

I didn't hear the rest as I made for the door. I knew Seb would grab the computer and be right behind me.

Luke was still on my comms, keeping the line open although he was on the phone with Cullins, our handler in Virginia. Will and Mila were in the background of comms as well as I grabbed Brian and we ran toward the Eiffel Tower. I knew they'd take care of the rest, I was only focused on finding Hensley.

Clearing the last flight of steep steps going down from the apartment, I flagged the first cab I could find and flashed my gun at him, telling him to get out of the car. Brian and Seb jumped in behind me, and I took off for the Seine.

Brian had the DC team on speakerphone as we raced along the streets down toward the landmark where Adrien had last been. 'I'm coming for you, Hensley, I'm coming for you.'

"Guys, I have a crazy idea, but I think it will work." I heard Mila's words, but they didn't register and I didn't care. The only words I wanted to hear were about Hensley's location. Anything else, I knew Seb or Brian would take care of.

The words flowed around me, yet I was homed in on driving. What should have taken me about twenty minutes was going to take less than ten. Rounding the corner, I saw the man of the hour running toward us in the middle of the street. Adrien Richard.

Not caring about anything but getting to Hensley, and that was through Adrien, I threw the little car in park and jumped out. Horns were blaring at me, the bird flying left and right from angry French drivers swerving around me, and then Adrien.

"Adrien! Where is she? Where is Hensley?" I was shouting, but the man was less than ten feet from me. Grabbing him as he collapsed from the exertion of running and screaming, I got in his face.

"Where is she asshole? I will beat it out of you if I have to." I yanked him up and pulled my fist back, ready to make good on the promise.

Seb was rushing me, Brian with him. A crowd had gathered,

phones were pointing our way. Time seemed to slow in the sinking sunlight.

"Tell me where she is!" I screamed again.

"Theo?" Adrien asked. "Theo?" he tried again, breaking through my bloodlust.

"Yes, tell me where she is or so help me God, I'll kill you." I whispered the words, yet he heard them.

"She's on the boat, I'll take you there. I got away, but they grabbed her again. I'll take you to her." His words were rushed out, and I gave him no time, simply starting running in the direction he'd come from, dragging him along with me.

Adrien's body had given out, so I threw him over my shoulder and was barking questions at him as fast as I could to get directions.

"The boat—it's anchored right under the Eiffel Tower. She's there. But Theo, there are bombs everywhere." Like a fucking bomb would scare me away from Hensley. I was a Marine Raider, trained in special amphibious reconnaissance, a fucking SARC. My life had prepared me for this inevitability, I knew that instantly, deeply true in my gut. Hensley and I had collided when we needed each other the most.

In my peripheral vision, I could see that we gained a crowd and that it was growing with every step we ran. Phones were following every movement and people were shouting directions at us, pointing us to the river.

"I don't give a shit. Adrien, tell me which boat," I roared.

He pointed toward one sitting low in the water, the walls on the sides making it impossible to see if there were guards on board.

"Theo, wait. Theo!" Adrien was yelling at me and fighting to be let down. Sparing him only a moment, I dropped him cold and made my way to the boat.

"There are bombs in the scanning devices. I can re-activate the detection aspect if you have a computer, I set it all up to go to one switch, I just need to get to my notes and a phone. I can re-arm them and highlight where the bombs are instantly," he said, wheezing the words out.

Brian and Seb were right with me, and Brian turned to him then, pulling up photos on his phones as he crouched along Adrien. His notes! Right, Tad had sent photos of the burned pages.

"We have your notes from London. Here!" Brian held the phone out to Adrien as he dropped to the ground alongside him and motioned for the laptop back from Seb. Pulling it open, he typed in a password and handed it to Adrien as well.

I turned to run toward the boat, the golden rays of sunset sparkling along the water. They could save the world, I didn't give a fuck. I was going for Hensley, and I was almost out of time.

"Theo!" Something in his voice made me turn. "There's a bomb under the boat too."

"So disarm it!" I yelled as I turned back toward the boat.

Adrien was frantic, but also typing. Tad and Brian were on the phone barking locations as fast as Adrien could read them off, both looking over his shoulders as he did so. We just had to hope they could all be disarmed in time.

"Seb! You're up. Get in there, I'm going for her," I said, and I took off running again. Hensley was my only focus. I'd either get her off that boat in time, or I'd die trying. I didn't know how much time we had left, but I was spending it with her. I hadn't been spared in Mosul for nothing. If the only reason I had been spared then was to save her now, I'd do it. I'd die a million times over to save her.

"God damn it Theo, go," Seb yelled at me as he ran past, diving off the stone ledge of the bank. I heard Brian coaching Adrien, the steadiness of his voice calming me as it faded into the distance as I closed in on the boat.

Trust. The crux of my life. Trust, now the only thing I had between a future with Hensley, one of love, life and joy. Trust that my highly trained brothers were put in this very position to shine, trust that I could get her off the boat in time, trust in myself to save the love of my life.

The boat was empty when I jumped onto the walkway, the guards apparently having fled for their own lives. The sun was almost completely set, the in-between of twilight upon us. The golds and lavenders were mixing, a dangerous concoction for a man who needed the sun to never set on this day.

Adrien had said she was in the portside cabin earlier, and I jumped down the galley stairs in one motion to get to that door. Lowering my shoulder, I rammed that fucking door for all I was worth.

"Hensley!" I roared.

"Theo! In here!" I heard her cries and lowered my shoulder again. The light in the galley was growing darker by the moment.

Splintering, the door still held. "Hen, step back!" I yelled and rammed it again and again. On the third try, I burst through into the dark cabin.

"Theo! You found me!" She jumped at me, wrapping her legs around my waist.

"Always Hen, I will always come for you. But, baby, we've got to get off here before this boat blows up. Now!" I was running and explaining, holding her tightly to me.

She wrapped her arms around my neck and tucked her face into me, wordlessly giving her trust. Trust. Again with that very crux of my life.

We'd just cleared the steps from the galley when a rumbling hit my ears. Seb had gotten the bomb off the bottom of the boat, but had run out of time to disarm it. I sure hoped he'd gotten clear.

That was the last thought I had before the explosion rocked the boat, sending Hensley and I deep into the Seine. Locked together, going under the water much the same way we'd met. Only this time, we were together until the force of hitting the water wrenched us apart.

Fighting through the dark river, kicking my legs as powerfully as I could, I burst above the water line screaming for her. Seeing no sign of her, I dove back down, reaching for her frantically. I refused to lose her in the way that I had found her. I dove again.

THIRTY-THREE

HENSLEY

I was seriously tired of being blown up. For a woman who loved boats, I was re-thinking that affection. My limbs were heavy, but this time when I had hit the water, there had been a very large body bearing the brunt of the hit. Theo. He'd twisted us around in the air so that he'd be the one to hit the water the hardest. My protector.

I broke above the water yelling for him, wiping the river from my eyes. The sun had set and the Eiffel Tower was sparkling overhead to usher in the night. The noise was deafening, crowds were everywhere along the banks of the river, yet his hoarse screams pierced the darkness that had just fallen across the City of Light. I swung around in the water at my name.

"Theo!" I swam toward him, dodging burning chunks of the boat littering the water around us. "Theo!" I yelled again.

"Hen, baby. I love you so much, I am so sorry. Are you okay?" His voice was hoarse, but his words were clear as his arms closed around me. Fireworks burst above our heads as tears streamed down my face.

"You came for me." Those were the only words I could think of.

"Always. I will always come for you. Every single time," he said, kissing me again. I was so lost in him that it took me a moment to hear the clapping and cheering from nearby.

Pulling back, both Theo and I turned toward the sound, toward the banks of the Seine. There was Seb, scratched and bloody, yet grinning like a fool and clapping at us.

"Oh good, it worked. Phew, I was worried about that one," he said. Then he saluted us and turned to swim the rest of the way to the bank. Standing there, I could see Adrien standing with Brian, who was giving a thumbs up to indicate all good, and about three thousand people cheering and waving. Their phones were all lit up, their cheers wild. The waving phone flashlights mimicking the sparkles of the Tower.

I turned back to Theo, finding him already watching me intently.

"I love you." He'd said the words earlier, yet they hadn't registered at first. They did now. "And, Hensley, I am sorry. I do trust you. I was an idiot."

"And I love you, Theo. Now, let's give them a show. We can talk about the idiocy later." I smothered his laughter with my mouth, kissing him this time.

The romance of it all was my happily ever after. In the dark waters of the Seine, the Tower sparkled above us, fireworks exploding in brilliant colors, the burning boat around us, even the lights of all the phones live streaming my rescue. I guess we really were always on camera these days.

Kissing me deeply for a while longer, he finally pulled back long enough to remind me that he was treading water for both of us with his legs, and that we should take this onshore. He whispered a few filthy promises about a hotel room and I giggled as he helped me toward the bank. Actually giggled, wow, I may be in shock.

The city of Paris had cleaned the Seine so that it was safe to swim in for the Olympics, and yet they hadn't accounted for a boat exploding in the swim lanes. It took us a bit to get to the bank, exhausted as we were, and dodging the debris. It didn't help that Theo had to carry me and swim at the same time, yet that seemed to work okay for us. It had kind of become our thing, but maybe a thing I never wanted to experience again. I was a strong swimmer, yet jumping from exploding boats took it out of me.

Fished from the water and enveloped in warm blankets, we were met with cheers from behind a perimeter the police were rushing to set up. Now that we were out of the water, I could see that some of the lights were that of ambulances and police cars. Interpol was there, and Brian was managing the scene as Seb was being checked out.

"What about Ken?" I asked Theo as his arms closed around me. We'd sat next to Seb on stretchers the ambulances had wheeled out. They'd brought one for each of us, yet Theo was having none of that. He sat behind me while the EMTs checked me out. I was fine, yet again because of Theo.

"Ken was exactly where you expected him to be, standing in the limelight of the Opening Ceremony. His greed did him in again. Had he run, we probably wouldn't have found him for a while." His mouth settled into grim lines. "We'd have eventually tracked him down, though not right away," Seb said.

"So he's in custody?" I asked. I wanted him to pay for what he did, even as I recognized that he was a monster made of pain.

"He can't hurt you anymore, Hensley. No one will ever hurt you again. I promise." Theo's words were whispered in my ear, hot along the sensitive skin there. My core clenched. Okay, apparently my protective alpha Theo was a major turn-on.

"Tad and Nate cornered him. He's with Interpol now. They were close when we pulled up the information in Adrien's apartment, and Mila got them on the line while we came for you. We never would have been in time had Adrien not gotten away," Seb said. Adrien had told them all about our plan as we were being checked out, and I was damn grateful it had worked. So incredibly grateful that my brother's only error in this had been his own naivety, and not a small amount of his own greed. We were going to talk about that. Later.

"So that's it, it's really over?" I asked.

"It's going to be messy. Ken will stand trial, and we need to ensure that his goon squad goes away with him," Theo said.

Seb agreed, and Adrien remained standing there, looking appalled with himself. Brian had just walked up and was nodding his head too. I think he meant to reassure me, but it didn't.

"How do you ever know when you have everyone?" This was the tricky thing for me to comprehend in all of this chaos. I needed to see for myself that Ken was in custody and would pay for what he tried to do. He'd been able to completely infiltrate our company, how did we know that everyone who helped him would be caught? There had been guards on the very boat that just blew up, where did they go?

"I need to see him." The statement brought all four men's eyes to me, stopping the relieved tone of the conversation.

"I need to see him, understand why he chose us, see with my own eyes that he is locked up."

"Hensley, he's definitely locked up. The Tad person is with him right now, Brian could show you a photo. And we know why he wanted our company—for the contracts and machines." Adrien tried to reassure me. "I fell right into his trap, and then it was too late to get out of it, and I didn't want you in danger, so I pushed everyone away or out. He was able to do this because I let him." The pain in Adrien's eyes matched the despair leaking from his words.

I jumped up from where I had been nestled into Theo on the gurney and went to Adrien, hugging him tightly. I was still drenched, the reflective blanket the EMTs had given me dropping from my shoulders as his arms finally closed back around me.

I didn't have the right words yet, because it simply felt too raw. He *had* fallen into a trap—he *hadn't* communicated with me. We had both almost died for it. I wasn't sure that a platitude of assurance was the right thing right now. I couldn't bring myself to say them, even if they were true to an extent. I loved Adrien, yet I was also pissed. I knew I would forgive him, yet we had to break this pattern. We had to work through this before I was willing to say that everything was all right. It wasn't all right. No, without Titan Group, we'd be dead, our legacy lost. Our family heritage wiped out.

I stepped back from Adrien, my eyes finding his . . . a mirror of my own. The Titan Group guys were quiet behind me, watchful of us.

"Adrien, I love you. I may not know you as well as a sister should know her older brother, but all of that is going to change. We are going to run this company together, fully, as *Grand-père et Gigi* intended. I am also going to communicate better. I can see my part in this too. But, Adrien . . . I do need to talk to Ken. I need to know he is locked up. We need to be sure, for the health of our company, the protection of our legacy, that there isn't some other angle that we didn't see. We have to know every aspect of this and not simply take the easy answer." His eyes closed briefly at my words. I knew I was right in this, and I would fight for it. I knew myself; I couldn't work my way to absolute forgiveness until we tore this apart together. That part, I had to say out loud, no matter how it practically gutted me to do.

"We need to get to the center of this together, Adrien. What happened isn't okay. We're alive now, the bombs were deactivated, Ken is in custody, but if we don't solve what led to all of that, we have nothing. I want to trust you. I want you to trust me. We aren't there now, but I'll fight like hell to get there, that I will promise you, *absolutement*."

Rather than voicing his agreement, Adrien nodded at me. Too choked up to speak, he crushed me to him in another hug, holding me tightly as his tears ran freely down his face. Adrien and I were going to be okay. Richard Companies was going to emerge stronger. Through all of it, I had Theo at my back. Stalwart, steady, safe.

THIRTY-FOUR

THEO

My God, she was incredible. Most people would have immediately given some empty words of everything being okay now that they were safe, yet not Hensley. Hensley was facing the hardest thing she'd ever faced with her brother, and she was doing so head-on. Fuck, she was incredible, and it was seriously a turn-on. I couldn't help it; everything about her was a turn-on.

Her courage was blowing me away. What was playing out in front of me was a version of the conversation that I needed to have with Max. I couldn't continue not facing what had happened in Mosul. She was making it look effortless, and yet her courage, where I had lacked it, was fucking incredible. If she was willing to stand strong in the face of what had happened, then so could I. But for right now, she sure as fuck wasn't going to do it alone.

"The lady said she wants to see Ken, and the lady gets what the lady wants." I stood up, dropped the reflective blanket back on the gurney, and stepped up behind Hensley as she turned toward me, water sloshing in my tennis shoes with every step.

"We'll take you to him now, Hen, let's roll." I settled my arm around her shoulders, bringing her as close to my body as I could while still being able to walk. She was cold; I could tell. I turned back to Brian and Seb, standing behind us and talking to the authorities.

Brian was shrugging out of his jacket before I even finished raising my hand. These guys, my guys. My team. Keeping my girl warm and making sure she didn't blow up.

"Seb, thanks man for getting the bomb off the boat, but also, what the hell man?" I mock-questioned him. Seb was not the team SARC, the 'special amphibious reconnaissance corpsman,' of our former Raider unit, but he did know how to defuse bombs, even under water, like all of us did.

"Not enough time, so I had to dive it down and then try to get out of the blast zone. Sorry about that, Baby Theo, but hey, you got your girl, the sparkles of the Tower, the live-streamed rescue. We were able to reactivate the scanners, so our friends on the force were able to find and disarm all the bombs, so everyone was saved. You're welcome," he replied, his blue eyes crinkling with laughter.

"I did get the girl. That's all that matters. I mean, that and that everyone was saved," I agreed. I didn't give a fuck about the rest now that people were safe and Hensley was going to be tucked against me tonight, although I wasn't looking forward to watching her talk to the absolute piece of shit Ken. I knew if she could do hard things, I'd be right there with her. No matter where she was.

The drive to the police station was quick, with the escort they'd given us. Streaking across Paris, we could see jubilation everywhere. None of these people would ever know how close they'd come to death. They'd evacuated the areas around the maps we'd found in Adrien's apartment, and Adrien had been able to re-activate the tech via those old-school handwritten notes Tad had taken photos of from his place in London. I guess it was a damn good thing that Adrien printed papers for when he had a migraine.

Reactivating the devices had sent Interpol, the police, all private security firms hired for the games. You name the agency, they'd all jumped on the screaming devices. Thankfully, every single bomb had been deactivated. Somewhat begrudgingly, I had to admit that Ken's plan was genius. Who would have thought of scanning the scanners themselves? If only he'd used his intellect for good and not diabolical shit. Thank goodness we'd been able to stop him.

This is what we did—the impossible shit that no one should ever know about. I preferred it that way. I liked knowing there were people like me all over the world, willing to sacrifice themselves for innocent civilians. I sent up a silent prayer of thanks that I had been sent to Paris to be on standby for this. If I hadn't . . . I shuddered to think about what would have happened to Hensley.

The car pulled to an abrupt stop in front of an ornate stone building, and as I glanced up, my eyes were caught on the *Liberte, fraternite, egalite* carved deep into the facade. Ken was sure a clever asshole, I'd give him that. His use of *liberte* would never have caught anyone's radar if we hadn't been searching for patterns.

I helped Hensley out of the car and walked with her into the station, Brian, Seb and Adrien trailing behind.

"Hensley! You made it after all, good to see you." Tad had come from one of the holding rooms to our left and stopped at the sight of us. He hugged Hensley as she greeted him and met my eyes over her shoulder. Tucking his chin against her, he snuggled her a little more. His eyes never left mine, the bastard.

"Okay, that's a nice reunion," I said, gently pulling her back against me. I couldn't help myself; that inner caveman was back, and he was already tense over what had happened in the last eight hours. The safest place for Hensley was back in my bed, and I intended to get her there as soon as possible. She laughed at my actions, throwing a soft smile over her shoulder back at me.

Speaking to Tad, but winking at me, "Forgive him, he's sensitive about touching." She laughed.

"I'm not sensitive about touching. I want to do so much touching. So. Much. Touching," I deadpanned.

"Baby Theo, good to see you, man." Tad came around Hensley laughing at my touching comment and embraced me. Tad was the quintessential older brother. Like Seb, he saw too much. Like Luke, he was incredibly organized, a natural-born leader. Like all of us, he'd seen some shit. Unlike any of us, Tad had been born with the proverbial silver spoon in his mouth. It was our money that enabled us to do whatever we wanted, but it was his connections that paved the way.

He hugged me tightly, as if we hadn't seen each other in a while, and I returned it fiercely. Tad was my brother; I loved him. In our team, we were genuine in our affection for each other. There was no pretense when you'd bled together, almost died together, buried brothers together.

"It's good to see you back, Baby Theo. It's been too long." His words were whispered, yet they rocked me to my core. I was back. It *had* been too long. I nodded into his neck. Loving Hensley had cracked the concrete casing around my heart for good. Now, I just needed to talk to Max. But first things first, we needed to get this part over with.

"Ken is locked in there. He's a chatty motherfucker, with absolutely no remorse. Interpol picked up the guys from the boat, and we are closing in on a few others. Once they're picked up, I'd say we are at mission complete. For now, consider the threat neutralized," Tad said to all of us.

"Are you sure this is what you want to do?" Tad asked Hensley. Brian had called ahead, so Tad and the officers we were collaborating with knew what we were there for.

She took a deep breath and backed into me ever so slightly. Drawing my hand up, I settled it on her shoulder, my thumb rubbing gentle circles there. I would always support whatever she wanted to do; she needed to know that. As it had been with

Hensley since the moment I met her, she understood me without words.

"I'm ready. We need to do this. We need to know if there are other aspects of this we are missing." Her voice was firm, and I felt her steel herself under my hand.

She turned to me. "You're coming with me, right?" she asked.

"Always," I responded. I would always go with her.

THIRTY-FIVE

HENSLEY

"I LOVE LEADING THE WAY, THEO. THAT'S PART OF WHO I AM." I was leaning on his chest, his very naked and very sculpted chest, tracing the initials in the little purple heart inked there as I spoke.

"Boss ass bitch, I know. It's sexy." His hand swept down my very naked backside until he got to my butt. He grabbed a handful and pulled me up more fully onto him. "Sexy AF, Hen. Just like I like you. Now lead the way," he growled at me, pulling me down to his mouth.

Theo's other hand tightened against my back, pinning me to himself. Our tongues melded, lips seeking each other, my nipples scraping against his chest. We were desperate for each other again, each reveling in the solidity of the other, even though we'd already done this once since getting to the hotel room Luke had arranged. Ken hadn't told us anything we didn't already know—that our own issues with communication and trust had been our almost downfall. And now, now I was focused on transparency and Theo. I'd been given the time I was craving, time to know this man, time to love this man. Loving him was exactly my plan for the next few days.

I wiggled until he let go of me just enough to scoot downward, kissing as I went, coasting my lips along the strong column of his throat. His throaty hum vibrated against me, rumbling straight down to my core.

I bit gently at his clavicle, nipping it the tiniest bit and then soothing it with my tongue. "Mmmm. Tasty, Theo." I kissed him again, dragging my tongue downward even further. I followed my tongue with my hands, fingernails coasting along lightly in the wake of my mouth. Theo was squirming beneath me, those little groans of pleasure a near constant soundtrack to what I was doing to him.

I had found that being with Theo, finally being safe, and being with Theo, made me playful. I was fully myself. A boss ass bitch as they say, but soft with him, my tender heart held securely in his calloused hands. I was practically buoyant with my joy, my gratitude for time with him infinite. We hadn't talked about the future yet, but I knew we would soon, and we'd figure it out together. Tonight was for pleasure.

I nuzzled his hip bones, then along that deep vee of muscle with the tip of my nose, my hands sweeping down to his hips and gripping him tightly. I swiped my tongue across the tip, just barely. I did that three more times, each taking slightly longer than the last. Theo's hands had found my hair, his pleasure making me wet. I loved having this control over him, the power to bring him to the brink. My mouth closed around him completely, and I swallowed him as deep as I could.

Flattening my tongue, I swirled it around him, my hands dug into his hips. His own hands were getting tighter and tighter in my hair as his desperation for more grew.

"Hensley, baby, that feels incredible," he rumbled.

Instead of replying directly, I took him as deep into my mouth as I could and I hummed an *mmhmmm* of my own. His hips bucked up sharply, and his arms were under my armpits in a heartbeat, flipping me to my back.

"Your leadership skills are superb, but I can't take any more." I laughed as he dropped his own head onto my chest. Laving my nipple, he swept one of his thick fingers inside of me, dropping his thumb to press down on my clit. The combination brought me to the edge, then back as he retreated, teasing me.

"How does that feel, Hensley, my sweet little tease?" I felt his smile against the hollow of my throat as he mimicked my actions from earlier, nipping and laving at my collarbone and then down to worship my breasts.

The difference was that his fingers had never withdrawn from my core. He was slow and sure in his ministrations, working me to the edge of the abyss, and then swirling me back.

I was starving for it, chasing that last burst, my hips moving of their own volition into his hand. He pressed against my inner walls and rolled my nipple between his lips, the wetness of his mouth coating me. That did it. I was soaring. I didn't know my own body in that moment, so owned was I by Theo. He never slowed, even knowing that my body had erupted.

Leaning back, he reached across me to his wallet on the nightstand, pulling a condom out. He had it on and was back pressing at my entrance in moments. My body was hungry for more. It knew he was so close. I rolled my hips upward again.

"I love you, Hensley." He pushed into me, his eyes on me, the pupils blown. When his body was flush against mine, he dropped down and nuzzled my neck again, bringing his lips up to my ear, whispering the filthy things he wanted to do to me, and interspersing those with adoration. The combination was heady, and before too long, I was right back on the brink, frantically chasing that burst.

"Theo, please!" My nails were dug into his back and I felt his dark chuckle against me before his lips claimed my own. Sweeping his tongue inside and tangling with my own, he ground into me, hitting my clit hard as he did so. He kept the motion rolling and pounding into me, my own body desperate for the release he could bring me.

"Hensley, baby, I'm coming. I need you with me," he ground out. He reached under me, his strong hands rolling us both. As soon as I was on top of him, his hands grabbed my hips and ground them down on himself. His hands working me along his length frantically.

I dropped my head back, coming undone around him as he roared out his own pleasure. Spent, I dropped down on top of him, barely coherent enough to feel myself tucked into his side, or his lips in my hair. I burrowed into his strength and slept.

THIRTY-SIX

THEO

"I MEANT WHAT I SAID EARLIER, LEADING IS PART OF WHO I AM. IT'S easier now too, knowing I have you at my back, my anchor in chaos, no matter what. You bring me strength you know." She whispered against my neck. We'd been talking in bed for hours, the time a sheer luxury for us both.

"Well, that makes two of us. Your courage leads me, it gives me strength too. I'll always be here for you, I'd follow you wherever you wanted us to go. But not, like in a creepy way. As in, I'm the luckiest bastard ever to get to be your person," I replied, the truth of my words resolute.

I reached for her again, bringing her more tightly to myself for what I needed to do next.

"Hensley, I need to tell you the whole story of Mosul, and why I doubted you. I am really sorry about that by the way, it had nothing to do with you, only my own stupidity. I've been working on trust since it happened two years ago, but the breakthrough I needed didn't happen until that morning in Lyon," I said. It was time, beyond time. I owed Hensley all of me, all of my story, even the ugliest of parts.

"Are you sure you want to talk about it?" she asked. "We need to eventually, but are you sure you are ready?"

"Not really, but yes. Actually yes, I am more than ready." The more that I thought about it, I was ready. Sharing the story with her was the next step to a whole life, one I wanted with her. She deserved it of me, and I deserved it of myself.

Settling into the pillows at my back and anchoring my hands around her, I started the story of the woman in Mosul. I told her about how my gut had been off all damn day that day, how the woman in the coffee shop tried to distract me, how I lost the informant. Brokenly, I told her that the informant was picked up by someone, someone who used the information that had been given to us to ambush us.

Tears were streaming down her face, spilling on to my chest where her head rested as she listened.

"We lost three men that night. Sam, Luis, and Alex. Sam and Luis were newer to our team, yet Alex was one of us. He was Max's little brother, and we almost lost Max with him. He was refusing to leave the house, but the place was an inferno. A beam had come down on Alex and Max tried to die there with him when he realized that Alex was gone. It was awful. We heard the whole thing on our comms."

She sat up to watch me, her hand resting over the purple heart inked on my chest. Those chocolate eyes of hers were like pools watching me, giving me the will to tell her all of it.

"We got him out, but he fought us the whole way. We were all acting on muscle memory to survive, and I don't really know how we did it. Luke had been waiting to fly us out, thank God he could. We were all a mess. But Hensley, I've never told Max that I lost the informant. We did a debrief when we were state-side again, but Max did his separately, in the hospital." I stopped there. Took a deep breath. It was a God damn tragedy, but I wasn't going to let it drag me under any more.

"I made a vow that night Hensley, to my team brothers, to Alex. My life for theirs. And until I met you, that seemed fine.

We all died there in the sand. But Hensley, you woke me up so fucking fast. I was a goner the moment you opened those gorgeous eyes at me in Normandy and immediately understood what needed to be done. Baby, your strength makes me want to live. To beg forgiveness every damn day if that's what it takes." Shit, now I was going to cry too.

"There will be days when I don't know if I deserve this life, or you. I get the beautiful life, and they get nothing. Now, I know it's not directly my fault. I know that-mostly. I'm working through it, but there will be days I don't believe I am worthy of you."

"Theo, you can have bad days. This is real life. We will live it together and I'm not going anywhere on your bad days. I trust you. Wholly. With my heart, and God knows I have lost too many people I love to give that easily, but you deserve it. You deserve a life filled with all the good things. You just have to trust me too, even on the bad days. Stay in it with me, okay?" She'd taken my hands in hers, her eyes solemn on mine.

Fuck. Her strength.

"Hensley, if you're willing to put up with me, I will spend every day trying to live up to that trust, to the honor you do me to love me," I swore to her.

"That's what I want, Theo. Time, time to learn each other more, burrow into this love that feels all-consuming, thrilling, beautiful, safe. You. I want you." She had crawled back into my lap, settling her hands on my shoulders. I brought my hands to her hips again, reveling in the smooth skin there.

"Now, I think you deserve a reward for being honest with me, even when it was hard. Or, maybe think of this as motivation to have the conversation with Max, even though it will hurt." She sank onto me, bringing her hands up to cup my face. "Together, we can figure anything out." Her words were solemn, but she was already breathless, her chocolate-colored eyes already going glassy with need.

"Together, that sounds perfect to me." I tightened my grip on her and ground her against me. Together with Hensley was perfection. It was my life. Was I completely sure I deserved it? Not really. But I'd spend every single day I had left with her ensuring that I did, and being honest with her about it.

EPILOGUE

THEO

I HAD A CALL TO MAKE. A CALL I WAS DREADING, BUT FORGIVENESS had to start with transparency, and Hensley had shown me that the road to forgiveness was worth it. No more avoiding reality, no more wallowing in my own self-imposed exile. If Max couldn't forgive me, I'd understand. It would practically kill me, yet I'd understand. As Hensley had said to me earlier this morning, I needed to 'hold him able.' I couldn't keep deciding for Max what was best for him to know.

He deserved to know what had happened in Mosul, just like Hensley had deserved to know what that had done to my ability to trust. I hoped that he had it in him to give me another chance, as Hen had done. I may not deserve it, but I wanted it. With all of my being, I wanted it.

Hensley and I had decamped Paris for the safe house back in Normandy yesterday. Neither of us were quite ready to deal with the crowds there for the Olympics, and we wanted space to enjoy each other for a few days and make a plan for where we would go next. Hensley was preparing to head to London to meet with the employees of their company, with Adrien. I'd go with her, as I had that flexibility. For now though, we both wanted to be here, in this space, where we had started to fall in love. I had already told Luke that I wanted to buy this house from the company and he'd laughed at me. He said, "Let's call it an early engagement gift." I'd laughed with him, although I knew that someday, I would ask Hensley to marry me. I'd ask today, but I knew we both needed more time together to work through my trust issues. She needed time to see that I would never leave her. Our future was together, wherever that may be geographically. I'd be asking as soon as it felt like the time, so I agreed that if he wanted to gift it, I'd take it.

Placing my laptop on the marble counter of the kitchen, I dialed into the command center back in DC. Luke answered, as he was working crazy hours ensuring that Ken and all of his associates were appropriately handled. Tad was leading efforts here in France with Interpol, and between the two of them, I knew they'd make sure Ken paid for his crimes.

"Baby Theo, I'm surprised to see you. What did you call that time in-between Hazel and I admitting our feelings for each other and the start of the new normal? Ah, yes, it was sexfest. Why aren't you at sexfest with the lovely Hensley?" he asked by way of greeting.

"You know why. It's beyond time, but I need to talk to Max," I answered. My lack of a joke in response was all he needed to read me. And hell yes, I'd way rather be at my own sexfest. But, this needed to happen before we could start our "new normal."

"Way to be, Theo. I'm proud of you, man. Let me get him," Luke said.

Moments later, Max's eyes met mine on the video feed. He'd sat down in front of the monitor, so I couldn't see if there was anyone else from the team there with him. What I could see, was that Max had his son strapped to his chest. Little baby Alex, there, with us both. I swallowed the lump in my throat, coughed to clear the suddenly tight passageway, gulped in some air and spilled.

"It's my fault Alex was killed. I lost track of the informant that day in Mosul, or I would have seen him being taken. I could have prevented his death too, and the setup we walked in to. I cost us Alex, Sam, Luis, the informant, all of them. It's my fault." Once I started talking, I couldn't stop. The admission just spilled out, long overdue. I went on about how I knew I shouldn't trust that woman, how I'd moved around her multiple times, how my gut had told me something was off all day.

When I was finished, I was met with silence. Like a thick, wet wool blanket in summer. Scratching my skin and suffocating me.

I felt Hensley's hand on my shoulder, then a squeeze, before she sat down next to me, her hand on my lap. Solid, there for me.

I couldn't look away from Max's eyes on the screen. Max, Alex's older brother, my brother in arms. His eyes were tormented, tortured.

"It's my fault, Max," I said again.

His eyes met mine over his sleeping son's head. "Theo, have you carried this with you since that night?" he asked.

"I made a vow that night, Max, my life for theirs. But I have to break that vow. I see that now. Dying right there alongside them doesn't honor them. I want to live. I want to love. I want my own son someday with Hensley, or daughters, whatever we can get. I want that. I want what you and Vi are building, but I can't do that without telling you the ugly truth," I whispered.

Max was silent. Confessions like this are a weight. I may become lighter by giving it, yet now that weight was Max's to carry. Only he could decide what happens with the weight of my confession. He can carry it, he can forgive it and melt the whole thing away, but only he can do it. I knew that, but sitting in the tension with my brother, and having his eyes boring into mine was brutal.

I did feel lighter, but if I crushed Max with the weight of my confession, then it was all for nothing. Now, the path was out of my control. I knew that, yet it was hard to wait, to sit in it. I wanted to be there, with Max, to make him understand how sorry I was. I was so damn grateful for Hensley's quiet support as we sat there, the silence stretching across the ocean separating us.

Max leaned down and kissed his son's head, then looked back up at me, placing his hand where his kiss had been. The baby's downy hair cradled in his dad's hands.

"Theo, I've read the reports. I knew what had happened, yet have been working through my own grief. I mean, I'm the one Alex followed into service, onto the Raiders. Do you think I can go one day without knowing that? Do you think I don't pay for that sin? Tax is always due brother. Tax is always due." His hand dropped to the infant's back, holding him to his chest, even though his carrier was supporting him.

"Dying there in that house that night doesn't honor them, you are right. It also isn't what Alex, or the other guys would have wanted. Believe me, I'd wrestled with this every day since that night, but . . ." His words trailed off as I saw Vi's hand come down on his shoulder, then the camera pushed back from in front of Max. I could see Max and baby Alex, with Vi standing behind her husband and son. As the camera was pushed back, I could see that Luke and Hazel were there, as well as Wills and Mila. The gang was all there, I guess.

"Theo, hear me now, man, and remind me when I need reminding, because I will too. Forgiveness is a journey. It's a hilly road, with valleys and peaks, nice weather and fucking storms. Storms that rattle the windows man, but then the sun comes back out. As long as there are people by your side to remind you that this forgiveness is earned, worth it, hard, necessary and so beautiful. I have my wife and my son now. I miss Alex every Goddamned day, and yet I forgive myself for his death every day too, because I can't take his decisions from him. There's no honor in that either. It can't be about me, and it can't be about you. His choices were his to make and . . ." He broke off, his own tears choking him.

"And he'd have done it a hundred times over if asked. He was a warrior, he signed up, and he knew the risks. His choices can't be ours."

"You don't need my forgiveness Theo, because you didn't do anything to need forgiven from. I'm glad you're talking openly with me now. I'm glad you're back to yourself, and I am sure as shit thankful to Hensley for that, but you don't need forgiveness from me of all people," Max finished.

I gulped again. Real fucking tears streaming down my own face. I couldn't help it. If any man told you it wasn't manly to cry, then simply fuck him. I lived a lifetime in those tears, the anguish of losing Alex and the others, my role in that day, what Max endured, what Hensley endured, all of it. I sat and cried while the others waited for me patiently, Hensley's hand never leaving my lap.

"Thank you. The words don't seem enough, but that's all I have right now," I said, wiping the wetness from my cheeks.

"You're welcome. Also, thank Hensley. She called Vi, Hazel and Mila this morning to talk to them about what you were planning to do. I didn't know it at the time, but now I see why Vi insisted I have a session with Doc this morning, and why she's been my shadow," Max replied. He was smiling, and it lifted the deadweight from my chest. I could breathe, finally.

"Hey Theo!" I heard Hazel in the background. There were a chorus of greetings from everyone in DC and Hensley's replies. Stupid tears were flowing down my face again though, now I was starting to feel silly about the sheer volume of them.

"Why? How?" I had turned to Hensley to ask, yet everyone on the call heard.

I was met with silence for a beat before she said, "Because when you let people love you, and you hold them able to handle everything that brings, with your truth, they get a choice. And the choice, my darling Theo, is to love you."

I crushed her to me as the cheers of *"Hear, hear,"* rang out across the line.

Forgiveness. Trust. Love. They were all intertwined. Was I worthy? I hoped so, because I wasn't letting them go, ever.

SECOND EPILOGUE

TAD

"Well, another one falls, Sebby. Another one falls," I said to Seb. We were with Nate and Brian in Paris, enjoying a late dinner after our last interview with Ken and Interpol. I loved Paris, but I was ready to head back to DC in the morning.

"Cheers to the happy fucker," Seb replied, lifting his glass in a toast.

Laughing, the four of us toasted to Theo and Hensley. I was proud of Theo for owning up to what that day in Mosul had done to him. That day had changed us all. Set us on a path to right now. A person could argue that we were all doing pretty well, with hundreds of millions of dollars in the bank accounts, the ability to do whatever we wanted in theory, each other. Some of us even had a happily ever after.

But none of us had the one thing I would never waiver from, vengeance. No one had seen the woman from the coffee shop in Mosul that day again, but I'd been hunting. We didn't have much intel to go off, but I would die before I gave up the search for her. She was the link. There was a mole, there was no other explanation to what had happened that day. Not a single other possible explanation other than a mole, and that woman was the only puzzle piece we had. Wherever she was, I hoped she was ready, because I would find her, and when I did, there would be hell to pay.

If you liked this book, please consider leaving a nice review on Amazon and Goodreads!

ACKNOWLEDGMENTS

Thank you to the men and women who serve and defend our country, and their families.

As always, thank you to my family for supporting me as I chase this dream.

More tremendous thanks to:
Margy Poer Hogarty for encouragement, beta reading and general all-around amazing support.
The team at Red Fern Booksellers for their endless support and sacred spaces for books and kindness in my home community.
My incredible friends who show up, support my dream, support me as a person, share my social media posts, like what I put out there, drive to book events, read what I write, live this crazy life with me. I'm grateful to be part of the puzzle with you.
EJL Editing, Glittered Pen Edits, Mayhem Cover Creations, Jen and the team at Greys Promo. You are all wonderful to work with and I appreciate your expertise more than I can sum up with mere words.

Let's connect! Please consider signing up for my newsletter at amy@amycolebooks.com and follow me on social media under Amy Cole Books.

ABOUT THE AUTHOR

Hi friends! I'm Amy. I'm an 80's baby who picked up my first romance book putzing around an antique store when I was 11 and I've been reading them ever since. Behind every romance writer lurks a devout reader...and that's me.

I married my high school sweetheart after dating for 10 years. Clearly, he's slow on decision making...yet it's working out so there's that redeeming factor. We have two teenage sons and two black labs. We live in the Midwest, and in the middle of our hometowns so that we can raise our kids around our families. We live where we swore we'd never move back to and regret nothing about breaking that vow.

I'm a small-town girl who was fortunate enough to travel domestically and internationally for years for work (and for fun). I love to be outside, and give me a campfire at the lake, a ski run down the face of a mountain or a beach sunset any day. I love them all. Equally, please ask me where to eat or what to do in cities across the U.S. and France and I will immediately produce a 10-page itinerary. I love food and I love people watching. There really is a story behind everyone, and the journalism kid in me wants to learn them all. Don't worry, I'll make up some details to add an element of romance or mystery to every story.

I love my family, my friends, dogs, books, love stories, traveling, Murder She Wrote re-runs, sports, history, trivia and food. I'm kind of a smart ass, which I like to say is better than a dumb ass. You want me on your trivia team and if you read my books, I'll happily be your friend forever.

Photo credit to the lovely and talented Suni Michaelsen, one of my dearest friends who always shows up for her people. I remain glad to stand in her light.

instagram.com/amycolebooks
pinterest.com/amycolebooks
facebook.com/61562893197128